Sweet

Iris Kain

ISBN: 978-1-957244-26-6

Also by Iris Kain:

Shadow Hunter

Eternal Spring

The Murphy Blackwell Chronicles

Sour (Book 1)

Sweet (Book 2)

The Blood Tribe Trilogy:

Blood Tribe (Book 1)

Blood Trials (Book 2)

Blood Treason (Book 3)

To Lou, the sweetest guy I know.

Sweet

Chapter 1

Maybe February wouldn't suck this year, but I wasn't holding my breath. It hadn't been too bad so far, but something was making my skin itch this morning. I sent a psychic feeler to the wards around Blackwell Manor, the building that housed my home and business, and felt slightly more assured when I saw they were still intact. I didn't feel ready to let my guard down, though.

Hanna—my best friend and coconspirator—tweaked the angle of a crystal heart candleholder to reflect prisms of light onto the shelf below it. She stepped back, pulling a wavy strand of hair the color of polished tigers-eye behind an ear with a tanned hand.

"What do you think, Murphy?"

I let out a forced laugh. "I think love is your specialty, girl. Not mine."

Hanna presented the stunning half-smile that kept her calendar booked with aspiring suitors and shook her head, her eyes twinkling. "It could be, you know."

So I'd been told. I could be any type of witch I wanted to be—or all of them. I was the Summate. That was my… well, I still wasn't sure if *gift* was the right word for it, but in the last five months, I'd learned not to hate it. It sure was a pain when I felt a magical itch I couldn't scratch.

The tinkling of bells hanging over the door drew our attention to the entrance, where my first-ever boyfriend, Conall Berry, entered. Tall, fit, with wide brown eyes and a ready grin, Conall and I had finally admitted our feelings for one another last October during a tornado. It was a pretty crazy month.

I came around the counter and gave Conall a fierce hug, and he returned my fervent embrace as he lifted me off the ground the way he liked to do. He smelled like he'd just stepped out of the shower, which he probably had taken after his day job working construction. I giggled, and he set me down and gave me a big kiss.

"'Love is your specialty, not mine,'" Hanna quipped with a saucy bobble of her head. I waved her off with a blush and a giggle.

I swear, I don't think I ever giggled or blushed before Conall and I got together. If I did, I don't remember it.

"Pretty display, Hanna," Conall remarked, his deep voice gentle and sincere.

"See? *Some*body can appreciate my decorative skills," Hanna said with a broad sweep of her hands that would have made Vanna White fear for her job. "You just don't like red because it clashes with that green and yellow spring display you're so proud of."

I kept my eyes fixed on Conall as he roamed the shop, casually snatching a cookie and pouring himself a steamy cup of coffee from behind the counter. If there was anyone with a knack for detecting peculiar, otherworldly energies lurking nearby, it was him. Yet, he displayed no inkling of such forces. Not even a twitch.

Hanna had a point about that whole matching thing, I guess. But then again, I was never much concerned about that. I was more of a Converse and T-shirt woman. I'd put on silver stud earrings or a silver necklace when I felt fancy. Small silver hoops if I felt *really* fancy. Unlike me, everything about Hanna matched: her rosy nail polish and lipstick, her striped sweater, her fashionable pants that showed off her fit legs, and her red shoes. She has that gift. My gift is making it to work in time to open the door without appearing like I just rolled out of bed. Jeans and T-shirts with a fresh-scrubbed face were more my vibe. I'd made a recent exception for a Claddagh ring Conall bought me for Christmas.

Conall pulled out a chair and strategically positioned himself so he could engage in conversation with both of us. He stretched his long legs out, crossed his ankles, and shot me an affectionate grin that melted my heart despite my current state of magical alert.

"Y'all are so cute it's dis*gus*ting," Hanna commented, her words dripping with sarcasm as she picked up the Windex and paper towels she'd used to clean the shelf.

"Hey Hanna, what are we doing for your birthday?" I asked to change the subject. Yeah, the universe had not only made February the month where Hanna's red-witch skills shone, and it was also her birthday month. She was an Aquarius: prone to a positive outlook, rebellious wide streak, and an unending drive to help global and local communities.

She set the glass cleaner under the counter and tossed the used paper towels into the trash. "I don't know. I thought—"

Clunk.

All three of our heads swiveled to the front of the store, where a resin deer figure now sat on its side on the cherry wood floor. I winced. My house and shop were in an older Victorian home, and there were rare instances when the timeworn framework, drafty windows, and general age caused mishaps like falling items. Unfortunately, I'd lost a handful of inventory to damage from these mishaps over the years. Occasionally Rex, my old black cat and familiar, was guilty of breakage, but rarely.

This time, though, the sound alerted me to an invisible presence. As my attention shifted, I sensed that a fourth entity had joined us at the front of the store. My brow furrowed as a sensation of pins and needles caressed my skin.

"Y'all feel that?"

"Feel what?" Conall asked.

Well, that answers that question. If psychic Conall was unaware of an otherworldly entity, it was my unique brand of energy that made it possible for me to sense it. I couldn't tell if the force was positive or negative, which made me wonder if Conall felt nothing because there *was* nothing. Still, I focused inward to my third eye, willing my relatively newfound psychic sight to work. I panned the store with my human eyes and my extrasensory one for energies or entities and saw nothing out of the ordinary, but the nagging feeling we weren't alone didn't subside.

Hanna tiptoed toward the resin deer figure as if she believed it might not be damaged, as long as she didn't frighten it. She bent over, gingerly picked it up, brushed it off with a long finger, and inspected it from every angle. Her hair now framed a look of confusion and concern.

"It's fine," she marveled. "Not even a broken antler. Funny, though… I don't remember it being close to the edge of the shelf." Her voice faltered as she pointed to where the figure had fallen.

I felt a shiver run down my spine as the crystal heart candleholder that Hanna had admired earlier rocked ominously, its facets casting prismatic beams of light across the room. I continued examining my shop surreptitiously for a presence, a cause for the movement, but saw nothing.

Hanna replaced the figure in the spot where he'd been on the shelf, placing him a tad farther away from the edge for safety.

Thump.

Our heads pivoted together again to an Imbolc wreath made of pine boughs, bright yellow and white ribbons, and flowers with a white ceramic stag's head fixed at the top. It had fallen from the hook on the wall behind a circular table and landed on its back. Not a petal or needle had separated from the wreath. The ceramic stag remained intact.

Stepping out from behind the counter, I approached the wreath, tiptoeing in much the same way Hanna had moments before. I eyed the hook embedded in the wall that had held the wreath. It was cast iron and still anchored sturdily. A wide ribbon woven into the wreath had kept it at an acute angle from the wall. There was no way that it had fallen unless the ribbon had torn.

I lifted the wreath and inspected the white silk ribbon positioned inside the bow behind the stag's head. I stuck a finger inside the loop and made a circuit of the fabric, tugging on it as I went. It was as unbroken as the day I'd gotten it from Miriam, the coven rose witch who'd designed it.

Our playful banter had become silent as I stood on a chair to hang the wreath back in place. Conall came to my side to spot me in case I wobbled. A lifetime of having the woman you love living as an accident-prone gray witch will have that effect on a boyfriend.

I draped the silk loop over the iron hook and hung the price tag so customers could easily see the price should they be interested in buying it. Conall took my hand and helped me hop down from my perch.

Click. Slap.

"What in the—?" I couldn't finish the statement, and the pins and needles were back. Conall and Hanna watched with knitted brows as I followed the sound to where a deer magnet had fallen from the display near the register. I picked up the antlered bust and returned it to the metal display backing. It stayed in place just fine.

The three of us stood almost equidistant around the room, scanning the shop for another falling item. Once again, I used my sight to search the room for unseen visitors, but got nothing. From the way Conall's lips pressed together as his wide brown eyes darted around the shop, he'd had similar results. The air felt thick with an unseen presence, but neither Conall nor I saw so much as a flicker of otherworldly spirits, even with our supernatural gifts.

After a couple of minutes of silence, every second of which had chill bumps dancing on my spine, Hanna spoke.

"What do you think that was about?"

Conall shook his head. "I didn't see anything or anyone unusual. But now I can feel… something."

"What does it feel like?" My heart beating faster now that Conall had confirmed that something wasn't right.

"Maybe I'm just weirded out right now from everything falling like that," he said, his voice sounded strangely hushed and his usual good humor replaced with a hint of fear.

"But this has to mean something," I insisted. "Three deer falling inexplicably in such quick succession?"

Hanna stood with her arms crossed protectively in front of her. "I don't like this. I'm getting really creeped out, y'all."

"The universe is telling us something," Conall said. "The deer are symbolic. Any ideas, you two?"

Neither Hanna nor I had an inkling of the symbolism behind the deer.

I studied my friends with concern. Three deer. Three of us. I had had too many supernatural omens during my life to believe it was a coincidence. But what did it mean?

Chapter 2

The jingling of the bells above the door announced the arrival of customers to Witch's Brew, my metaphysical shop and coffeehouse. This time it was two of my favorites. Jake, the tall, soft-hearted metalhead musician, and his slim, shy girlfriend Cadence strolled in, their hands intertwined. I couldn't believe they'd be celebrating their four-year anniversary as a couple on Valentine's Day. They were only juniors in high school. Longevity in relationships at that age is unheard of, but those two made it work. From what I'd seen, their communication with one another was mature beyond their years. I'm not sure about reincarnation, but if it exists, I'd wager these two were soulmates from another timeline.

"Murphy!" Jake hailed with the lift of a solidly built hand and smiling blue eyes.

"Jake!" I hollered back in kind. He grinned, and I pointed two fingers at them. "Salted caramel mocha and a skinny vanilla latte?" I asked, and they nodded.

"And an Irish crème coffee, too!" chirped Betony, trailing in behind them. Last week, her hair had been peacock blue. This week, she'd tied her shoulder-length red hair in low pigtails that framed her round face. Her hazel eyes with gray centers smiled as she saw the three of us.

Betony was the reason why until last year I'd thought I was a gray witch—a chaos witch. Blackwell Manor was the only place where I felt safe. For years I lived upstairs, ran Witch's Brew out of the downstairs, and protected the world from my destructive power by staying behind my home's heavily warded doors as much as physically possible.

Turns out, I was only reflecting the chaos energy of one of my regulars, a sweet local high school junior. Betony Yarborough.

Only, I say. As if reflecting Betony's chaos wasn't enough. When Betony found out she was a chaos witch, she did *not* take it well. Like, uprooted trees, caused a tornado, knocked out streetlights, nearly killed my boyfriend, *did* kill her father, and wound up in a juvenile detention center bad. Not that he hadn't deserved it. Her dad, that is, not my boyfriend. The way her god-awful father abused her... well, no kid deserves that. No *human* deserves that. And it was easy enough to forgive Betony, since most of that damage happened while her horrible dad's spirit possessed her.

It was a wild Samhain. The whole last half of October was pretty insane.

"Sure thing, Bet. Irish crème coming up," I replied, swiftly getting to work on their coffees. They grabbed a couple of chairs, situating themselves at a nearby table where we could easily chat. A few more high schoolers sauntered in right after them, prompting Conall to rise and lend a hand in taking their orders.

Betony officially became my apprentice in the craft once she was released from the juvenile facility. Currently, she resided with LaDonna Whelen, my former foster mother and the esteemed high priestess of the Lughaidh coven. Fortunately, the court recognized Betony's actions as self-defense in the case of her father's demise. Now, she dedicated her days to refining her skills as a gray witch under LaDonna's guidance, while I continued my journey as a burgeoning Summate. As part of her training, Betony delved into the depths of shadow work, aiding others in confronting their darkest moments, traumas, and tragedies. Her progress was nothing short of remarkable, thanks to her own experiences with personal healing and her innate talent for connecting with people as a compassionate gray witch.

After our small after-school rush, I wrapped up pricing my herbs, shelved them on the storage racks, and joined the kids at their table. The fourth member of their crew, Lorina, had joined them during our rush and was tapping drum beats on the edge of her chair with reed-thin fingertips. Once fire-engine red on one half and coal black on the other, Lorina's hair had been cut into a messy, asymmetrical bob and dyed a more natural brown color. Her curls, previously weighed down by length, now waved in adorable abandon as she swayed to the rhythm.

Rex had curled up into Betony's lap and was purring contentedly. He'd come a long way from the crotchety old cat who had nothing to do with her when her chaos energy was untamed.

"How y'all doing?" I asked.

"Betony is worried that she won't have anyone to take to the Valentine events at school," Cadence said.

"Valentine… events?" I said, puzzled.

"Nobody really does dances anymore," Jake explained. "Our school has a pep rally for the spring athletes and passes out chocolates with little cards attached to them as a fundraiser for cheerleaders."

"Lots of folks get prom invitations in the Valentine cards," Cadence added.

Lorina snorted with laughter. "V-card," she said. The three of them giggled at that, and it took a second for me to understand they didn't mean Valentine. *Virginity. Right.*

"Oh." I felt so out of touch between the slang and the missing rite of passage of high school dances. The Gryphon High Valentine's Day dance had been a big deal when I was high-school age, which wasn't that long ago. Not that I ever went. LaDonna home-schooled me as a safety measure after too many catastrophes in middle and high school. Which was fine for me. "Awkward teen" didn't even begin to describe my high school years. Try hell on fiery, emotional adolescent, accident-prone wheels.

Hanna helped herself to a cup of coffee and a cookie from behind the counter. She added a touch of her sweetened rosewater stash to the mug before joining Conall at the table next to ours. She leaned over to Conall and me and as her brown eyes watched Cadence and Jake, she muttered, "They are so cute together. And everything about them complements one another." She motioned at them with a hand full of oversized cookie.

"Huh?" Jake asked, his eyebrows raising as he noticed her observation.

"Nothing," she said with a flirty smile, and she turned back to face Conall.

The door chimes rang again, and as I started to stand, Conall gave me an "I've got this" hand motion and darted behind the counter.

"God, is it prom season already?" I said to no one in particular.

"Not yet," Cadence said, a long-fingered hand smoothing back her wiry curls, "That's not until April, but some people plan way in advance."

"Which is stupid," Jake said. "I mean, who wants to think that far ahead?"

"Well, just because *you* know who you're going to take already doesn't mean the rest of us do," Betony chided.

"You haven't officially asked me," Cadence reminded Jake.

He frowned. "Do you need me to? I mean…" Cadence's wry expression seemed to knock the breath from him. He took her hand in his and looked her in the eyes. "Cadence Mackenzie Hemingford, will you go to prom with me?"

"Yes, you dork. Of course, I'll go with you." She grinned and bopped him on the head, ruffling his shoulder-length hair as she did so.

Finished with the customer, Conall stepped out from behind the counter and strode toward Hanna's table. As he passed a display of crystal balls, he faltered. His eyes locked on a clear crystal ball posed on a rose quartz lotus flower. He froze, then blinked, transfixed by whatever had drawn his interest to the ball.

Conall is an orange witch with the gift of prediction who has supernaturally powerful insight. In the evenings, he often hangs out at my shop. He has a regular clientele that he sees who love getting tarot and oracle readings from him. I'm not sure if it's the readings they love, since he's typically spot-on, or if it's getting the chance to hide behind a curtain in a walk-in closet-size room with my hunky boyfriend, but whatever. I trust him, and it's a great side gig for him. Plus, it gives us an excuse to hang out most nights.

I sat up, concerned with the way his unblinking eyes and furrowed brow studied whatever he saw in the crystal globe. "Conall? Everything alright?"

He swung his head from side to side slowly. "No. No, it's not." He blinked, tore his gaze from the ball, then strode purposefully to his reading room and retrieved his satin drawstring bag of tarot cards.

"Conall, what's wrong?" Hanna inquired.

Conall fetched my purification spray and a black satin tarot spread cloth from my cupboard. Muscles tense, the corner of his mouth tight, he cleaned off the table where Hanna sat and wiped it with a cotton rag before spreading the satin cloth atop it. The rest of us sat silently, watching my typically laid-back boyfriend move with an uncharacteristic intensity.

"I saw a deer," he explained, his voice cross. He withdrew his tarot cards from the midnight blue bag. His traditional Rider-Waite deck was worn and lovingly dog-eared from years of use.

"What the fuck? *Another* one?" I said. The teens at my table shot each other a confused look, but there wasn't time to explain.

When cards are laid for a tarot spread, the seer sends their requested answers to the deck, and if the dealer has the gift of prediction, the way Conall does, the deck responds. To my surprise, Conall opted not to do his preferred five-card spread or the more elaborate Celtic cross arrangement. After a brief shuffle with his eyes closed, Conall flipped the cards he needed into place with practiced flicks of the wrist. He laid three cards down: center, left, right.

"Past, present, future?" I ventured as I surveyed the cards.

"Situation, action, outcome," he replied, his thick brows meeting in the center.

I took in the cards on the table, and my face mirrored his concern. "Mmm. That's, that's not good."

To those unfamiliar with the tarot, the three cards on the table might not mean much. Normally, I'd never assume how another witch interpreted their spread, but these cards left little to decode, even for an inexperienced reader. To Conall and me, it spoke volumes.

The situation card was the Tower: danger, destruction, crisis, or unforeseen change.

The action card: Death, inverted. Tumultuous change. So not just change, but turbulent change. *Great*.

The outcome card: the Hanged Man. Trials. Heroic Sacrifice.

"Damn, that's a lot," I said, concern thickening my voice.

"Yeah." Resting his palms on the table, his fingers draping over the edge, Conall studied the cards with an intensity suitable for a complex Celtic cross spread, rather than a simple three-card reading. Leaning in closer, he shifted his weight to his right leg, gracefully crossing his left behind him in a pose that resembled the Hanged Man. The sun emerged from behind a cloud, casting a radiant glow around Conall, completing the eerie likeness.

Chapter 3

Betony stood at Conall's elbow, ready to learn as usual. Conall and I explained the tarot spread's significance to her. As she took it all in, her attention intermittently shifted to the young man whom Conall had previously served. He sat alone at a table, engrossed in his phone, rapidly tapping the screen with agile thumbs. With dark skin, short, curly hair, heavy-lidded brown eyes, and a strong jaw with a surprising amount of stubble for a teen, he was everything that Betony was not typically attracted to: lean, fit, and male. Even his clothes—a leather racing jacket and black jeans that ended in black leather brand-name athletic shoes—screamed masculine. Betony's taste usually ran into androgynous males or other young women in her class.

"Bet?" I ducked my head to interrupt her distracted inspection of the newcomer. "You OK? Is he bothering you?"

Her hazel eyes, with their gray-ringed pupil, refocused on me. "What? Oh, no. I'm just…" She blushed adorably and dropped her eyes to the cards. She fidgeted with the hem of the silk spread cloth, caught herself fussing with a magical item that wasn't hers, and stopped. "His name is Rene Basilio," she said. "He's new, and he's in my econ class. I heard he moved here from Atlanta." The way she gushed *Atlanta*, like it was a far-off place, reminded me how little Betony had seen of the United States.

Conall put up his cards, giving Betony and me a chance for some girl talk.

"He's very masculine," I remarked.

"I *know*," she said, her voice as confused as I was at her atypical crush. "I don't get it. He's not my type at all!" She caught the way her voice had shot up, and her eyes grew large as she drew up a hand to shield her face. "Oh my god. I'm sorry. Is he looking?"

I snorted, glad that I wasn't facing Rene squarely, so he didn't see how I was smothering a laugh. I stole a glance in his general direction.

"I can't tell if he's looking at you or Cadence," I said softly.

She sighed. "Better not be Cadence," she said. "I'll be so upset. She's already got Jake. She doesn't need Rene."

"Neither of you *needs* Rene," I said, trying to appraise the newcomer without making it obvious. "He is cute, though." The way the late afternoon sun came through the window made his dark skin look golden.

Betony made a frustrated sound and flopped into the nearest chair. I heard a *crack* and instinctively grabbed Betony's elbow and jerked her upright as the chair under her collapsed with a broken leg.

"How did you know—? Oh, wait. Summate witch," Betony said. She was right—my orange witch intuitive skills had grown dramatically with lessons from Conall.

My mind spun back to the card reading. The tower card suggested damage or possible jeopardy—events that typically happened when a gray witch did not focus her power the way Betony had recently learned to do. Unfocused chaos power can cause minor damage, like a broken chair, or worse. Much worse. Like death worse.

"Bet," I said, "please tell me you're still concentrating on your shadow work."

"Yeah, why?"

"Have you been working with others and their self-reflection, too? Kids at school and stuff?"

"What? Do you think I might be losing control of my chaos?"

"I'm not saying that for sure. You can't risk letting this guy derail you from the progress you've made." I gave Rene a more earnest appraisal. He *was* pretty darn cute. I totally got why he'd be a distraction. Betony continuing to channel her gray witch skill was far more crucial than a high-school romance, though.

"I won't let him distract me," Betony promised. Rene peered up and met her eyes, and he gave her a sexy, lopsided smile from under his heavy brow. Her mouth opened in surprise, but she regained her composure to offer him a nervous smile. She was utterly twitterpated.

Oh, shit. She's a goner.

)O(

"We'll have to keep an eye on Betony," I said to Conall after the kids had all left and the after-school rush had passed. He grabbed a broom from behind the swinging doors separating my shop from the kitchen and started sweeping the floor. I took my blackberry and clove spray from under the counter and began wiping crumbs and coffee rings from the tables. Rex slinked in from the kitchen and rubbed his ribs along the doorframe before perching on the tall wooden stool behind the counter to supervise.

"Is that the kid she was eyeballing earlier?" Conall asked.

"Yeah. His name is Rene. I'm afraid he's going to distract her from her gray work," I admitted. I accidentally pushed some carrot cake crumbs onto the floor, and Conall added them to his growing debris pile.

"What's his story?"

I told him what Betony had shared with me, which wasn't much, and he laughed.

"New kid in Gryphon where nothing new ever happens? He's bound to get attention at first. His shine will wear off, eventually."

"Speaking of new kids," I said, wrapping up my cleaning and dumping my palmful of crumbs into the trash by the counter, "what are your thoughts about training Jake up so he can join the Lughaidh? With the Wildes moving back to New Hampshire, we could use a new member to keep the coven at the same power level. Betony's filled the one slot, and Jake could take the other if he wants to he and demonstrates enough skill. I've seen his aura—it's impressive. LaDonna likes to keep the number around twelve or thirteen, and I think he might be ready."

After the chaotic events of last October, I found myself immersed in the Lughaidh coven, a clan of witches that Conall, Hanna, and I had been a part of since birth. Our parents, excluding my father, raised us within its folds. The coven became our anchor in the aftermath of a tragic event where our mothers were killed during a coven ritual. I'd only recently understood a little about the reason for their deaths. Betony's parents believed that by seizing power from the local coven, they could grant their daughter the power of the Summate—a witch possessing the ability to harness the powers of every witch archetype. They were unaware the universe had already chosen one among the Lughaidh.

Yeah. It was me.

Ten-year-old me had no idea I was a different. Like most witches that age, I was still discovering where my talents lay. Unbeknownst to me then, Betony's birth that year threw the ability to uncover my gift beyond my reach for the next fifteen years.

Conall paused and propped the red broom on its bristles. "Jake seems interested in the craft, sure, but it'd be unusual to bring in two outsiders in less than a year."

I knew what he meant. Most coven members were descendants of previous Lughaidh coven members. I couldn't say for sure when the last time a non-blood descendant had been brought in before Betony, but I didn't believe it was in my lifetime.

"It might take him a while to get comfortable with the idea, anyway. Meanwhile, I'll ask LaDonna."

"Ask LaDonna what?"

As soon as my high priestess crossed the threshold to Witch's Brew, the energy rose. The Source power that linked me to the pulsating life force coursing through the universe thrummed with renewed intensity. Even the bells above the door sounded amplified with the strength she carried. Her coffee brown locks cascaded to the center of her back, and every item of clothing she wore flattered her Mediterranean skin and deep green eyes. Striding with her customary equanimity, she exuded a confidence that never bordered on arrogance. LaDonna always struck me as a regal hippy, if such a thing existed.

With her was a woman I had never seen before. Tallish for a woman and curvy, her closely cropped blonde hair exhibited a tasteful blend of stylish flair and untamed spirit. She wore a perfect Southern upper-middle-class outfit that included an oversized turquoise sweater that drew out her matching eyes and a cashmere scarf draped elegantly around her shoulders.

"Murphy, Conall, this is Ericka Moore. Ericka is in town looking for a coven to join, and she's considering the Lughaidh. She's also mulling over the idea of hiving off and making her own nearby."

"Pleasure to meet you," I said in Ericka's direction as LaDonna engulfed me in a hug, but the words sounded less than enthusiastic. Maybe I should have extended my hand to Ericka to be polite, but I tried to make up for the feigned sincerity in my voice with a polite dip of my head.

So much for Jake joining the coven.

Conall took the handful of steps to shake Ericka's hand. "Nice to meet you, Ericka. I'm Conall Berry."

"You must be Paul's son!" Ericka chirruped. "We were just having coffee at his house. Your father is so nice. And his house—wow!"

"Thank you," Conall said. "I think he's pretty great, too."

Ericka broke away from LaDonna and Conall as she perused the displays with great interest. "Murphy, LaDonna tells me this is your shop."

"Yes, it is. I opened Witch's Brew six years ago, with a lot of help from LaDonna and the coven."

"It's lovely," she gushed. "I love how you've interwoven the Imbolc theme into everything. Oh, and look! Valentine's Day! How *cute*!" She picked up a packet of tea wrapped with a red ribbon and ooh'd and ahh'd over it. "Oh, and a rose quartz heart! And pink candles. That's just perfect. I love it."

Depending on how Southern folks are, "cute" can be the worst compliment. Especially in Alabama when you get it from a Southern belle like Ericka. At least she didn't call it *nice*. My lip curled, and I turned the gesture into a fakey grin.

"That display is courtesy of Hanna, my friend, and the red witch of the coven." I bit back the defensive tone by the end of the sentence, but she likely caught the sting in my first few words.

"Where do your strengths lie, Ericka?" Conall inquired, which was a polite way for one witch to ask another what type of witch they were.

"Gold," she replied with a smile. Her eyes twinkled with a flirtatious sparkle that I had no doubt she used with most humans of the male gender.

"Good fortune with money and financial success," Conall said with a reciprocally flirty hint in his tone. "I'll bet you've been a real asset to your coven."

Ericka made an "aw shucks" motion with her hand, wrinkled her nose in Conall's direction, and returned to LaDonna's side.

That explained why everything Ericka wore carried an expensive label. *Ericka must be practicing her craft on herself.* There wasn't anything wrong with that—most witches do if it benefits them. I thought of how another coven member, Miriam, had lost her job and struggled to make ends meet by selling her crafts at fairs. It was her wreath that had fallen in the shop earlier. Perhaps having Ericka in the coven could turn life around for Miriam. That'd be an upside.

"It was a *real* pleasure to meet you, kids," Ericka said, her voice positively syrupy in its sweetness. "Murphy, this is one *heck* of a store you've got. I can't wait to shop here."

"Come back anytime," I said, not even attempting to meet her enthusiasm. I'd have to have eight cups of my strongest espresso to match that level of perk.

The bells jingled again as Ericka and LaDonna made their way out. I was relieved to have ducked the question LaDonna asked earlier about what Conall and I had been discussing. Asking if Jake could join the coven might be moot, and I sure didn't want to bring it up in front of Ericka in the event she joined us. No sense in starting a working relationship with friction.

Conall let out an amused chuckle after the door closed. "What was *that*?" He said with a sweeping hand toward the door.

I wagged my head back and forth. "I have no idea," I admitted. "But I don't believe a word of it."

Chapter 4

Witch's Brew was adorned in celebration of Imbolc, the spring equinox's cross-quarter sabbat that falls between Yule and Ostara. Yule coincides with Christmas, while Ostara aligns with Easter. Saint Brigid's crosses and attractive displays of bear, deer, and groundhogs sprinkled with acorns, daffodils, and pine boughs had taken over the wall opposite my register. I'd kept the theme rich in greens and whites to represent the waning winter and coming spring, and even added green matcha and Irish crème flavors to the coffee menu for seasonal flavors.

The front portion of the store was like the rest of the three rooms that encompassed the store. Witchcraft supplies lined shelves along the walls. Mismatched tables and chairs salvaged from curbs and repaired with nails, screws, and spray paint were scattered around the room's centers so coffee drinkers could enjoy their brews and baked goods. At the moment, only a half-dozen people populated the tables while another three or four shopped.

Friday after school let out, and the usual gaggle of teens descended on the coffee shop. Jake showed up without his usual crowd, his guitar case in one hand and a suitcase-sized amplifier in the other, a dark knit cap pulled low over his forehead. He often played guitar on Friday nights and had a standing invitation to squat in the corner and perform whenever he pleased. The amp's presence told me he and Lorina—who provided the vocals and drums via a drum box—hoped for the chance to get louder as the evening progressed.

Jake plugged in his amplifier, sat, and plucked a few strings until the guitar was in tune, and set his guitar in a metal stand in a corner near the window. He waved to a couple of classmates en route to the counter where I was reviewing a book called *To Run with Spirits*.

"You're early," I commented as Jake laid a hand on the counter and gave me a grin. Jake's typically anxious personality always relaxed a bit before his performances. It was as if he tapped into a side of his nature that allowed him to appear more extroverted. Tonight, however, he struck me less at ease than was typical.

"I wanted to talk to you," he said.

"Need a bigger tip jar?" I asked, and he chuckled. It was a running joke. Months ago, after hearing Jake and Lorina perform for the first time, I'd told him the two of them would hit it big one day in Nashville. He said they'd need more money if they were going to move up there. I said, "No problem. Just get a bigger tip jar." Now, when he approaches me for anything before a performance at the Brew, I'd ask him the same question.

"Not today," he joked with a lopsided grin. "Actually, I wanted to ask you about something I saw here in the shop yesterday."

Glad he was showing a continuing interest in the craft and still hoping he'd join the coven instead of Fakey Ericka of the Unsettling Vibes, I slid a receipt between the pages of my book and set it aside. "What caught your eye?"

"Um… it was in the Valentine's Day stuff." He walked over to the display, his thick-soled boots quiet on the wood planks. He withdrew a raspberry red fabric drawstring bag and brought it to the counter with an inquisitive, hopeful face. "This."

"A love potion?" I asked as I took it from him. I cocked my head and paused as I deliberated Jake's possible need for the contents. "Are you buying it for a friend at school or something?"

He shook his head and swallowed something back. His pride, I guessed. "It's for me."

I blinked twice. "Come again?"

"It's for—"

"No, I mean, I heard what you said," I replied. "I'm just not sure why you said it. Jake, Cadence adores you!"

"Do they work? Love spells?" he pressed. He leaned in and put his elbows on the counter, and his downturned blue eyes studied its surface. His beard and eyelash hair had a distinct red tint. Why do guys have such long eyelashes? It's not fair.

I placed my hand on top of his, which was probably twice my size. His frazzled energy radiated through my fingers all the way up to my elbow. Jake had a lot of untapped magical power, and tonight, it vibrated like one of his plucked guitar strings.

"Jake, you don't need this. This is more for people trying to save something they have or give an already blossoming romance an extra push."

His gloomy eyes grew cloudy. My gentle giant was trying not to cry. "Murphy, I might need it to save me and Candace. I think she might be starting to like someone else."

Recalling the way Betony had difficulty focusing because of the new guy yesterday, I ventured a guess. "Rene?"

His shoulders slumped. "You knew?"

Squeezing his hand reassuringly, I sat up. "I know he's caught Betony's eye, but I still don't think you have anything to worry about."

Hanna passed through the swinging doors from the stockroom that linked my store to my kitchen, brushing her hands onto a flour and spice-spotted apron. She smelled like cinnamon rolls. "Murphy, do you have any cardamom?"

Hanna is half red witch, so love is one of her two talents. The other half is brown, or kitchen witch, which is fine with me. I sell her pastries and other baked goods in my coffee shop, and they bring in many of my repeat customers. Witch's Brew is only a stone's throw away from Gryphon High, and teenagers love a sugar rush after school lets out.

"Pantry shelf, on the right, in the drawer with the rest of the spices," I responded. "Or maybe with my new stock on the shelf to the left. Before you go back to the kitchen, though, I have a question for you, my red witch friend, if Jake will allow me to ask it."

Jake's eyes reflected panic for a moment, then softened. I would never intentionally hurt him, and he trusted me.

"If Jake is maybe a little concerned about Cadence's feelings toward him, what do you recommend he do to strengthen their love?"

She saw the love spell under his hand and hurriedly stepped around the counter with a businesslike air. She swept it away and returned it to its spot on the shelf. "Don't use that," she said with a wrinkle of her flawless nose. "You don't need it. Have you seen how she looks at you?"

"She's been looking at me like that a lot less lately," Jake mumbled, refusing to be persuaded.

"As a red witch, let me tell you this: you don't want to force her emotions. It's never a good idea to use a spell to manipulate anyone," Hanna stressed. "A love spell might be too strong for where you two are right now."

I took in the contents of my store shelf by shelf and landed on the display of love-inducing items Hanna had assembled yesterday, among them a bag of candy hearts with phrases like "Twin Flame," "You're Magical," and "My Goddess."

"Why don't you make her some candy?" I suggested.

Hanna's eyes lit up. "Murphy Blackwell, you're a genius!" she exclaimed. "That's perfect! Jake can infuse the candy with his feelings, and she's sure to respond to that, and Jake won't have to resort to heavy-duty hocus pocus. We can include some lovey items in the box, like little pink and red candles and a rose quartz, maybe an inexpensive ring or something blingy. Cadence loves to accessorize. It's subtle enough to be a gentle charm, and sensible."

The slight upturn at the corner of Jake's mouth said he was willing to give it a try, but the clouds at his brow showed he felt doubtful. "I want to do it soon. She said she might go to her dad's this weekend. I think she leaves tomorrow?"

"Will she be here tonight to watch you play before she goes?" I asked. He nodded. "We'd better get started then. Hanna, will you help me get a few ingredients together from the front and then watch the store so Jake and I can put the recipe together before she gets here?"

"I could help him make the candy," she offered.

"Nah. I'm working on my brown witch skills," I said. "This will give me good practice. Plus, I need to learn my way around my kitchen better."

"*That's* the truth," Hanna teased. "If you need help finding a piece of kitchenware, just ask."

I snorted. I might do the shopping, but Hanna did the baking, and neither one of us doubted she knew her way around the pots and pans in my enormous commercial-quality kitchen better than I did.

My mother, Nora Blackwell, had been a brown witch, and the kitchen past the swinging doors into the "home" part of my house was exceptionally efficient—if you enjoyed cooking, that is. Until recently, I hadn't used the trove of appliances and gadgets besides the microwave and the occasional pot and spoon to heat a can of food. Since uncovering my Summate status, I'd made it a goal to learn at least a few of my mother's kitchen spells and to study them well.

Hanna bustled around the shop with a wicker shopping basket collecting items for Jake's love-infused recipe. "Hmm… Pink and red candles to use while you make the candy. The flame will symbolize the fires of love. You'll use honey in the recipe to keep yourselves 'stuck' together. Maybe add a tiny touch of hot pepper for heat. A tiny dash of lavender syrup mixed in with the sugar would be helpful, too, to represent drawing sweetness to them. Murphy, you can use one of your mother's hatpins that she kept in her utensil drawer to draw a sigil into the top of each candy. Something simple, like 'love' should do. Or you can just make a heart. A piece of parchment to write words of love for her to read—"

"I can't write a love poem!" Jake exclaimed, his eyes wide. "I'm no poet."

I shrugged. "You're a musician. Imagine you're writing her a song," I suggested.

Jake let out a snort and laughed curtly. "Murphy, you really are a genius."

"Rose quartz," Hanna continued. "And you can wrap it all up in pink silk. You have some of that, don't you, Murphy?"

I withdrew a square of pink silk from a drawer I kept near my wrapping paper. "This should be big enough."

"Perfect," Hanna agreed. She handed the basket across the counter to me with a flourish. "There you go. Happy sort-of spelling."

"You got the counter, Hanna?" I asked her, and she shooed us through the swinging doors and into the kitchen.

Chapter 5

My kitchen is an eclectic mix of materials—dark wood floors, zinc counters, a copper sink, and an enormous butcher block island in the center, above which I hung herbs on a long drying rack in season. I made it across the room to the Wedgewood stove before realizing Jake hadn't followed me in.

"Jake? You coming?"

"Sorry. I got distracted by something in your storage room." Jake passed through the low doorway, ducking his six-foot-three-inch frame under a bough of drying rosemary as he did. His energy was still off, but I resisted the urge to use my magical sight to investigate. It was Jake. Probably an overdose of teen angst.

"It's OK. Come on," I said. I pulled out a thick, faded leather book held shut with a thin strip of leather. The parchment pages were messy, some loose to the point of falling out, and many stained with various ingredients spilled onto them over the years. One page had a recipe for coffee cake and what looked like a thumbprint in a berry juice; the berry juice page was my favorite. I couldn't have requested a more wonderful, personalized grimoire to inherit from my mother.

Jake joined me at the countertop to the side of the stove. His furrowed brows showed he was doubtful but willing to try anything to hold on to Cadence, who already thought he hung the moon.

"I'm sure my mother has something for candy in here. Oh—and look—Hanna has baking chocolate on the butcher block already. It's like the universe knew we would need it."

Jake's smile didn't reach his eyes, but he headed to the butcher block and dutifully returned with the chocolate. I sent him through the kitchen and pantry searching for the ingredients Hanna had prescribed while I paged through my mother's book for a recipe that would tie them all together.

"Here's one," I said, pointing my finger at a truffle recipe. "We can weave Hanna's ingredients into the filling if we're careful. What do you think?"

He shrugged, impatient to get started. "Sure."

I searched for a mold to use for the candies. Thankfully, Hanna had left one behind from Christmas that she hadn't taken back to her dad's place yet. I had Jake light the candles—pink on the left, red on the right, while focusing on his intentions—and then set him to assembling the ganache. I gave him a few silent minutes of reading, measuring, pouring, and mixing while I watched from a distance and answered the occasional question. His brows knitted with focus and he paused, checking over his shoulder to make sure I was still there.

"How's it coming, Jake?"

"Um… OK, I guess."

The smell of melting chocolate ganache mixed with honey and lavender syrup soon filled the kitchen. I ensured Jake followed the recipe correctly while melting another chocolate candy on a separate burner for coating. As we worked, I coached Jake to keep his thoughts on Cadence and the strength of their love.

When the ganache was complete, Jake followed me to the island at the kitchen center, where I instructed him to fill the molds with the melted chocolate. Then he tipped the mold over to spill the excess out, leaving behind what would be the chocolate coating. The result was a mess that was fun to sample, and Jake finally grinned for real.

"When it cools, you can add a sigil or a heart on the inside, if you want," I suggested. "Or you can decorate the outside."

Jake shook his head. "My handwriting is too messy. Inside is better, so she can't see it."

"Better add a bit more to the tops to keep it from cracking when you press down, then."

He did, and when he finished the last mold, he stood tall again.

"You can put them in the fridge to chill for a few minutes. Not much to do until the coating cools. You good if I head to the shop for a bit?"

Jake nodded, and I left him to stay with the candy and play with his phone. Hanna was captivating the customers with her charm, as usual. I swear, she's the only person I know who loves the month of February. It's like her version of Christmas.

When we had a moment between customers, Hanna leaned in and presented me with a concern.

"This isn't like Jake," she said, her features fixed on me. "Cadence's love is as strong as ever. I can tell. Do you think something might be wrong?" Hanna had a soft spot for Jake, as she did with most sweet guys.

"You mean other than the usual teen drama?" I asked.

She frowned. "Yes."

I used my hand to brush a few crumbs from under the domed cake stand and brushed them into the trash. "They're teenagers, Hanna. It's not likely they'll last forever."

"I hope they do, though."

I gave her a hopeful smile. "Me, too," I admitted.

Returning to the kitchen, I dug through my mother's many utensil drawers searching for the hatpin Hanna had mentioned. I finally found it, gave it a quick wash, and handed it to Jake.

He nodded solemnly and took the hatpin as if it were a grenade pin instead.

"Murphy, can we say a spell over it? I feel like this won't be enough."

I frowned, but agreed. "Nothing crazy, though, OK? Just a little added charm to help you see your love for each other more clearly."

He agreed, and the enthusiasm he'd been lacking returned.

"You're going to put a heart inside the cap of each candy, and as you do, repeat after me. *Goddess Aphrodite, help us see how beautiful our love can be.*"

After repeating the words, he looked at me for more guidance.

"That's it?" he said, surprised. "Those are all the words?"

"It doesn't have to be fancy to be effective," I pointed out. "It's a charm, not a spell. And you should know by now that it's all about intent."

He hunched over the candy and gently carved hearts into a couple of the caps. He was right. His writing was atrocious, and working with a hatpin didn't help. But his heart was literally and figuratively in the right place. He stepped back, observed his labor with a critical eye, shrugged, and moved on to the next cap, making sloppy hearts and mouthing the words as he did.

I poured the ganache into a piping bag for him and left him to fill the caps with the sweet filling. Returning to the store, I found Hanna wrapping up someone's purchases.

"How's he doing?" she queried.

I leaned against the shelf of bulk herbs in glass jars behind the counter.

"He's doing OK, I guess, but he's stressed."

Jake's deep voice called from the kitchen. "Murph? Can I pour the rest of the chocolate over the tops now?"

"If they're nice and full, go ahead, that's fine," I said. "Then put the other half of the mold on and set them in the freezer to harden."

"OK."

Hanna chuckled. "He's like a regular Alton Brown in there."

"He's trying so hard."

Hanna noticed something in my eyes and tipped her head to face me more directly. At five-foot-eight and wearing boots with pump heels, she towered over me.

"I'm thinking maybe too hard."

I crossed my arms and sighed.

Jake emerged from the back, wiping freshly washed hands on his jeans to dry. "They're in the freezer. I think I'll play for a few minutes while they cool."

"Sounds good, Jake," I said.

He headed to his regular corner and folded the small wooden bistro table and chairs I kept there so he could easily clear a spot. He kept one chair aside for himself to sit on and then began plucking the strings of his instrument almost randomly as he decided which tune to play first.

As he strummed the last string, Lorina and Cadence paraded through the door, wiggling their fingers at him so he noticed their newly polished, glittery red nails. Cadence's nails were almond-shaped and feminine. Lorina's were more like mine—shorter and functional, barely reaching the fingertips. The two of them kind of reminded me of Hanna and me—one stylish and feminine, one a tomboy, but still very much a girl.

After showing off their new nails, Lorina ducked back outside to her car. She carried in a drum box and set it next to Jake before strolling to the counter to order some coffee. Whip-thin and confident, she eyed the chalkboard featuring the specials as she squinted and wrinkled her freckled nose.

She set both bony elbows on the corner and bent her tall frame down to lean on them, much as Jake had earlier. "What's good?" she asked. I knew she wasn't referencing the menu.

"Not much. How are you?"

We made small talk while I prepared Cadence and Lorina cups of coffee. As we did, Jake started singing. Lorina cringed.

"He should have waited for me," she said.

Admittedly, Lorina was by far the better singer—probably few people on earth sang better. But Jake's voice was deep and heartfelt as he sang a song about an angel, directing the melody in Cadence's direction. From the enchanted look on her face, spell or no spell, Jake had nothing to worry about.

"I think he's doing alright," I said. Lorina gave me a look from under her brow, and I backpedaled with my hands up defensively. "I mean, you're clearly better, but look at Cadence's face."

She scoffed as I handed her the cappuccinos. "Yes, we all know," Lorina said with an eye roll, "They're grotesquely in love."

Lorina glided away with their drinks, and the next woman at the counter giggled, her black, spiraled hair waving as she did.

"Sounds like she probably isn't a big fan of Valentine's Day," she observed.

"Lorina?" I said with a casual wave of my hand. "She's fine. She probably just needed her coffee fix. What can I get for you?"

"Do you have any of your Eros oil?" she asked. "You had some on your display up front yesterday, and it smelled amazing, but I don't see it today."

Hanna had strolled around the counter as we chatted and verified that the display she'd put together yesterday was out of her Eros oil.

"I think I put some in the stockroom," she said. "Hold on a tick."

A tick? She watches too much British TV, I thought with amusement as she headed into the closet-sized stockroom between the sets of swinging doors. Who am I to complain if my best (and only) supplier of pastries was addicted to *The Great British Baking Show*?

"Huh," she said, her voice slightly muffled from around the corner. "I don't see it. Murph, did you restock the display today?"

"No, I didn't." I pulled one of the swinging door panels back and flipped on the single overhead light, which we rarely needed. The space was so small that my arms could touch both sides when I stood in the center. The light from the kitchen or the store was usually more than enough.

"I had one more bottle right here, I thought," Hanna said with a frown, tapping a narrow strip of shelf about chest height.

"Maybe Conall sold it?" I suggested. She shrugged.

"You really should get a modern cash register with an inventory tracker," she scolded, not for the first time.

"And ruin my vintage vibe?" I retorted with a sassy hand on my hip.

Hanna gave an unladylike snort and headed back to the customer to gather her information so I could call her when Hanna had another batch prepared.

I turned my attention back to the group of teens at the front of the store—Betony had joined Cadence at the nearby table, and the two friends were chatting away. If I had to guess, Lorina was talking to Jake about the next set, but he was looking at me with a new type of concern.

What's wrong now, Jake?

I felt my lips press together as I contemplated why he might be stressed. And then I recalled how he'd paused before joining me in the kitchen earlier and said something in my storage room had distracted him.

Did you take the Eros oil, Jake? Thievery, deceit, and manipulation are never a good place to start a spell, my man. Not good at all. I tapped my foot and considered saying something, but it was just a guess and not a likely one. Jake was a good kid—stealing was not in his nature. Was it? My next question was, if he was responsible for the oil's disappearance, how was he planning to use it?

Chapter 6

Saturday morning dawned with powder blue skies and bright winter sun streaming through the windows of Witch's Brew. Several cars on Oberon Street had tracks scraped through a thick frost film on their windshields, evidence of drivers braving the morning hustle. On days like this, I was extremely glad my short commute consisted of descending the staircase and strolling through the kitchen to my shop. Driving on ice—a rarity here in Alabama—has never been one of my favorite activities. When bad luck strikes you on the daily, adding ice to the mix is downright treacherous.

The wooden floors in the downstairs kitchen were chilly under my bare feet. Chocolate, honey, and lavender lingered in the air from the night before. The brown paperboard take-out box Jake had put together for Cadence sat wrapped with a red silk ribbon on the butcher-block table. Inside were ten adorable chocolate truffles adorned with a parchment sheet containing a short poem in Jake's charming but messy left-handed scrawl. He'd made a dozen candies, but had broken two as he'd cracked them from the mold. He grew more cautious after that. He'd put off handing the treats to her until today, when they'd had more time to solidify.

I passed through the storage room into the shop and kicked the thermostat up a couple of degrees in anticipation of the heating game my old house would play that day. With each customer entering, a gust of chilly air would sweep through the door, causing the front rooms (originally intended as the parlor and sitting rooms) to cool down when business was thriving. The rearmost room, what the blueprint called the dining room, would become toasty at the raised setting, but better that than chilly. It's hard to shop with numb fingers.

Unlocking the cash register, I stocked the till out of my tiny safe, then started my first batch of coffee in the percolator for the morning regulars. The air soon grew full of the smell of freshly brewed coffee. Maybe I should be used to the fragrance by now, but it never got old. My routine and relaxed movements allowed my mind to wander.

I reflected on yesterday's events, the multiple encounters with deer that appeared to be orchestrated by a mysterious force. Was it a message? Could it be related to Betony's preoccupation with the new boy, Rene? Was Betony's control over her chaotic gray energy faltering, posing a danger? My power and her chaotic energy had found a delicate equilibrium, but we were still navigating uncharted territory. If she tipped the scales, there was no predicting the result.

Perhaps it was linked to her abusive and murderous father. Though the coven had banished his spirit with a powerful spell, it was also possible that Betony's mother was involved from her prison cell. After all, they were both part of the coven responsible for the deaths of my mother, Conall's, and Hanna's.

It had been five months since we'd uncovered the truth about the murders on that horrible night over sixteen years ago. The courts deemed her father's confession to Betony as unreliable hearsay. None within our coven had seen the faces of the assailants. While Betony's mother, Virginia Yarborough, was found guilty of criminal child abuse for failing to protect her child from her husband's harm, the sentence she received felt woefully inadequate. Her mother could be spelling from jail. As far as we knew, she didn't have a coven to help her. But things change. Virginia claimed she'd converted to Christianity in prison, but nobody familiar with Virginia's history believed her.

Does the deer tie in with Betony's dad? Was he a deer hunter? My heart clenched in my chest as I recalled the way the hunter's blade looked in his hand when it pierced my mother's skin. I remembered a little from the night my mother had died, but not enough to convict either of Betony's parents.

The promising cool spring night took a dark turn on the fateful night of our mothers' attacks. We'd hiked for what felt like miles to my young legs before assembling a bonfire with logs, branches, and sticks, which soon reached the starlit sky above us.

I remembered how the fire popped and crackled as LaDonna and her partner, Luke, opened the rites. Luke prepared a wide ring of sacred salt. LaDonna used her athame to cast the circle enclosing the coven within. The short blade and its moonstone-embedded handle caught the glint of moonlight as she moved clockwise to begin the ritual. Her dark green robe, darkened in the dim light of the forest, flowed like liquid coal. I recalled the coven assembled, hands clasped inside that circle, their faces blissful as they stood, eyes closed, faces skyward, bathing in the moonlight.

Hanna and Conall stood between their parents and clasped their hands the same way I'd stood next to my mother, clinging to hers. Hanna's father stood on my other side. I've never met my father, but I've never lacked for a family, thanks to the coven, even despite my isolation and penchant for introversion.

As usual, we three kids stole peeks at each other more than we paid attention to the ritual. We made silly faces while the others closed their eyes and struggled not to snicker or wiggle too much. It's hard to take such a solemn activity seriously when you're ten and look forward to hollering and gallivanting in the woods with your best friends once the rites are concluded, and the grown-ups start eating the picnics they'd brought. Our favorite game was playing Knights of the Round Table, using large sticks as swords as we rode invisible horses and jousted invisible opponents.

"Mother Goddess, Father God, we kindle this fire in your presence tonight and beseech your blessing upon this rite."

LaDonna's throaty, earthy voice petitioned deities as she took her place at the west end of the coven, facing Luke, stationed at the eastern side. A dark velvet cape covered his muscular frame and wavy hair.

LaDonna's voice was a pleasant drone in the cool night air. The bonfire warmed my front, and the cool spring air chilled my back and calves. LaDonna and Luke raised their eyes skyward and closed their eyes like the other adults. I did the same, trying, for once, to stop farting around and pay attention to the words. When the central part of the ceremony started, it was time to act mature.

Heady with wood smoke and the lull of the ceremony, I wavered on my feet as the invocation carried on. I heard the snap of a twig behind me, but that wasn't unusual for our woodland ceremonies. Deer and other wildlife often passed by as we conducted our rituals. I remember hoping it wasn't a cougar. I'd seen one of them as we retreated from the Beltane rites at sunrise earlier that year, and the beast had about scared the pants off me. Fortunately, the cougar paid us no mind—likely thanks to someone's protection spell. Or maybe it didn't like its odds against thirteen witches, even if three were on the smaller side.

"Under the light of the Goddess Moon, full with the sun's glow, its source of light...."

A sudden pull jolted my hand, followed by an eerie sound from where my mother stood. The noise reminded me of the breathless gasp I had let out after an unfortunate tumble from a tree. Then she made it again. My eyes snapped open as an intruder forcefully wrenched my mother's hand away from mine. My mother convulsed as if struck by a whip's lash as a shadowy arm and gloved hand ensnared her torso. Dark blood trickled from her mouth as she turned to face me. I saw a second gloved hand tightly clutching a knife lodged in the back of her neck.

She couldn't speak, but she mouthed the word "run." Hanna's father, realizing the ceremony had gone horribly awry, swept me from my feet and shoved me toward the woods, yelling the word my mother could not utter.

I thought my heart might stop.

I ran.

I remember nothing except the sound of my breath, my heart hammering in my ears, and Hanna and Conall directing my steps through the thick, shadowy woods. My eyes stung with tears that blurred my vision. My lungs burned until they felt like balloons about to pop, and my legs pumped nonstop; they were exhausted within minutes. Something dripped into my eye, and I wiped it off. The back of my hand came away colored with my sweat and mother's blood.

Then my memory was blank until I woke up sitting on an uncomfortable plastic and metal chair in the police station. I was covered from shoulders to mid-calf in a scratchy wool blanket, clutching a Styrofoam cup of cocoa. The blanket was green. My shoes and the hem of my jeans were soaked. A kind, young officer in a gray uniform knelt before me, checking to ensure I was OK. My eyes hurt from crying.

Betony's mother and father had killed Conall's and my mother instantly. Hanna's mother hung on for part of the night, but she passed away before dawn.

Maybe I'm reading too much into this. This whole deer thing might not have to do with Betony or her parents.

Drawing myself back to the present, I wiped unshed tears from my eyes before pulling the keys from their hiding place under the register and unlocking the door. I set to work, roaming through the store and fussing with the displays in the bright morning sunshine. The coffee urn was reaching the final stages of its gurgling and percolating, and the sound made my stomach growl.

How long had I stood in my reverie thinking about that terrifying night? It felt like I'd relived the whole thing. My heart still beat double-time, and I would have sworn the hems of my jeans felt damp.

Coffee. I need coffee. Coffee solves everything.

I grabbed my favorite coffee mug from behind the counter (the one that read Witchy Woman), carefully rotated the urn, and poured a steamy cup of brew, grateful for its warmth in my chilly hands. The door bells jingled, but I didn't look to see who had come in, not wanting to spill and make a mess as I poured.

"Let me know if you need any help," I hollered over my shoulder as I finished pouring. I got no reply, but that wasn't unusual. Plenty of folks like to be left alone as they browse. I turned the urn back around, added some standard coffee creamer—nothing fancy for the boss, thanks—and turned to see who'd entered as I grabbed a spoon. I stirred the creamer in a clockwise direction (what my mother had taught me to call deasil), mentally saying my morning thanks as the spoon clinked north, east, south, then west inside my cup.

Whoever it was stood out of eyeshot across the new display rack from me, and I wanted to make sure they didn't need any guidance. Maybe they hadn't heard my greeting.

"Would you like some coffee as you look around?" I approached the shopper from behind the counter and saw a crown of conscientiously mussed platinum blond hair beneath a plaid green newsboy cap. Turquoise-blue eyes met my brown ones, and a toothpaste-commercial smile grew wide as Ericka saw me.

"*Murphy!*" she exclaimed. "What a treat! I was hoping you'd be here this morning. LaDonna spoke so highly of you and your shop. I just *had* to come back to see what all you've got. If I join the coven, I imagine I'll get most of my supplies here!"

"Most coven members do," I said, trying to keep the wariness from my voice. That wasn't true. All of the coven members bought any supplies they didn't raise, make, or find in nature at my shop, but I didn't want to sound like I was bragging.

What was it about her that grated on my nerves so much? She wasn't doing or saying anything wrong. Her energy wasn't confrontational, even though LaDonna had undoubtedly told her I was the Summate. That alone might make some witches eager to prove themselves and their power. One of us came along only once every three hundred years or so.

I took a drink of my coffee and felt its warmth slide down my throat like a sip of liquid heaven. I focused on that so my following words didn't sound cagey.

"Would you like me to show you around?" I didn't mean a word of it. It would have suited me just fine if she marched out the door and I never saw her again. But I couldn't treat a potential new coven member like that.

Breathe, Murphy. Learn more about her before you draw conclusions.

"Oh, no, that's alright. I can show myself around just fine. You seem to have everything well organized." Her hand waved in tandem with her words, showing off her manicured nails and enormous wedding set. I can't tell genuine diamonds from fake, but I'd wager they were a couple of carats of the real deal, her being a gold witch. Funny, she hadn't mentioned a family.

"OK. If you change your mind, you know where I am." I tipped my head toward the counter area, where I planned to stand and surreptitiously monitor her.

"Thanks, Murphy."

Nothing about our exchange was unusual, yet it felt like we were tap-dancing around each other like two challengers from rival gangs who had handcuffed themselves to one another before a knife fight.

The old Murphy, who reflected chaos, would have dismissed her feelings as acting irrational and overreacting. But New and Improved Murphy skillfully tapped into an additional dose of the Source. With its power, I surreptitiously trailed her throughout the store, my consciousness fully present while my physical body mechanically grabbed a notepad and aimlessly stared into space. It wasn't an astral projection; instead, it felt like an intensely intimate connection to my surroundings. I perceived every subtle breeze and observed every object Ericka interacted with.

Ericka strolled through each room, taking in the displays of candles, incense, oils, and books. A few things caught her eye along the way, and she often picked up an item, checked it out, and, more often than not, replaced it on the shelf. When she reached the odd center portion of the house, an inner four-foot closet converted into a display of tarot and oracle cards, she paused and tilted her head like a dog hearing a strange noise. Hunkering down, she explored a few decks, staying on one in particular: the Sun and Moon tarot.

Interesting. There was nothing particularly spectacular about the cards alone—I had a couple of dozen decks just as good. What was unusual was Ericka picked the deck I'd used to distract myself moments before Conall and I had… consummated our friendship. The two of us had taken shelter from a tornado in the card space last October. After some wine, realizing I wasn't a chaos witch, and twenty-plus years of crushing on one another, things escalated quickly.

Ericka examined the deck, and while she may have been staring at the description on the back of the deck, it didn't seem to me the words were what she was reading. After a few moments, she replaced the deck, stood in the slow way middle-aged folks often do, and continued her deliberate review of the shop.

When she returned to the front room, I dropped my Source sight and began writing bogus notes in the notepad as if it was a Very Important Ledger.

"Find everything?" I asked, as if it was the first time I'd seen the few small items she'd selected in her hand.

"I *did*," she gushed. "This store is *so* charming."

"Thank you." I took her purchases and rang them up, noting her selection. Black tapered candles. Wolf hair (bought from a friend who owns a wolf sanctuary in Indiana). Deer bone (from a local hunter who told his renderer to save them for me). A poppet.

"Interesting selection," I observed as I rolled the poppet doll in purple tissue paper. "Are you hexing?"

"Maybe," she drawled with the arch of a professionally styled eyebrow. Microbladed, maybe. They looked too perfect.

I decided it was best not to question her further; I didn't want this woman's negative energy to stay in my shop. More than that, I didn't want her in the Lughaidh.

Chapter 7

An hour later, I was still sitting on my tall stool behind the counter, planning to tell LaDonna that the woman who may want to join our coven needed to be turned away. She would take me at my word regardless of my reason, but those words needed to be more substantial than "Ericka gives me an icky feeling, and I don't like her. She's weird." Middle-school popular-kid judgment was not the way to handle this.

It wasn't that she wanted to hex someone; I'd hexed plenty of folks in my time. Some people—an abusive spouse, a judge who took bribes in exchange for leniency, a local high school teacher who misused her role to be inappropriate with her students—deserved it. And while I believe in karma, giving karma a little jumpstart or a start in the right direction never hurts. Well, never hurts *me*, anyway. One of the fundamental differences between witches and wiccans is that witches don't believe in the Rule of Three—the belief that energy you release in the world comes back to you threefold.

No, the hexing wasn't the problem, nor were the words she used. The energy coming off her wasn't malignant so much as fishy. And fishy wasn't a substantial reason. Fishy could be because of insecurity or the possibility that she was putting on airs to impress me. (It still felt weird thinking of myself like that.) But that wasn't it. I didn't know how I recognized it, but I did.

I headed into the kitchen to refill my glass of sweet tea, and when I returned, Jake stood before me with Cadence on his arm and a proud, goofy grin on his face. The problems of my morning vanished at his irresistible enthusiasm. His restless energy had been replaced with a glow of pride.

"Mornin', Murphy," he said and shot Cadence a look that said she was sort of in on their reason for arriving, but not entirely.

"Hey, you two. What brings you here so early, Jake? Don't you usually sleep until noon when you don't have a percussion competition?"

"I wanted to give Cadence her present," he said.

"Valentine's Day isn't until Monday!" I protested.

"Come on, Murph. I want to give it to her while it's... um... new."

"What the hell, Jake? New? It won't be new Monday?" Cadence laughed in confusion and crossed her arms warily across her slight chest. I assumed what he'd wanted to say was "fresh," but he managed to not give it away just in time.

I gave the teens a wry smile and waved them back into my kitchen. I heard Cadence ask why we were heading into my house, and Jake just said, "You'll see," as he led her back.

We met at the center table. Jake stood across from Cadence, and I faced the doors to my shop. He retrieved the little takeout box wrapped in pink silk from the pantry and presented the gift to her with a flourish and a shy smile. He was blushing a little, and I found it adorable that this sturdy, six-foot-plus metalheaded black belt was brought to such helplessness by the petite young woman with an impish grin.

"What is this?" After pulling the box from its silken wrap, Cadence tucked a strand of wild curls behind her ear. "You bought me Chinese food?"

"Open it," Jake urged.

With nimble fingers, Cadence untied the ribbon and opened her gift. She found the parchment page on the top and lifted it out between two fingers.

"Is this like a card? Should I read it first?" she asked. Jake nodded.

I hadn't seen what he'd written the night before, since it wasn't any of my business, but it must have been exceptional. After a couple of minutes of scanning the page, her face growing more sentimental with each pass of her eyes, she put the page down. Tears glistened on the verge of breaking.

"Oh, Jacob. Oh, baby. Wow."

They met at the opposite end of the table and embraced. She almost disappeared into his arms as they wrapped tightly around her. He gave her a swift kiss on the top of her head and returned to the box, pulling it toward them.

"Have a chocolate," he said. "I made them."

"You *made* them? Oh my god? Really? Murphy, did he *really* make these?”

I affirmed Jake's claim, glad his efforts blew her away, and pleased I'd suggested it.

Cadence dipped into the box and pulled out a piece of chocolate. She eyed Jake warily.

"Have you had any?" she asked.

Jake scoffed. "I sampled some last night when I was making them. They're good. Hanna gave me the recipe. Well, her and Murphy."

That seemed respectable enough to persuade her, and she smiled coyly as she took a bite, placing a hand under her mouth as a small piece of chocolate broke off. "Oh, my god, this is so—"

"Hey, y'all back here?" a familiar female voice called, and Rene Basilio trailed Betony through the swinging doors. Betony's red hair was tied back in low ponytails, and she'd drawn hearts by the corners of her eyes with black eyeliner. She'd dressed in black and red with tall black boots. Standing next to Rene, who'd once again dressed like an upper-class, otherwise average, high-schooler, Betony looked dressed in a Valentine goth costume.

"No Lorina today?"

Betony snorted. "No. She's grounded. Again. Her mom found some stuff on her phone she didn't like."

I didn't press. Knowing Lorina, she'd manage to get out soon. She always did. Thankfully, her mother understood her need to play music, if nothing else, and often allowed her to pause her grounding to perform.

Cadence chewed and swallowed her chocolate, her bright eyes showing appreciation as she worked the cloying candy.

"Jake made me candy!" She crowed.

"Can I have one?" Betony asked.

Jake opened his mouth, but Cadence spoke for him. "No! He made them for me, and they're mine." She drew the box to her chest like a little kid and clutched it possessively with a joking grin.

Betony rolled her eyes and changed the subject. "Jake, Cadence, have you met Rene?"

Introductions were made, and Cadence glowed with a bit of smug happiness as she downed another chocolate. Jake stood beside her and beamed in pride at his success. Betony eyed the box and opened her mouth as she eyeballed the candy. I sensed she was about to ask for a bite and hastened to curb the request.

"Come on up front. I'll give y'all a couple of Hanna's latest cookies," I offered before she could speak. I was not too fond of everyone else gobbling up the handmade sweets that Jake had created for his Valentine.

Jake shot me a look of unspoken appreciation and took the lead in the pack, followed by Betony. Rene followed, trailed by Cadence, who seemed to realize the new boy was there for the first time after swallowing her second candy. Her eyes panned the lithe young man from head to foot and back. Her head tilted, and her eyes grew appreciatively. Rene, who faced the opposite direction, had no idea Cadence was eyeballing him.

Does she recognize him from someplace? School, maybe? Why would identifying a new classmate invoke such a drastic response? It looked almost like she was ready to eat him next.

"So, um, Rene?" Cadence said, her voice tentative, "You're new, right?"

Rene turned, his dark eyes meeting hers. "Yeah, my folks moved here from Buckhead."

She batted her eyes. "That's outside Atlanta, right?"

They made small talk as they headed back into Witch's Brew, and for the second time that week, my gut told me something had happened beyond what human eyes could see.

Chapter 8

The teens grabbed their usual spots near the register, and Betony ordered coffees for everyone. She'd gotten generous with her money since LaDonna had started paying her for housework. Betony made money, and LaDonna no longer paid for a maid. It worked well for everyone.

Jake helped Betony carry the mismatched cups to the table. Everything in Witch's Brew was mismatched: the mugs, tables, chairs, and even some curtains. It added to the eclectic feel of my store, which I loved.

What I didn't love, however, was the look that Cadence had begun giving Rene. As she sipped her coffee and munched on her chocolate candies, she seemed entranced by his stories of living in the Atlanta suburb.

Not cool, Cadence. What the hell? Only minutes ago, you were weepy-eyed and clinging to Jake over the poem he'd written, and now…

She popped another candy into her mouth, and recent incidents clicked into place like gears. The missing Eros oil. Jake left alone to stir the ganache as I tended my store with Hanna. Cadence had been head-over-heels in love with Jake until she'd had about her second chocolate. Jake stood by her side while Rene stood before her as the candies performed what should have been a minor charm.

"Jake? Can I talk to you, please?"

Jake's attention shot up from where he'd been watching Cadence, his face simultaneously painted with sadness, confusion, and guilt. My voice reflected the sternness I felt—the kids didn't call me Mama Murph for nothing. I was, at times, like a mother hen to them, even though I only had maybe eight or nine years on them.

Jake stood slowly, his thick, boot-clad legs unfurling from under the chair as if moving through molasses. He'd barely reached his full height when a screech followed by a loud crash came from outside the shop.

What in the hell?

I darted from behind the counter and threw the shop door open. Two cars had collided on the street in front of Witch's Brew. Steam rose from the radiator of the rear vehicle, an old Honda. The driver of the Lexus in front emerged like a CEO late for a meeting, now forced to deal with a terrible inconvenience. He held a cell phone in his hand, undoubtedly to take pictures of the rear bumper damage.

"Betony, call Officer Hendricks," I said, tossing her my phone. She caught it deftly and began pressing my code to unlock it. That I had one of the local police officers' phone numbers saved in my phone under my favorites probably tells you a lot about how my life was back when I reflected Betony's chaotic energy.

I dashed out to the cars and checked on the driver of the Honda, a paunchy middle-aged man with dark, greasy hair and glasses that had gone askew from the airbag. He looked at the billowed, powdery cushion before him as if it had decked him for no reason.

"Sir, are you alright?" I asked. He blinked, dazed, and took in my presence as if he'd expected someone else to be there.

"What happened?"

"You just back-ended someone," I replied. The guy in the Lexus was clicking away, taking photos with his mobile phone. Judging from the robotic voice coming through the speaker, he had already called his insurance company and was waiting on hold.

"I did?"

"Are you OK?"

"I—I think so." He tried to stand, and I helped him sit at the curb.

"Might want to stay put until the EMTs get here. They'll probably want to check you out. I have a friend inside calling emergency responders."

I turned to the man taking pictures.

"It looks like you're doing alright," I observed.

He scoffed. "Better than my car," he said dryly, but without a touch of humor.

I shrugged. "Better your car than you?" I offered, trying to sound placating. He tilted his head in disapproval and frowned as if I was the world's biggest idiot, but he snapped to attention when the person on the other end of the phone picked up.

Betony descended the veranda, bringing my phone with her. "Kenny's coming, and he said he'd call the ambulance and stuff."

"I don't need an ambulance," the greasy-haired man protested, eyeing the damage to his Accord's hood. I held out an impatient hand.

"You look a little shook up to me," I said. "Better to be safe than sorry."

Several minutes ticked by before the sound of sirens emerged from the distance, and Officer Kenny Hendricks' familiar patrol car came into sight. Confident that everything was in professional hands, I returned to the shop where the kids were rubbernecking out the window.

"Get away from the window," I scolded. "Why in the hell are you looking? Do you know those people?"

The kids eased away from the bay window and trailed back to their chairs. When Jake tried to join them, I snapped my fingers for his attention and beckoned him back. He trudged to my side like a chastened puppy.

"What did you put into those candies?" I asked, my voice low so only he could hear.

"Um… I didn't—"

"Jake?"

He licked his lips and stared at the floor. "Eros oil," he said, his quiet voice heavy with regret.

I breathed heavily, like an angry bull, and Jake's face shot up, pleading.

"You're not going to tell her, are you?"

"Jake, are you sure that's edible? Not all of the oils are food-grade!"

Panic washed over his face. "It isn't?"

I pulled my cell phone from where I'd shoved it into my pocket. "I'll call Hanna and find out. In the meantime, you're going to get that box of candy away from Cadence and start praying to any god you believe in that Eros oil doesn't have unexpected side effects." My gaze trailed to where Cadence sat across the table from Rene, thoroughly enchanted.

It most *certainly* had unexpected side effects.

Hanna's phone rang only twice before she picked up. I

explained the circumstances to her, and she started cursing under her breath.

"No, it's not meant to be consumed. How much has she had?"

I looked to where Jake was coaxing the box from Cadence's hands. She barely noticed, so engaged was she with the story pouring from Rene's mouth. Rene sat holding court at the table, clearly thrilled the two pretty young women at his table were engrossed with his every word and clueless about the reason for his effect on Cadence.

"I'm not sure," I admitted, "but Jake just got the box away from her."

"Good. I'll call Miriam to see if she knows the Eros oil ingredients' toxicity levels. Thank the stars we have a rose witch in the coven. She'll probably have a better idea than I do what the side effects are and if we need to do anything to flush them out of poor Cadence's system."

I watched the yellow, blue, and white ambulance wheel up to the crash site. "Well, the EMTs are already outside the house. If she says it's really dangerous, the paramedics are close. There was a car wreck in front of my shop."

"Damn. That's never happened before. I take it you didn't extend your protection ward to the street lately?"

My attention turned from the ambulance to where Betony sat happily at Rene's side, oblivious to Cadence's sudden and inexplicably deep fascination with the boy. "I thought I did," I mumbled. *And maybe Betony isn't channeling her chaos energy the way she should, and it's running loose all around her.*

I hung up with Hanna, took a deep breath, and let it out in a not-so-impatient sigh. With Jake pulling crap like this, maybe strange, fishy-acting Ericka was the better choice for the coven, regardless of how much she weirded me out. And if Betony didn't pull her head out of her butt and stop obsessing over Rene, I'd have to talk with her, too.

Jake carried the box behind the counter and stashed them out of sight, his shoulders stooped, his movements heavy.

"I'm sorry, Murphy," he murmured. "I don't know… Something just… I felt so… it's like…" He trailed off, unable to defend his actions.

I frowned, my mouth pressing into a tight line. "I'm just hoping you didn't mess things up with Cadence while doing something crazy to hold onto her," I said.

Jake sniffled and pulled a paper towel from the roll, using it to blow his nose. "Me, too."

He turned his attention to where Cadence and Betony sat. His girlfriend's mouth hung slightly open, and she appeared engrossed in Rene's every word.

"It didn't even work, did it?"

I scoffed. "Oh, it worked—but it did exactly the opposite of what you wanted. Instead of making Cadence fall for you, I'm pretty sure she fell for Rene."

Jake's heart appeared to implode where he stood, and his hands pulled into fists. "No."

I rubbed his back between his shoulder blades, and he wavered like a large tree with no roots. I had the feeling if his friends weren't there, he'd have requested a hug.

"Yeah. We'll figure it out, big guy. We'll fix it. Somehow."

Chapter 9

Hanna called me back within a few minutes and said Miriam was researching one of the ingredients, but so far, Eros oil didn't appear to be too unhealthy, at least in small doses. We verified with Jake how much he'd added to the recipe and decided Cadence would probably be in the clear if Miriam said the final ingredient was relatively safe, at least physically. Psychologically, however, she was under the influence of the spell Jake had inadvertently wrought.

She seemed fine, other than the ridiculous mooning she was doing. Even Betony had caught on to how Cadence's gaze had riveted on Rene and was shooting daggers in her friend's direction. Cadence, however, had no clue; she wasn't looking at anyone but Rene.

"We need to monitor her, though, just in case," Hanna said. "Is there any way you can make her stick around until we hear from Miriam?"

I thought about it. The EMTs had cleared out with the greasy-haired man in the back of the ambulance, and tow trucks were pulling the damaged vehicles onto their beds. The thumps of the loading cars and the groans of the winches distracted me from my thoughts.

"Why don't I ask Cadence to watch the store for me while you and I head out to the graveyard for a bit? Betony and Jake can stay with Cadence and make sure she doesn't get sick while we're gone."

"That'll work. I'll throw together a picnic and meet you there in a few minutes."

I clicked the button to hang up and sighed heavily. Getting Cadence out from under the Eros oil's influence would not be easy. Hanna's love spells worked—almost too well sometimes.

I wiggled my fingers to catch the kids' attention.

"Hey, y'all, Hanna and I want to go to the graveyard to get some dirt from my mom's grave. Cadence, would you mind watching the store while she and I go out?"

Cadence looked confused, as if someone had startled her. She blinked and tore her eyes from Rene. "What? Did you say something?"

"Would you watch the store for me? Just for a bit? Do you mind?"

"I'll stay with you, Cadence," Betony said, reading the need in my expression. "Between the two of us, we know the store pretty good. Her register's easy—everything is priced, and you just punch the numbers in. We can have fun looking at all the spell books while Murphy and Hanna are out." I'm sure her motivation was more than just sharing a chuckle with her friend, but that was fine.

"Thanks, Bet," I said. "That'd be great."

Jake, catching on to my plan, followed up with, "Rene, why don't you and I play that new game I got today while these two giggle at what skyclad is in Murphy's spell books."

Rene's brow furrowed. "What *is* skyclad?" he asked. I shook my head. Teenagers.

The four of us shared a laugh while Rene looked from person to person for clarification. Betony motioned with her arm, and Rene followed her to the books, looking at her behind the entire way. Cadence trailed behind them, and the mournful look on Jake's face broke my heart.

"You can't mess with magic," I reminded him. "It has a way of backfiring if you aren't careful."

"You think?" Jake said. He looked like he wanted to follow the others to the back room where the books were, but he couldn't stand to watch Cadence make puppy dog eyes at Rene.

☽◯☾

Once Rene's education on defining skyclad was concluded—complete with pictures of nude witches performing rites—the girls took their spot behind the cash register. Jake coaxed Rene out the door and to his place, where the video game awaited. As Cadence watched them pull away in Jake's Eclipse, she looked almost ready to cry or pounce at the door. Whatever Jake had spelled in those candies, combined with Hanna's oil, worked fast and well. Or not so well, given what he'd been trying to do.

Betony's jaw clenched tightly, and her hands balled into fists as she watched Cadence's puppy-sick frown.

"Bet," I whispered. She either didn't hear me or ignored me—her fixation with Cadence didn't waver. The surrounding air grew warm.

"Bet!"

It was more of a stage whisper from behind clenched teeth than a whisper, but it got the job done. Betony finally turned in my direction. I crooked my finger in a "come here" gesture. Frowning, she met me behind the register.

I leaned in close so Betony knew our conversation had to be stealthy.

"She's bespelled," I explained.

"What? How?" She noticed the candy box stashed behind the counter, and I could see her coming to the same conclusion I had recently. "Jake's candy? But why?"

"Ironically, because he thought he might lose Cadence's love to Rene."

"That's so *dumb*. She'd never."

"I know that. You know that. But for some weird reason, Jake was feeling insecure. Unfortunately, Rene was the first person Cadence focused on once the spell kicked in, and here we are. So be patient with her—she can't help it. We'll fix it soon."

Hanna burst through the door, a large picnic basket in her hands. "Ready?" she asked. I nodded, grabbed a small jar for graveyard dirt, and joined her on my wide veranda.

"What time is it?" I asked Hanna, remembering Conall had said he would come by after finishing a job that morning. Almost in reply, I heard his Camaro growling up the street before pulling up next to the curb. My face lit up. I felt as charmed as Cadence was as Conall emerged from the driver's seat with a smile.

"Y'all fixing to go have a girl's lunch or something?" he inquired, noting Hanna's basket.

"We need to discuss how to handle a problem that's come up," I replied. "You should come with; I'm sure you'll have some ideas on how to fix this."

He hustled to our side. "Where to?"

"Walker Cemetery. I'm going to get some dirt from Mom's grave while we're there." I held up my jar.

Conall took the picnic basket from Hanna and tested its heft. "Damn, Hanna. What'd you put in here? An old encyclopedia?"

Hanna snorted, a noise that might have sounded obnoxious from another person but was feminine coming from her. She ticked off the list on her finger. "No. I brought sandwiches, potato salad, a couple Mason jars of sweet tea and…."

"You cleaned out your dad's fridge," Conall joked. "Got it."

As we strolled the two blocks to the cemetery, I filled Conall in on the morning events, and Hanna interjected periodically with her understanding of the story.

Conall shook his head in frustration once I concluded. "Damn fool teenagers. He could have killed her."

"Yeah," I frowned. "It's irresponsible and out of character, and I'm surprised he did it. Cadence clearly adores him."

"Never underestimate the insecurity of a Gemini," Conall said. "They love like crazy, but sometimes they love so much they drive the person they're in love with crazy while they're at it."

We reached the gate to Walker Cemetery, over eighty acres of rolling hills, tombstones, and mausoleums, and crossed the brown winter grass to where our mothers and their fathers lie in side-by-side graves. My mother lay in a solitary plot. One of these days, I plan to get around to buying the plot next to her. Part of me wondered if I'd be buried next to my husband instead. Would that be Conall? I looked where my sweetheart stood, staring mournfully at his mother's tombstone.

"Anyone hungry?" Hanna asked, taking a seat cross-legged on the brown grass. Thankfully, it was a sunny February midday, and the temperatures had broken into the fifties. It was chilly for a picnic, but not intolerable.

"You should've brought coffee instead of sweet tea," I joked. "I could use the warmth."

Hanna laughed. "You don't get enough coffee at the Brew?"

I scoffed. "Never."

Conall and I joined her cross-legged on the cold ground and helped her unload the food. Hanna didn't mess around when it came to her picnic basket. Hers was designed with loops in the lid specifically for holding silverware and glasses, and there were additional loops inside to secure plates, matching cloth napkins, and plastic food containers. Hanna had taken the basket on probably a hundred dates, but it'd never show. Hanna took great care of her belongings.

We spread a tablecloth on the ground, set out the dishes, and scooped generous helpings of potato salad, baked beans, and veggies onto our plates, adding the egg salad sandwiches Hanna had assembled last.

"Thanks for bringing lunch," I said. "Sorry it's last minute, but I need some ideas about what to do with this mess Jake has put us in."

Conall gave me a half-shrug and said, "Simple. Unspell Cadence, and don't let Jake into your kitchen again."

"It's more than that, though," I said. "He ruined my trust in him, and now I'm not sure if I want Jake in the coven."

"Might be a moot point if LaDonna decides Ericka is the next member," Hanna remarked. I frowned and told them about my last encounter with the odd blonde that morning. My friends listened attentively but seemed as perplexed as I was.

"Her energy wasn't off, you said," Conall mused, "but you still feel like she's not a good fit."

"Do you think it's a mental health issue?" Hanna asked. "Maybe that's the problem, and if she got some help, she wouldn't ping your 'weirdo' radar so much."

"Maybe," I said doubtfully. Could it be a mental health issue? The negative feeling I had made me believe that something more alarming was at play than a chemical imbalance, but the reason why was unclear. Why did I not trust her? Ericka's demeanor resembled that of a twenty-first-century realtor who had transformed into a Stepford wife rather than a serial killer.

We finished our lunches and put all the contents into plastic grocery bags Hanna brought before loading everything into the basket. I gathered a handful of graveyard dirt from my mother's grave and thanked her and my ancestors for their guidance and love. Perhaps one of them would visit me in a dream with a solution. My ancestors were good at that.

After deciding to heal Cadence, the three of us returned to Witch's Brew. However, we were still uncertain about how to approach the coven initiation process. Should we speak with LaDonna about it or not?

As soon as we opened the door, a blast of warm, incense-laden air hit me, making me glad I'd turned the thermostat up that morning. The heat felt great after the chilly walk back.

Cadence stood behind the counter with a wide grin on her face. "You'll never guess who came by while you were gone," she said, clearly proud to deliver some positive news.

"I give up. Who?"

"Your father!" she chirruped.

"My—my father?" I said. "That's not possible."

"Why not?"

"Because my father is dead."

Chapter 10

All of us stood there staring at each other, each of us waiting for the other to say they were kidding or unsure. My father had passed away; my mother had kept in touch with him until he died from cancer at a relatively young age—twenty-something, I'm not sure what. She'd not asked for his help to raise me. He'd never requested to see me, as far as I know. I often wondered if inclusion in the Lughaidh coven might have saved him.

"He said he was your dad," Cadence insisted.

I tugged at an earlobe, choosing my words so she knew I didn't doubt her conviction. "That might be what you think he said, but it can't be right."

Betony tried to intervene. "I didn't see him, but I heard Cadence talking to someone. He didn't buy anything, whoever he was."

This didn't bode well. Was Cadence seeing and hearing things? Might the spell Jake inadvertently cast cause hallucinations? I needed to find out. More than that, I needed to get Jake's spell out of her.

"Oh, and this broke while you were gone," Betony said, holding out an eye of Horus chime. My shoulders stooped as I accepted the broken item from Betony. Its bells tinkled mutely against my palm. "I'm sorry," she said with solemn eyes similar to how Jake's had appeared earlier.

What is going on? Is Betony's gray growing? I haven't had this much shit going wrong in such close succession since I started learning my Summate powers. A few broken pieces of inventory weren't a big deal. Neither was the broken chair, the car accident, or Jake's poorly executed spell if taken one at a time. Thankfully, none of the chaos has been too bad so far. Even so, this was a lot of crap going wrong in close succession.

"It's alright," I sighed, examining the chime. One of the chain loops hung open, which was odd. How did a chain loop pull open without someone tugging on it? Maybe it had been faulty and somehow slipped past my inspection when I checked in the shipment. I could try to repair it, but chances were good it wouldn't look the same.

"You could take it to Luke," Hanna suggested.

"Good idea. Maybe he's got something in his jewelry tools that will do the job." LaDonna's partner, Luke, made a living crafting and designing jewelry.

"I'd better go," Hanna said, her hand on my arm. "I have—"

"A date?" Conall ventured, his eyebrows raised.

Hanna swatted at him. "Not all of us have the perfect fucking relationship, mister," she retorted. She collected her basket and flounced out the door with a hug and a see you later to all of us. She acted playfully enough, but I sensed hostility in her spirited comeback toward Conall. I made a mental note to check in with Hanna later.

"There's my mom," Cadence said as a maroon minivan pulled in front of the shop. "Murphy, I'm telling you, it was your father. He looked a little taller than me. Like, strong jaw? Light blue eyes? Does that sound right?"

I ran a hand through my red-brown hair. Could Cadence have suffered a hallucination from the candies? Was this some convoluted side-effect of Jake's spell? Did we need to keep her longer? She seemed to be doing alright. Surely, if she was in physical danger, she'd be showing signs by now.

"That doesn't help, Cadence. I've never seen my dad." It was true. My mother didn't even have a photograph.

She frowned and snatched up her purse, heading to the door briskly. "I'll prove it," she said, holding up a finger to emphasize her point, "but I've got to go."

She crossed the room so fast that I barely had time to say anything before she opened the door.

"Cadence! Hey—I need to talk to you soon. Come back, like, soon, OK?"

God, sound like an idiot, why don't you? But it worked. Cadence stood in the doorway with the knob in her hand as cold air blew into the shop, waiting to hear why I needed her to return.

"She wants to offer you a job," Conall said, filling in where I'd lacked details. I hadn't thought about hiring Cadence, but it gave the young woman a reason to come back. "She's going to have more business soon, and she'll need the help. If you want the job, she needs you to fill out paperwork," he added.

"OK," Cadence agreed, somewhat mollified, and dashed out the door. "Thanks, Murphy!"

"I'm going to have more business soon?" I said after the door closed and traffic was down to Conall, Betony, me, and a couple of milling customers.

He nodded, and I smiled. Who was I to doubt the word of an orange witch and his gift of prophecy?

And with that, the lights went out.

☽○☾

Betony and I helped the three customers who were in the midst of shopping when the lights stopped working. We wrapped up their purchases (let's hear it for my antique, non-electric cash register!) and guided them out of the store before locking the door. It wasn't fully dark inside, but gray clouds obscured the horizon, and I sensed an early winter twilight.

Conall and I ventured around the house, he to the back and me to the front, trying to pinpoint the cause of the blackout. My phone pinged, and I saw he'd sent me a message.

Conall
It doesn't look like the fuse box.

Do the neighbors have power?

Conall
Let me check
Yep, looks like Titania and Oberon Streets both have power. You're the only one dark. Do you have a ladder?

Yes, should be in the carport

Conall
OK. Going on the roof for a sec

The roof?

Nothing inside the house presented any clues. I threw a thick fleece blanket over my shoulders and stood on the chilly veranda with Betony, my hands wrapped around a warm coffee mug while waiting for the verdict of Conall's roof inspection. I was glad the wind had held off until after our return from the graveyard. The air smelled like pending snow.

"We need to get Cadence back and deprogram her from Jake's spell," I observed, shoving a free hand inside the blanket in a makeshift hand muff.

"The sooner the better, as far as I'm concerned," Betony said. "I was really doing well with Rene. He even started texting me between classes."

"Well, that's promising," I said. The temperature was dropping, and the wind was picking up quickly. I wished Conall would hurry.

I heard footsteps descending an aluminum ladder from the back of the house, where the roof was less steep. The rattling of the collapsing ladder was followed by more footsteps as Conall put the ladder away and hiked around house.

"Looks like something damaged the weatherhead," he said as he appeared, worry wrinkling his brow.

"I don't even know what that is," I admitted.

"It's where power and phone wires drop into the house," he explained. "And damned if I can figure out how it happened. Those aren't easy to damage, and it's not like we've had a storm or falling branches." He eyed the sky. "Yet."

I liked how he didn't say "your" house or "your" weatherhead. Like he thought of it as home. Maybe I was reading into his comment, but it implied that he took a little ownership of Blackwell Manor. OK, a very little.

Don't jump the gun, Murphy. It's only been five months. He's your boyfriend, and he's staying over damn near every night—of course he wants the house to be operational. Chill.

I ran a hand through my hair, and it tumbled right back into place over my shoulders.

"Well, shit," I sighed. "I guess I need to call Gryphon Utilities."

Once inside the darkening house, the power company explained, to my dismay, that the earliest they could get over would be Monday. There was no guarantee they'd be able to fix it right away, even if they were able to determine the best way to fix it. They put in a work order, or whatever they called it, and said they'd call me when the service folks were en route. They said the repair alone would take about five hours, and that was if they had what they needed on hand.

This whole crappy luck shit is getting old.

This would be an unfortunate string of events for most folks, but not out of the question. Life happens, and sometimes life sucks for all of us. However, I had turned things around and improve my life by harnessing the guidance of the Source. Through its influence, every step in my life has been improved. The Source has become my ultimate guide, shaping every facet of my existence, and leading me towards a more enjoyable and successful life.

The falling inventory, Betony's breaking chair, me helping Jake with a charm that went wrong, the car accident, the oddly broken Eye of Horus, Cadence claiming she'd seen my father, and now the damaged weatherhead, all happening in such close succession added up to one thing—chaos had returned to my life. But why?

Betony hugged me and said her farewells when a classmate came by to pick her up and take her home to LaDonna's. I watched them pull away with an odd sense of relief. If the chaotic mess swirling around me was linked to Betony's inability to control her own chaos, perhaps putting some distance between us would alleviate at least some of the influence she had on my life.

I pulled out my phone and dialed LaDonna's number so she'd know to keep an eye out for… well, anything.

Chapter 11

I peered out of my darkened shop window and watched headlights passing back and forth on Oberon Street. Thoughts tumbled through my mind in search of answers, questions on a repeating loop. Jake's misguided spell and its failed impact on Cadence. The traffic accident outside of my shop. The falling objects intended to send a message I couldn't divine. Ericka's possible inclusion into the coven. The broken weatherhead. Cadence saying she'd seen my father. This had been one helluva—shit. When had everything started? Wednesday? Only four days.

Conall approached me, and I watched his reflection grow on the mirrored surface. He raised a firm hand and rubbed my back before pulling me close.

"What do you want to do now?" My hair muffled his voice.

I shrugged as frustrated tears sprang into my eyes. "Mind if I stay at your place?"

Conall laughed, amused that I felt I had to make the request. "Of course you can stay at my place."

He joined me upstairs as I wandered through the dark house, using my phone as a flashlight. I threw a few items into a bag, enough to last for a few days. As the beam of light sliced through the rooms upstairs, my heart swelled with love for my old home. Despite its flaws and imperfections, I cherished every part, from the creaky floors to the beautifully stained wood trim around the doors and windows. I headed to my private dressing area in the back corner of my bedroom. I stored my clothes and shoes inside the room—essentially an oversized walk-in closet. A fancy accessory for a house, given that I'm a jeans and t-shirts woman.

Rex, my sweet kitty boy, joined me as I shoved a couple of shirts, bras, underwear, socks, and jeans into a navy carry-on suitcase I'd pulled from a shelf. I gave him a few head scratches and picked him up for a long, soft hug before crossing the hall to my bathroom. I set him down on the tile, and he wound around my ankles.

"It'll be OK, buddy," I told him. "It's only for a couple of days. I'll be back soon. I wish I could take you, but Conall's apartment is a no-kitty zone."

I made my way to the bathroom and barely had time to scoop my toothbrush, hairbrush, and deodorant into the bag before my phone died. The battery indicator had read 25 percent only seconds before.

Damn, damn, double damn.

I dropped my overnight bag in my frustration. The topmost contents slid out and clattered on the floor. I closed my eyes, placed my hands on either side of the pedestal sink, and stopped moving. Rex pressed himself against my ankles, and the soft fur of my familiar grounded me a bit, for which I was thankful. So what? The battery to my phone died. No big deal. It happens. There'd still be enough murky light coming through the windows, once my eyes adjusted, to get the job done.

It's not about the dead phone that shouldn't be dead already. It's about everything. About how I'd lived my life sheltered from the world because every time I ventured out from beyond my warded home and business, the world fell apart around me.

I'd never heard the word Summate before. When I did, it was to discover that I was the only witch alive with the ability to harness the powers of any color—prophecy, hexing, healing, love, and anything else. Unfortunately, only one of us emerged every few hundred years, so it wasn't like I had a tutor. LaDonna and the coven surrounded me to help me learn their powers, but they were only ten of... how many colors were there? I'd forgotten that gold was one until Ericka arrived.

Even though I was still discovering how to fully use my newfound abilities, a hint of the constant stream of universal understanding remained with me. Rather than forcing things to happen, it flowed through me, serving as a subtle guiding force that enabled life to unfold with minimal disruptions.

Keeping my eyes closed, I rocked gently from heel to toe, bringing my awareness to the cool tile under my feet, the sound of my breath, the smooth porcelain under my hands. The sound of traffic on Oberon Street became hypnotic. I pulled my awareness in, focusing instead on my connection to the Source, that warm, soothing energy that allowed me to sense the connection of everything on the planet to the universal energy field. It was no surprise to learn that it had slowed to a trickle.

OK, you've found the problem; you've allowed your connection to the Source to become choked off. Now fix it.

Setting my jaw firmly, eyes open but gaze softened, I sent my thoughts outward until I sensed a fraction of the infinity of the cosmos. I revived the awareness of my divinity, my ability to harness the power within the earth under my feet, the air that blew outside and flowed through my lungs, the water in both the clouds overhead and the tap near my fingers, the fire of the sun, and the spark of the spirit within me.

The power swelled, and I pulled it in with my breath, feeling a tingle in my fingertips and a lightness swelling in my filling lungs and heavy heart… and it stopped.

What?

My eyes sprang open wide and shot around the bathroom as if searching for something physical that I had dropped.

That's impossible. That's impossible!

Forgetting the suitcase, I dashed from the room and whipped down the darkened hall to my study, what I called my Room of Power. Rex trotted after me, his paws silent on the floor, his tail swishing in stimulation. The walls appeared less colorful in the dimness, but I had lined them with shelf after shelf of my personal book supply and spelling equipment. More than any room in my house, my Room of Power was where I felt most like myself—my sanctuary within my sanctuary. It was here where I spent my private time casting spells and allowing myself to pour my heart into them. This was where the universe always felt most open to me, and I to it. While casting a spell, the only thing that limited me was the fear that I might take on too much. I'd never thoroughly tested the limits of my power.

Once inside my Room of Power, I closed my eyes again, harkening back to the lingering energy of past spells, the smell of old books, crushed herbs, fragrant candles, and oils. I pulled the memory of previous experiences on starlit nights when the Source had driven me to the point I thought my fingers could ignite, and my body would levitate. I willed my spirit to connect to that flood once more. Or open even a tiny bit more. A drop. Anything.

The connection wasn't broken, but I sure as hell didn't feel like

I had Summate strength, either. I felt like Samson after Delilah tricked him into cutting his hair. He wasn't dead, but his potency was completely gone. (Yes, we witches can be familiar with Bible stories, too.)

My knees weakened, and I sank into the cushy floral chair. Rex jumped into my lap, and I clutched him to my chest like a life preserver.

"Murphy?" Conall's voice called up the stairs from the landing. "You alright up there?"

"No," I said, my voice feeble and shaky. Conall's steps picked up their pace, and he called for me again once he reached the top of the stairs.

"In here," I said miserably.

He came to my side and crouched to face me. "What's wrong?"

"I can't… Conall, I think I've lost hold of my power."

Chapter 12

Conall took my hand, but it wasn't enough. He coaxed me out of the floral chair, sat in my place, and encouraged me to join him in the seat so he could envelop me in his arms. Together, the three of us sat, Conall behind me, Rex in my lap, and it was like being sandwiched in a soothing ball of love. Their calm caressed my heart like a salve. My heart stopped racing, and my panicked thoughts slowed to a reasonable pace.

Assured I wasn't prepared to jump from the second-story window, Conall stood, careful not to disturb Rex much, and set us both back into the flowery chair. He found my suitcase in the bathroom. I heard him shuffle around in the medicine cabinet, adding a couple of items I'd missed, probably his toothbrush and razor, which I had forgotten in my haste. When he returned to my study, he found me in my chair, still in a fetal position, still clutching Rex to my chest.

Conall held out his hand, and I took it, allowing him to pull me to my feet. I gently put Rex on the floor. Conall led me down the stairs and through the kitchen to fill Rex's bowl.

"Litter box?" he asked.

"I just cleaned them. He should be OK for a little while." My voice was small and pitiful, and I hated it.

He nodded, and I stood there, unmoving like a frightened child as he proceeded through the house and locked the doors. He found my laminated "Closed Until" sign, added the date for Tuesday on it in dry-erase marker, and hung it on the door. Damn, it was only Saturday. The utility company wouldn't come out on a Sunday just for me. If they made it out on the earliest business day, it'd still take almost all day Monday to repair the damage. He was right. It was likely that it'd be Tuesday before I could open back up. Tuesday felt like an eternity away.

Rex found me again and wound his way around my feet, and I cherished the affection from my cranky familiar. I let out a sob that sounded like a choked hiccup and bent to pick him up again, holding him once more to my chest. Conall put his arms around the two of us, pulling us close. I half expected Rex to throw a hissy fit at being enveloped again, but he understood my need to have both of them close.

"We could bring him," Conall offered, his chin resting on the top of my head and his neck and body making a canopy over Rex. "I could turn into Rolf and play with him. He'd like that."

I let out a curt laugh. Conall had the power to turn into a squat little dog we called Rolf that looked like a wolf and a Corgi hybrid, thanks to a spell LaDonna had given him. I wagged my head back and forth and sniffed. "You'll get in trouble with your apartment people."

He blew out scornfully and made a dismissive gesture. "Fuck'em. If you need him, we'll bring him."

I loved Conall's disregard for petty rules when it came to preserving my mental health, but I shook my head and set Rex down. Job complete, he scampered off in search of shadows and dust kitties to chase.

"Anything from the fridge you want to salvage?" he asked.

"Shit, I hadn't thought about that." I slapped my forehead and moved my palm down to bury my face.

I half expected Conall to joke about how I should be more experienced with power outages. We live in Alabama, where spring and fall tornados are not only common but expected. He refrained from any attempt at humor.

I dug out a mountain of cloth grocery bags from my pantry, and we loaded them with salvageable food, discarding any out-of-date condiments while we were at it. It didn't take long. I'm not much of a cook.

The work was a welcome distraction, and after we'd added the groceries to the trunk of his Camaro, we drove through the small town of Gryphon to his apartment. He took my hand in his while he steered with the other, the way he often did, and his warm, firm hand felt like an anchor to reality. I feared if I let go, I'd float off and remain in this hellscape where events went awry all the time again. *Dammit, I'd thought I'd left that world behind me.*

Conall slowed down and turned onto Hamlet, the main road through town. Many of the quaint storefronts were decked out for Valentine's Day with hearts, flowers, or other goods for sale in red, white, or pink in the window. The secondhand clothier had red and white outfits, my favorite being a red sparkly gown with a long side slit that reached the thigh.

The story behind the naming of Gryphon's streets had been passed down for generations. The story was that the town founder, Charles Gryphon, wanted the village to be a small hamlet, so that's what he named the first street. From there, the town names grew into other Shakespearean characters. I'm not sure if the story is true, but I've always loved it.

My house is going to be dark on Valentine's Day. Hanna's most recent batch of love spells and decorations would sell late, if at all. Conall and I hadn't talked about doing anything special besides going out to dinner. He said he had reservations at a restaurant in Huntsville, which was a bit of a drive, but not too far. I'd bought him a fancy new opalite dowsing pendulum and board, since he wanted to explore that realm of divination more deeply. He had said nothing about wanting to exchange gifts, but I couldn't let our first official Valentine's Day together go by unrecognized.

Conall's apartment was tucked away behind a small shopping center, a two-story brick and beige-siding complex dubbed Arden Apartments. The name always reminded me of the word "ardor," which I found incredibly adorable when he moved in as a lifelong bachelor. It's amusingly fitting now. The building comprised eight units, with four in the front and another four at the back, offering a pleasant view of a small pond. Conall parked in the designated spot for apartment 2, and we unloaded his car and squeezed my food into his refrigerator.

Conall's upstairs apartment offered around 1200 square feet of functional living space. Unlike my sprawling Victorian house, his place had a minimalist aesthetic with very little clutter. A few framed family pictures adorned the entry table, along with a small altar dedicated to Brigit, the Celtic goddess of arts and prophecy. It wrenched my heart to see the photo of 10-year-old dark-headed Conall next to both of his parents. It was adorably pre-braces, showcasing his charmingly crooked smile and youthful innocence. I couldn't help but wonder if it was the last photograph taken of his mother.

It always struck me as peculiar that the first thing you noticed upon entering Conall's apartment was the dining room table and chairs. Given the open floor plan, I suppose the location of the dining area was trivial. The set, constructed from black and brown wood, was most likely acquired from a run-of-the-mill furniture store in Huntsville with a convenient delivery service. The token piece of décor in the dining room was a mirror that may have been hung on the wall before he'd moved in. Beyond that, the galley kitchen was a pristine white. Casting my gaze to the living room on the right, an unremarkable piece of art hung above a couch that could best be described as a dusty mauve. Conall had acquired the artwork from a home improvement store, and he had purchased a chair to match its unique hue. Hanna accompanied him during the selection process and confided in me she had tried her best to talk him out of them. I couldn't help but agree—the color was a wee bit funky.

His apartment barely looks lived in, I mused, surveying the spotless floors and surfaces. Other than a couple of discarded clothing items on his bedroom floor, the place was remarkably clean—especially for a bachelor. But I guess keeping his apartment tidy was easier since he'd been spending so much time at Blackwell Manor.

Conall set my bag down in his bedroom and met me in the living room. He glanced from the couch to the television and back to me. "Want to watch some TV?" he offered with raised eyebrows.

I shook my head.

"Want to… go for a walk?"

I shook my head again. "Too cold."

"Wine?" he offered, and I laughed.

"I don't think a depressant is a great idea right now."

He pulled me in, his taut arms encircling my waist and drawing me near until our bodies pressed against one another. I buried my head into the crook of his neck and inhaled the clean but masculine smell I knew so well. My hands reflexively clutched his firm back. He drew back and gave me that wide, wicked smile, took my hand, and swung it back and forth playfully.

"Bed?" he said with an arched eyebrow and a sexy smile. I swear every inch of me flushed at once.

I grinned like a fool, my troubles forgotten. "Bed."

He pulled me eagerly down the short hall to his room and turned the light on in his bathroom, leaving the door open a crack. Conall's bedroom was as practical as the rest of his house. With the lights in the bedroom off and only his closet light shedding a faint amber glow into the room, the ambiance was perfect.

Normally, our lovemaking was full of passion and energy. Tonight, Conall posed me at his bed's edge as he slowly eased my shirt over my head and discarded it to the floor, his eyes fixed on mine. He unfastened my brassiere. His coffee-brown eyes fixed on mine as his rough hands caressed my shoulders, breasts, and back. He kissed me gently but hungrily, making my legs shake. I moved to touch him, and he grasped my arms and moved them back to my sides, directing me without saying a word to stay put. He found my waist and followed it to the front of my pants, unfastening them as he kissed my neck and shoulders and nipped my skin playfully. Easing my clothing from my hips, he backed me onto the bed before pulling the last of my clothes off with a softness that made their removal feel like caresses as well. He shed his clothing as I watched, making a show of exposing every part of his muscular frame and his lengthened member before joining me on the bed.

His apartment was warm, thank the goddess. No need for blankets. I wanted to see him in the golden light, feel his well-built body under my hands, the way his shoulders tapered to his waist, and how his ass looked as I gripped it. I wanted to urge his chest to my lips, to taste him. We pressed together, enjoying the sensation of flesh on flesh, weaving our legs together, hands exploring, thrilled with being naked and together. I couldn't get him close enough.

His body was perfect, breathtaking. *He* was breathtaking. When he touched my intimate parts with his solid and practiced fingers, it took no time before it felt like my body was trembling and my breath gasping. I couldn't wait any longer to have him, and I pressed a hand to his chest, urged him to lie down, and he obliged. I straddled his hips and guided him into me. My breath caught as his entire length slid inside, and his groan only heightened my pleasure.

He grasped my hips with powerful hands and urged me, guiding them to a fervent rhythm as his hips thrust upward to match my movement. Gone was the gentleness from moments before; my need had broken through any reservation or docility.

He sat up and clutched me to his chest, kissed me aggressively, and kept me moving along his length as I rose and fell in cooperation with his leading hands, my back arched against his supportive arm. He kissed my neck, my lips, my breasts. Our pace grew more frantic, and I gripped his headboard and clawed it as he drove into me, urging me to an explosive, loud, vocal climax.

Recognizing I had reached my peak, he eased me back, my head facing the footboard, never leaving my body as he did. He placed his arms astride my body, clutched the bed linens, and continued thrusting, my body reaching the heights of pleasure with every push. I gripped his arms, back, and shoulders, encouraging him, wishing this could go on forever, but understanding it could not.

"*Conall!*" I cried, and as if he was waiting for that moment, he pushed inside with one last powerful drive and moaned, a sound that turned me on every time.

Moments later, sweating and entangled in his sheets, we wove our hands the way we often did, and he caressed my palm with his thumb, staring into my satisfied eyes. I nestled my head near his shoulder, resting on his As Above, So Below tattoo, and kissed his chest.

"I want to make you feel better," Conall said.

I laughed and pulled my hand away from his so I could run a finger down his body. "Believe me, you just did," I teased.

He flushed, which I always found so loveable. "No, I mean… you've had so much going wrong lately, and I'd like for one thing to go right. And I think that I might have a way to make one thing go right. At least, I hope I do."

Confused, I cocked my head and regarded him. "What are you talking about? You always make me feel great. You're my one bright spot in this crazy freaking world. You and Hanna."

He propped on an elbow, eager and anxious energy coming off him in waves, his eyes bright. "I… I was going to wait until Valentine's Day, but now I don't think I want to."

He leaned over to get something out of his nightstand and turned on the bedside lamp. I eyed his flexing body in appreciation, wondering what he would say if he saw my unabashed thirst for him. The man was built like a superhero.

When he sat back up, he had a small green box with a gold border in his hand, which he offered to me with an odd sense of reluctance.

"Um, happy Valentine's Day?" he said.

He looked nervous. Why did he look nervous? One side effect

of being a chaos-power-reflecting-witch-turned-Summate: I was the one person on earth whose future Conall found impossible to forecast. Even if he tried to predict how I'd respond to his gift, he couldn't.

It resembled a ring box, and I accepted it with my fingertips. His tension brushed off on me, and I wondered what was eating at him. The container was light, and I resisted the urge to shake it like a little kid with a mystery Christmas present. My eyes darted from it to him and back. I pried it open.

It was a ring box. Inside lay a gorgeous emerald ring with a delicate Celtic knotwork band in an unusually coppery shade of gold. My jaw dropped.

"Conall, it's beautiful! I've never seen anything like it. How on earth did you find it?"

"Luke," he responded. The jewelry maker. Of course, Luke would help. LaDonna undoubtedly also knew about Conall's gift, and neither of them would have said a word to me if Conall had told them it was a surprise.

"It's Welsh gold. And I know how you feel about diamonds, so I thought an emerald would be more fitting, since it's your favorite."

Diamonds? Wait, diamonds are for—
Seeing the revelation dawning on me, Conall gripped my hands as if he feared I'd run away, forcing me to put the box down on the bed and peer into his tense eyes.

"Murphy Blackwell, will you marry me?"

My body grew hot again, this time in astonishment, and my heart nearly stopped. I couldn't stop blinking from all the ecstatic tears rushing to my eyes.

"You—ah, this is an engagement ring?"

"If you want it to be," he said in a rush, as if wishing he could retract his words. "Size six and a half, right?"

I could hardly think. I hadn't expected this. Not in a million years. I had always adored my sweet, smart, funny friend Conall and thought he was mind-bogglingly attractive. But I'd always considered him off-limits because my life had been a total mess.

Conall wanted to marry me. Conall wanted to *marry* me!

I pulled in a shuddering breath, trembling for an additional reason now. I couldn't talk. I felt lucky and terrified and cherished and in love and terrified all over again. But more than anything, I needed to say something soon.

"Murphy?" The strain in his handsome face was painful to see, and I wanted to talk, but a million words fought to be first.

All that matters now is one thing. Do you want to be with Conall for the rest of your life?

Yeah, I did. It didn't matter that I'd never been with anyone else. Conall had been my best friend for twenty years, and I wanted to be with him for the rest of this lifetime and any that might come after.

I lunged at him and knocked him back onto the bed, careful not to drop my beautiful ring. My beautiful *engagement* ring.

"Yes! Yes, oh my god, Conall, yes!"

His eyes lit up, and he let out a pleased laugh as I peppered his face with kisses. He took the box from my hand and slipped the ring onto my finger. It fit perfectly. I laid on my stomach next to him and admired how it sparkled in the glow of the bedside lamp.

"Don't scare me like that again," he scolded.

"Really?" I teased, cocking my head. "What will you do if I do?"

He growled and rolled me over, lifting my arms over my head and pinning my body to the bed with his legs.

"That is not motivation to be good," I laughed. I wiggled my legs out from under him and wrapped them around him. He dove for my neck and nuzzled it fiercely, and I giggled and noticed as I did, he was ready for another round. So was I.

Chapter 13

Sleep wouldn't come. Two rounds of intense lovemaking the knowledge that Conall and I had a wedding in our future had charged me like a lightning bolt. As Conall dozed lightly nearby, his arm slung possessively across my middle, I admired the sparkle of the emerald in the dim rectangle of light from the bathroom.

Blessed. Loved. Contented. Emotions that had been absent from my life for the past few days came back in a rush that left me elated, floating on the proverbial cloud. *If someone had told me a year ago that this would be my life, I would never have believed them. Not in a million years.*

I had a wedding to plan. Wow! Hanna would be my maid of honor, of course. Maybe Betony could be a bridesmaid. And La-Donna would perform the wedding—the handfasting if we stayed traditional, which was customary within the coven. How soon did Conall want to get married? And where? Did he want a big ceremony? I didn't have many friends outside the coven and my customers—a side effect of living as a recluse when I'd thought I was a chaos witch. He had his coworkers and his family on his dad's and mom's side. My family was the coven.

You'll never guess who came by while you were gone. Your father!

Cadence's words returned to me as What will life within Conall's extended family would be like? I knew his father and remembered his mother, but I had met little of his extended family, not being one to observe regular American holidays.

It wasn't my father Cadence had seen. Which meant that either someone was posing as my father—which wasn't likely—or Cadence was hallucinating.

There was no way I would solve any of these questions tonight. I'd meet Conall's extended family when I met them, and if they were anything like he was, it'd go just fine. Thank the goddess, the candy Cadence ate hadn't been poisonous, so that wasn't a problem we'd have to face. If she had hallucinated, Jake's spell had created an odd and unpredictable magical side effect. It was strange, but it shouldn't be a problem for me to heal if it lingered. I'd have to ask Hanna later what all she'd put into her Eros oil and note it for future items I made for the store. The combination of ingredients might have been the trigger for the weirdness.

I caressed Conall's arm, careful not to wake him. Lying in bed beside him was my favorite thing on the planet, but I needed something to do, and sleep was out of the question. Now that I had a small measure of the Source to wield, I could use the time to enhance my magical skills. Although Conall and I had practiced my prophecy at my house a lot, it wasn't a talent I hadn't tested outside of my house. With Conall, one of the most talented orange witches I knew, lying beside me, it seemed as good a time as any.

On a whim, I reached for the Source to see what would happen, and I was thrilled to see the flow had grown more substantial than when I'd last tried at home. It was not the significant flow I was used to, the downpour that swept me away into the wave of the universal force—it felt more like a gentle flow, like from a slightly turned tap—but the information and power were there. One more sign life was looking up.

Still and alert, I let my thoughts get fuzzy, increasing the space between them until the absence of distractions allowed my psychic vision to open. Although the strength of my perception was dimmer than average, I observed how my indigo aura and Conall's aquamarine wove and surged together where we connected, making a beautiful meeting of blues and purples. It was so beautiful I wished I could touch it. Instead, I centered on Conall's aura and his gift of divination, recalling the brilliant blues and golds and diamond-bright stars that danced around him when he did readings. Conall loved helping people see everything—from the joyous occasions to the dangers ahead. He put a trace of himself in every card flip and willed it to show the experiences ahead of his clients. Through the Source, it was like I was reading a recipe and understanding how every ingredient he used played a part in his gift.

I closed my eyes and turned inward, envisioning a single flame at the tip of a light blue candle. The flame burned bright and tall, undulating on a faint breeze that blew only in my mind. As I freed my vision to follow the current into the future, the flame color morphed from gold to yellow, yellow to green, green to royal blue, and then to turquoise, where it stayed.

The turquoise color transfigured into a thick smear of paint on an empty canvas, then a painting of an ocean on a starless night that grew stormy and turbulent, the heavy surf and frothing white-caps crashing violently against a midnight blue coastline. At the far end of the shore, the silhouette of a two-story building emerged from the land. The building solidified into a haunted and forlorn Blackwell Manor, standing alone on the coast. The surf coalesced and expanded into an enormous tsunami that crashed against the walls of my home, wiping it into shambles and sucking it under the colossal wave.

With a gasp, the connection broke. My heart hammered in fear, and my mouth had gone dry. I sat up and gripped Conall's arm, needing his strength.

"Murphy?" Conall said, thick and groggy with sleep. He sat up and brushed my hair out of my face. "What's wrong?"

"I think… I think I'm in danger."

☽○☾

Moments later, Conall had shed any semblance of sleep, and we mulled over the meaning of my prediction together. Interpreting the significance of another witch's vision is often challenging. Emotions and gut instincts that emerge while interpreting the images revealed play a significant role in unraveling their implications. What's felt is every bit as important as what's seen. However, Conall and I shared a bond of love and lifelong friendship, giving him exceptional insight into the workings of my mind. Also, you know… orange witch.

Conall paced the floor at the foot of his bed, hand on his lean hip, as I sat with my arms wrapped around my knees. I seemed to be doing that a lot—curling in on myself like a pill bug protecting its soft parts.

"You said it started as turquoise paint on canvas and turned into a dark sea? Did you have any strong feelings about either the paint or the water? Did a name come to mind as you looked at either one?"

"Not the water," I said with a cock of my head. "The turquoise kind of reminds me of Ericka, though."

"Kind of reminds you, or really reminds you? It's important."

I bit my lip and rocked back and forth on his soft mattress as I strained to remember. Had Ericka come to mind when the color appeared? Or was the color reminding me of her because of her eyes and clothing choices the two times I'd seen her?

"It's hard to tell. I just met her a couple of days ago, and it all happened so fast."

He stopped pacing and stood before me, clad only in a pair of low-slung flannel pajamas. "You could try the Source. You said it was working better now."

Letting go of my knees, I extended my legs, jiggled my shoulders and arms, and forced myself to loosen up. "OK."

I pulled in a deep breath and extended the energy from my body so it connected more intensely with the universal force linking all things. The light stream of energy I'd felt earlier was there—it hadn't grown any more substantial, but it was enough.

Whenever I have a question, my initial instinct is to inquire using words. However, this time, I resisted the urge to verbalize my thoughts. Instead, I let my emotions do the talking, the way La-Donna had taught me. Instead, I drew to mind a single color, like a square paint sample found on home improvement store racks, and I allowed that color to overwhelm my mind.

Turquoise.

That was all it took. The color, previously associated in my mind as a bright, cheerful desert mineral hue, instead triggered thoughts of shattered walls, broken glass, suffocation, devastation, and corruption. The smell of stagnant water and putrid, rotting waste overwhelmed my sinuses, and I choked on the imagined stench. Behind all of it surfaced a monstrous pair of turquoise-blue eyes, wide, unblinking, and oppressive.

"Murphy!" I was unaware I'd hidden behind my hands until Conall dove to my side and peeled them away from my face, his wire-strong grip bordering on painful in his effort to see my expression. "Are you alright?"

My eyes were hot, and I wasn't sure if I was angry, upset, miserable, or terrified. "It's Ericka. It meant her."

"Shit, Murphy. We definitely need to talk to LaDonna about this. This is not good."

I took a deep breath, and my lungs hurt like I'd been running a sprint in sub-zero temperatures.

"It will keep Ericka out of the coven, for sure. But Conall, what does it mean? What is she doing that's so bad?"

He settled on the bed and wrapped an arm around me, resting his hand on my hip. He didn't say it was too bad that I didn't get a clearer picture while I was connected, but I thought it for him. And now, when I reached for a fuller portion of the Source, the flow came in drips and drabs. When I tried to go deeper, the only impression I received was those unblinking turquoise eyes staring at me.

I shuddered, and he pulled me in, so I buried my face in his chest. He smelled like masculine deodorant and sex, and in a heartbeat, I got a little turned on despite myself.

"What can I do to help?" he asked.

He put his fingers under my jaw so we were face to face. His five o'clock shadow had grown in a little more. Did I mention my boyfriend was hot?

"This," I said. "This is what you can do. Listen. Help me think when my mind doesn't want to work right—which is a lot right now. Mostly just be there for me."

He clasped a hand under my chin and drew it nearer so he could kiss me.

"Always," he said.

Oh yeah, we're getting married. A feeble smile rose, and Conall kissed me again. Even his lips were strong. Fiancé. He was my fiancé. Damn, that was going to take some getting used to.

"Tomorrow, or later today, rather, we'll talk to LaDonna," he said. "I don't want to wake her up in the middle of the night, but we need to tell her there's something sketchy about Ericka as soon as we can."

"Yeah. Good idea,"

"What do you think about going back to Witch's Brew first so I could do a reading for you? My favorite deck is in my reading room, and I want to use my best equipment for this."

I pulled at a tiny piece of fuzz from the blanket and let it drift to the floor, watching it as it coasted down to the carpet. Just the thought of returning to my place made me nervous after watching it reduced to rubble in my mind.

"You've never been able to read me before," I reminded him.

Not that he needed reminding.

"It's been a while," he said. "And I've improved my skills since then. Plus, now that you've learned you're the Summate, things have changed. There's something else that probably affects us too... you know..."

"That we've been intimate?" I suggested, arching an eyebrow with a half-smile.

His expression switched from concerned to positively wicked in a flash.

"Yeah, intimate," he said, his voice lower than before. "It might make a difference."

I touched the outside of his thigh, caressed it, and said, "Well, maybe we should be intimate again. In case it helps."

He positioned himself in front of me, a hand placed on either side of my body, leaning in like a predator.

"Well, if it helps."

Chapter 14

The coffee smell was nearly as good as the coffee itself; Conall always sprang for the good stuff. This morning, the flavor I chose (from his selection of bags with *Witch's Brew* printed on them) was Highlander Grog, one of my favorites. The aroma of coffee blended with butterscotch, rum, caramel, and vanilla notes. I pulled two mugs from the cupboard and topped them off with coffee creamer from his refrigerator, which now held more of my food than his.

I tiptoed to his bedroom, wary about spilling the dark beverage on his light beige carpet. One benefit to having wooden floors—even old, squeaky ones—is that they don't stain.

Pausing in the doorway, I admired Conall as he slept. He snored lightly, and after the first night when he'd stayed over, I found it to be a soothing white noise. Now I struggled to sleep without it on nights he stayed at his place. One arm lay draped over the blue and white striped blanket, a brawny shoulder ending in hands I loved well, hands that had explored every part of my body.

I perched on the edge of the bed and set the coffee cups on his nightstand. Either the movement of the mattress or the smell of coffee roused him, maybe both. His sleepy brown eyes opened with a smile as I sat up.

"Morning, beautiful," he said.

"Morning," I murmured, feeling my face color in pleasure.

He sat up and accepted the cup I offered, the blanket falling to his waist. I couldn't help it—I looked. He noticed. I gave him a meaningful smile, which he returned with interest and a waggle of his eyebrows. If we kept going like this, we'd never leave his apartment.

We've never had a day off together. Either he'd had to go to his nine-to-five construction job, or I was running the store. It was the weekend. He didn't work, and my store was closed until the weatherhead was fixed. *Oh, the potential.*

"Why don't we talk to LaDonna this morning and get that out

of the way, and then we can come back here," I suggested.

"And do what?" he teased, his eyes flirty over the rim of his coffee cup.

"Oh," I said, leaning in. I tilted forward, my eyes on Conall's lips, my body craving the rest of him. I took his cup away and put it on the nightstand next to mine. "I can think of a few things."

)O(

After we shared a shower and I changed clothes, we contacted LaDonna and inquired if we could come by her place for a few minutes. Sure, telling her over the phone would have been quicker, but news like this was better delivered in person. She invited us over for brunch, which we happily accepted. Conall and I loved LaDonna's cooking. The woman even made grits taste good—and despite being born and raised in Alabama, I'm *not* a fan of grits. Maybe saying that as a Southerner is right up there with confessing I don't go to church. But hey, I don't do that, either.

The winding roads up to LaDonna's unique architectural masterpiece—half treehouse, half cathedral—were more fun in Conall's sportscar. The Camaro took the corners much better than my Corolla would have dreamed. We sped up the winding wooded road that hugged the hillside of Ladonna's neighborhood nestled in the Appalachian foothills. I could smell the spring lurking just beneath the chilly late winter air. After an evening—and a morning—spent in Conall's arms, I had a hard time believing anything could go wrong. The heaviness lingering on my chest eased in the crispness of the morning air and the rev of his car's V8 engine. The drone of the tires on the road, damp with early morning rain, soothed my frazzled nerves.

A massive buck darted around the corner in front of the car. Conall slammed on the brakes, missing the deer. Not fast enough, though, to avoid the enormous silver SUV coming from the other direction that had swerved and crossed lanes to evade the deer. It smashed into the Camaro's front quarter panel and driver's side door with a terrifying crash. Conall propelled toward me as his side airbag deployed. I winced as glass from Conall's window sprayed into the car and across my face. The seatbelt painfully restrained my body. The SUV had too much momentum to stop after impact, forcing us into the guardrail. With the screech of metal on metal, the Camaro tilted toward the passenger side, and I realized with horror the railing wouldn't hold.

"Conall!" I screamed, reaching for him in fear and discovering he'd done the same. Helpless until the car stopped moving against its will, we gripped each other's glass-scraped hands like lifelines. For an instant, I thought we would tip over onto the roof, maybe roll several times, or collide with a tree, or both. With a metallic grind, the car slid to a halt, and the twisted guardrail stared at me through the windshield. A spiderweb of shattered glass on Conall's side obscured my view to the SUV's crushed hood, which was embedded in Conall's door. The airbag also blocked my view, and I could not see how the other driver had fared. What it did not block, however, was the treacherous drop-off on the other side.

"Murphy?" Conall said, his voice remarkably calm.

"I'm OK." My voice shook, and my nerves sang with adrenaline. "Are you OK?"

He licked his lips, his eyes shooting around as he gathered his thoughts. "I think so. Listen, honey, I need you to do me a favor."

"What?"

"You need to be super careful when you get out and try not to open your door any further than necessary."

His request confused me. I checked the view out the window. There was a steep drop-off, but I thought I could handle it if I was cautious. "Why not?"

"I'm pretty sure we're just hanging here."

I peered out of my window and reevaluated the portion of the car on the road versus the part hanging over the edge. He was right. *Shit. Shit. Are we going to tip over? How steep is this hill? I can't even see where the ground starts from my window!*

"Let me… let me try something first."

He swallowed hard and waited, anxiety evident on his tense features.

I pulled in a shaky breath and tried to summon the Source. Then I tried again. All I needed was enough to stabilize the vehicle long enough for us to climb out. But it wouldn't remain steady—the flow was still stop and start the way it had been at Conall's. Definitely not enough to trust with the weight of a sports car.

"No good," I told him. "Should we wait?" My strained voice

struggled to be as composed as his had been, but failed.

"No," he said. "No, I'm not sure we won't fall before help gets here."

I made a slight noise intended to be an "Mm-hm" that wound up being a whimper.

He squeezed my hand. "Murphy, hey. Listen. You got this. Undo your seatbelt, crack your door slowly, and ease yourself out. When you get out, move where the car can't roll toward you if it falls. I'll be right behind you."

"Make sure you're behind me so you can take the door and it doesn't fall all the way open, OK?"

"OK. I will."

Every part of me quaked, but he squeezed my hand again and gave me that ridiculously calm expression he did so well. For the first time, I saw the terror behind his steady brown eyes.

"You got this," he assured me again.

Treating the car as if made of dynamite, I undid my seatbelt and cautiously pulled the door handle. It eased open instead of falling, and I breathed a little easier. The smell of oil, burned rubber, and cold woodsy air hit me at once, and I almost coughed, but I fought it back in the fear that it might rock the car.

I braced myself on the doorframe and eased one Converse-clad foot out onto the steep slope, probably around sixty degrees, and added the other foot once I thought I had sufficient purchase on the wet ground. My feet slipped on the muddy hillside. My first impulse was to grip the car to keep from dropping, but I let go and slid about ten feet before my hand wrapped around a sapling.

"Murphy!" Conall's voice held a panic I'd never heard before.

"I'm fine!" I called back. The door had slipped from my grip, and it and the car moved more than I was comfortable with. My palm was scraped, my pants were soaked, and I'd skinned the hell out of my cheek, but I was okay.

"Holy mother goddess," I heard him say, his deep, relieved voice carrying on the cold air.

It wasn't until I saw how the Camaro dangled off the edge that I understood how accurate Conall's deduction was. Climbing out of the driver's side window wasn't possible for him; the SUV had wedged into the door. He'd have to clamber over to the passenger side and exit like I had. My throat tightened in fear.

How much does Conall weigh? A hundred and eighty pounds? I ventured. Maybe more. Muscle weighs more. And the door's hanging wide open now. What if he tips the car?

The vehicle rocked in place a bit as Conall switched seats. If it fell, I was in precisely the wrong place to avoid being crushed. Clambering on my hands and feet and slipping on the wet brown leaves, I crawled to the left to get out of the path. I watched as Conall eased to the passenger's side with my heart in my throat. My mouth hung open, and I watched as his once-beautiful blue sports car wavered precariously with every one of his cautious movements.

Please, mother goddess, please father god, keep him safe. Keep him safe. Keep him safe.

The balance of the car tilted like scales with every movement he made. I wanted to clutch my stomach, place my freezing cold palms together, and run up to help him, but I could only watch with my heart hammering in my chest.

He made it to the doorway and paused, evaluating the angle of the slope. He noted where I was in relation to the car and seemed satisfied.

I wondered again how the other driver had fared. I hadn't seen or heard from them.

Conall extended one leg and then another, as I had, only he didn't slip the way I did. His height gave him an advantage. His feet found a slanted, but firm, foothold on the ground, and he edged his body from the car and took a few hunched steps toward me. Satisfied that he'd successfully escaped, he raised to his full height just as the car tipped and dislodged from the guardrail.

Chapter 15

The sound that issued from my mouth was not a warning so much as a scream of terror. Conall whipped around to see what had happened and fell, landing heavily on his side as the Camaro dropped onto its passenger side and slid toward him, tilting onto its roof as it traveled directly for my tumbling fiancé.

"Noooo!"

Without conscious thought, my actions unfolded. In less than a heartbeat, I lifted my hands, using every cell in my mind, body, and spirit as I reached for the Source. The surge overwhelmed me, threatening to sear through my very nerves. Focusing my will, I channeled it all into the car and my partner. With the authority of the universe mine to wield, I encased Conall in an impenetrable shield of earth while simultaneously unleashing a tremendous burst of air to lift the car from its current trajectory. The Camaro flew as if launched from a catapult over Conall and bounced down the hill, only to slam with a loud crash into a short-leaf pine.

"Conall!" I scrabbled on my hands and knees to his side, my every muscle aching as if I'd just finished a marathon. Had I acted fast enough? Was he alright?

"Conall!" Dirt covered him from the collapsing wall I'd built. His lungs were heaving, and he was coughing. That was a good sign. "Are you hurt?"

"No. Holy shit, what the hell happened?" He blinked and saw where his car was lodged halfway down the steep hill, having taken a path that defied the laws of physics. He turned to the street and pivoted back around, doing the mental math as he did.

"How—?"

"I—I did it," I admitted, almost embarrassed to say it. It felt like bragging to say I had hurled a vehicle over Conall's head to save his life.

"What exactly did you do?" We reached for each other as we spoke, taking comfort in one another's presence, grateful that we were both still breathing.

"I saw the Camaro was falling, and I shielded you and lifted the car over you." I winced as something broke off the Camaro with a crack. I saw the wheel, the CV joints, and some stem I didn't recognize still attached at the center on the pine needles below the car.

"You did?" Conall cried with delight, bringing my focus back to him. "That's great! You touched the Source, then."

"I did," I admitted. "I needed it, and it was there. A lot of it."

Movement emerged from the top of the hill. The driver of the SUV, I assumed, peered his craggy face over the edge warily. "Y'all alright?" he asked. I fought back a biting retort when I saw the massive bruise forming on his broad forehead and noticed that his forearm was bleeding where it protruded from the cuff of his flannel shirt. I wanted to be angry with him for almost killing us, but I was also sure it resulted from a knee-jerk reaction from trying to avoid the deer.

"We'll be fine," I assured him.

"I've called nine-one-one," he said. His non-bleeding hand held a cell phone at his side. He scanned up and saw where Conall's car leaned against the pine farther down the hill. "Well, that's a damnable thing," he commented incredulously. "I'm sorry about your car, man. That deer—"

Conall held up a hand to stop him. "It's just a car. We're all alive, and that's what matters."

The man at the top of the hill nodded, grateful at Conall's understanding, and turned his attention to the emergency operator on the other end of the phone.

"You're back in touch with the Source? Physically intact?" His fingers brushed the scrape along my face, and worry painted his handsome features.

I laughed, surprising myself at the relief that had washed over me now that the worst was over. "It must have been the panic that plugged me in. And I'm not the one who almost got squashed by a car!"

"Thank you for saving me." He took a deep breath, and I noticed he was still shaking: the fingertips at my chin trembled with lingering fear. Not that I blamed him—my nerves felt jangled too. His expression softened, and he embraced me so tightly I could barely breathe. I didn't say anything, but I hugged him back tightly, grateful for his beating heart and the air filling his lungs. Conall was still alive.

He leaned back, and when he shouted to the universe, I heard it from deep inside his chest where my ear pressed against him.

"Thank you!"

)O(

Conall made his way to the car, surveyed the damage, and returned with his cell phone, which he found in the leaves on his way down. He brushed it off on his jeans, which weren't much cleaner, and called LaDonna to tell her what happened. I heard the concern in her voice over the speaker from where I sat. Within minutes, her vintage green Mercedes pulled to the side of the road as the police, two fire trucks, and an ambulance arrived.

Two ambulances in less than a week. It felt like when I was back in high school and went through a brief stint of rebelling by trying to live everyday life outside the warded walls of LaDonna's house. She'd tried to be supportive, but it had to be hard for her to watch me making disastrous choices. Literally. Chaos followed me everywhere, and I caused car accidents, broken bones, lost friendships, indescribable weather oddities, broken relationships… the list was a long one. Well, technically, Betony caused it, but since she was not even old enough for kindergarten, I don't hold it against her.

LaDonna approached the broken edge of the guardrail as the firefighters disembarked their vehicle. She followed the trail from the broken railing to the ravaged ground and traced the path to the undisturbed grass beyond us. She saw where Conall's car had lodged against the tree, saw where he and I were still sitting, crouched in the wet dirt together. After doing the mental math, LaDonna cocked her head at us and smiled with her timeless, perceptive smile. Without a word, she stepped away so the emergency responders could do their job.

)O(

Conall snapped some pictures of his car and the damaged guardrail from the base of the incline and called his insurance company. I wondered what the insurance company would make of the odd path the car had made to wind up where it did. I don't think his policy covered "My fiancée is a superpowered female who hurled my sportscar through the air to save my life."

Satisfied he'd captured the requisite images, he studied how the car was positioned against the tree. He cocked his head, furrowed his brow, and disappeared from my view for a moment, reappearing once more with my tiny purse. I let out a choked laugh, and he beamed like a child proud of his crayon art.

"Thought you might need this," he said as he dangled it before me from the long straps.

"Thank you," I said, accepting it with an odd sense of relief. The familiar weight of my cell phone and wallet were in there. I pulled the phone out, and it came alive just fine, no cracks in the screen, thank goodness. It was one of the few positive outcomes since the deer darted in front of Conall's car.

Another damned deer. Is this one connected to the others? What in the hell does it mean?

The firefighters rappelled down, and we allowed them to take what I felt were drastic measures, buckling us into an odd safety harness to aid us back up the ledge. LaDonna waited impatiently to embrace us. Her body, although curvy, felt tiny after holding Conall in my arms so often.

The cops had taken everyone's statements, and we had swapped insurance information with the SUV driver. The tow truck operator provided the contact number for the towing location. We waited until the firefighters and tow truck driver were winching the Camaro up before we joined LaDonna in her car.

An odd sadness settled over me as I opened the Mercedes' creaky car door and sat behind LaDonna. After moving out of his father's house, the Camaro had been Conall's first big purchase, and he'd loved it. No thanks to whatever mysterious forces had been trailing me again, it was destroyed. I flashed back to my premonition and the destruction it had predicted. Was this the first of many things destroyed in my near future?

We pulled away from the curb as the car crested the hill. The guardrail had been reduced to a large lump of useless, twisted metal.

I resolved to make it up to Conall somehow.

）O（

Brunch became a late lunch at LaDonna's. Conall fielded phone calls with his insurance company and the rental car company as my foster mother put together plates of leftovers drawn from what she and Luke had eaten for dinner the night before. The smell of warm turkey sandwiches on whole-grain bread with sides of tossed salad and kettle-cooked potato chips and stuffing was delicious, but my stomach wasn't so sure. Luke and Betony joined us, dressed in casual winter clothes. I don't think I'd ever seen Betony in sweatpants before, but she made them stylish with her hair in an elegant braid and her makeup applied with polish.

We gathered in the soft high-back chairs around the long table in her dining room and made small talk. LaDonna offered Conall the use of her Mercedes while he waited for the insurance to pan out, and he said he'd consider it. I tried to eat. My stomach felt hollow, but my nerves were still too frayed and raw from the narrowly-escaped danger that morning. I ate the stuffing, which is my favorite food in the entire world, and a bite or two of turkey, but picked at the rest of the food, wishing for more of an appetite.

Since Conall had wiped out everything on his plate, I offered him what remained on mine, and he placed my plate on top of his and dug in. I swear, the man is unflappable and always hungry. I guess he's got to feed his muscles. Not that I'm complaining.

LaDonna noticed I'd finished my food, and she brushed her fingers off on a cloth napkin. "You two were heading over to talk about something before the accident. Are you ready to have that conversation, or should it wait for another day?"

"Does it have to do with that ring on her finger?" Luke asked, his eyes quick and his mouth turned up at the corners.

I pulled my lips in and bit them to suppress a grin as my high priestess's eyes shot to my left hand. "Conall!" she exclaimed, slamming both palms on the table.

"I couldn't wait for Valentine's Day," he fessed up. "She was having a rough week, and I hoped it would make her happy."

"Is that what I think it is?" she asked. "And did it make you happy?"

"An engagement ring? Yes," I said. "And yes, it made me ecstatic

She and Betony squealed so loud I thought I'd go deaf for a

moment.

"Blessed Lord and Lady! Congratulations!" LaDonna verily leaped from her chair to embrace both of us, followed closely by Betony. Luke gave Conall a handshake and a brotherly pat on the back before hugging me and kissing me on the cheek. Everything was all smiles for a few sweet moments, and we settled back into our chairs.

"Did you come to plan the wedding, then?" LaDonna's eyes sparkled with eagerness.

"Not yet," I said. "There's something else we need to talk about first."

For the next few moments, I unraveled the events that had transpired since Thursday. LaDonna and Luke took it all in, and Luke, also an orange witch, posed insightful questions about the vision much the way Conall had. The high priestess's eyes narrowed, and her jaw tightened as she heard my conclusion that Ericka harbored a destructive secret. She rested her chin on her hand as she pondered.

Conall laid a hand on top of mine as I wrapped up my story. "I suggested I do a reading for her to see if I could gain some insight."

"I could help," Luke offered.

"I'd like to go back to Murphy's place to do it," Conall added. "My deck is there."

LaDonna agreed. "Using a deck with the energy you've imbued is always good. I want to go with you as well."

"Can I help, too?" Betony offered.

"Whoa, whoa, whoa," I said with my hands up in protest. "I saw my house *collapse* in this premonition. The last thing I need is for all of you to come with me and put yourselves in potential danger. If Conall is set on using his deck, he should run in, grab it, and run right back out. We can do the reading here if y'all want to be part of it."

"I disagree, Murphy," LaDonna replied. "The premonition involved your home. It is the last place you saw Ericka, and it's where all the misfortune has come to pass—until this morning's incident with the car. That's where Conall will find the most power in his reading. The closer, the better."

"I don't have power," I reminded her. *In my house, at least. In my mind, body, and spirit—well, that seems to be hit-or-miss.*

"We can bring my lanterns."

"I don't want anyone inside!" I insisted. "Whatever is causing all of this is manipulating the physical world. It bent my— whatchamacallit?"

"Weatherhead," Conall said, finishing the last of his—my— lunch with a bite of crunchy potato chip.

"My weatherhead. It killed my electricity. It has hurt my house, which in turn hurts my finances and my customers. There was a car wreck in front of my building, where the street should have been magically warded. What if this power is what gave Jake the idea to act recklessly? Cadence could have *died*. It's probably what caused that deer to trigger the car wreck—"

"It's possible," LaDonna conceded.

"I'm just—I don't want anyone else to get hurt. I'm wondering if I'm putting y'all in danger just by being here."

"We could compromise," Betony said. "Go to Murphy's place, but do the reading outside. You have a firepit in your backyard, don't you, Murph?"

"I have dry firewood in the den," LaDonna offered.

I mulled over Betony's suggestion, trying to poke holes in it. We could always die en route to Blackwell Manor. The building could collapse while Conall was inside or tilt over on top of us while we were in the backyard. One of us could catch fire.

It was as if the chaos in my life had never left.

Conall shook my hand, jolting me from my somber thoughts. His furrowed eyebrows and determined expression, a blend of concern and conviction. He believed a card reading using tools infused with his own energy would give us a glimpse into our future. Although he'd never had success reading me before, it was easy to tell how important this was to him.

"Fine," I said. "But Conall, you go in, grab your cards, and get your ass out. Don't stay in there. I don't trust that house right now. Not after–" The memory of seeing my home and business wash away made me shudder.

He nodded, and we set to work.

Chapter 16

The five of us loaded into LaDonna and Luke's SUV and drove down the hill to my house. As we passed the broken guardrail where Conall and I had crashed only a short time ago, I tried to peer over the drop-off to view the damage, but the drop-off was too steep to see anything but the mangled guardrail. The only other evidence of the accident was the rubber tire track marks and the disheveled gravel by the side of the road.

The drive through the woods set my teeth on edge. A sense of foreboding turned every shadow into a demon, every tree appeared skeletal. Every trick of light filtering through the bare tree branches became a sinister being come to release turmoil in our path.

We arrived at Witch's Brew an hour after we'd set our plan into motion, and the hazy golden sun was already low in the cloudy, gray sky. LaDonna, Betony, and Luke went to work grabbing logs, kindling, and newspapers from the Whelen's vehicle for the back-yard fire pit. I wanted to help them, but more than that, I felt compelled to observe Conall during his brief trip into the store to get his tools. Maybe I was being paranoid, but it wasn't a risk I was willing to take.

We trudged up the short staircase and crossed the veranda, where Conall unlocked the front door.

"I'd prefer it if you stayed here," he told me, his hands gripping my upper arms to ensure I faced him. "It's twenty steps there and back, and you can watch me through the window and see that I'm alright."

I concurred. If things took a turn for the worse while Conall was inside, it'd be easier for him to dash out the door safely alone. He kissed me on the forehead and hugged me.

My face was inches from the front door glass, so close my breath left oblong patches of fog that obscured my view. It felt al-most anticlimactic as Conall strode through the shop with familiar ease, drew back his navy privacy curtain with the constellations on it, withdrew his cards from his walk-in closet-sized office, and met me again outside.

"See?" he said, "Piece of cake."

Piece of cake, my ass. Conall's voice told me he was as relieved as I was that his quick trip was uneventful. I smirked. Conall chuckled and he took my hand as we descended the steps. We followed the stepping stones around the carport to join our friends in the backyard.

Another feature I loved about my old house—I had a wide veranda in the front, a side porch, and a back porch. My back porch led to a large concrete area where I did my outdoor spelling. I'd spared no expense to have a colorful compass professionally painted onto the concrete with accurate cardinal and ordinal directions. I had positioned my firepit at the southerly point, close to the porch overhang, but not dangerously so.

My friends had created a teepee of wood and paper in the firepit and were trying to light it. The wind fought them with every flick of the lighter, and the set of LaDonna's mouth reflected an uncharacteristic impatience.

"May I?" I asked.

LaDonna stepped back, motioning to the fire to show I was welcome to try whatever I had in mind. "Do you need the lighter?"

I swung my head back and forth with a suppressed smile, and Luke and Betony stepped back to watch.

Peering past the logs, I fixed on a spot at the center of the cone and imagined it smoking hot, with crackling flames, the molecules racing as they gained energy. The hold I had on the Source felt shaky, as if I was trying to direct a thin metal rod that had expanded and begun to bend. Perhaps a holdover from the car accident this morning? I had no way to know. I ignored the sense of instability and thought, *Cool as water, hot as fire, let my will ignite this pyre.*

A white-hot glow appeared in the center of the wood and paper, and from there, a loud *pop!* told me it had combusted, but with a little more power than I'd intended. The log teepee had turned into a blazing sunburst with waist-high flickering flames. I was relieved everyone had stepped back; if they hadn't, we might have had a couple of injuries.

"Um…fire's lit," I joked weakly.

Betony, always the first one to make light of a situation, giggled, and the rest of us joined in her infectious laughter. Luke grabbed the tongs and set to righting the logs inside the metal basin instead of around the edges.

"Hello?" a familiar voice called. "Murphy, are you home? Conall?"

Cadence?

"Back here, Cady!" Betony shouted.

I was relieved to hear the cheerful tone in Betony's voice. Either she'd forgiven Cadence for mooning over Rene or realized the poor girl wasn't to blame for falling into a love spell.

The creak of my gate hinges sounded from behind me, and I turned as Cadence joined us with a radiant smile and a bounce to her gait. "Murphy! Hey, I came by to tell you something I re-membered about yesterday, so you knew I wasn't crazy." She glanced around the yard at each of us, and then her eyes lit up. "Oh hey, good! Your father found you!" she exclaimed, her eyes aiming at a spot of empty air. As far as I could tell, she was staring at the fence at the back of my small patch of yard.

"My—father?" Why I turned my head to see what Cadence was seeing, I don't know. I allowed my third eye to open and pan the yard for ghosts, but came up empty. The lack of energy that another entity would have emitted told me that there was no one there, but my head still swiveled to see what she meant. "Cadence, there's no one there."

"Murphy, c'mon! Stop messing with me." Cadence laughed nervously, her expression begging me to tell her I was playing, that she didn't imagine him.

"She's not messing with you," Conall insisted. "Cadence, we don't see anyone."

Cadence's cheerful gait screeched to a halt, and she studied each of our faces to see if we were joking with her. Our somber ex-pressions convinced her we weren't.

"He's… he's right…" she lifted a hand and motioned to a spot between Betony and Luke.

"Cady, honey, there's no one there," Betony whispered.

"I can prove it!" Cadence insisted with a frustrated stomp of her foot. "Murphy said she's never seen her father looks like. Did anyone else know him? Conall? LaDonna?"

"Luke and I do," LaDonna said, resting a hand on Luke's arm to point to whom she meant. It wasn't much in the way of an introduction, but it'd have to do for now.

"He's tall," Cadence said, eyeing the empty space, "Dark hair, like Conall's, only he's whiter. Um… lighter-skinned. And blue eyes. His hair is short but wavy like it'd be curly if he grew it out."

LaDonna and Luke concurred, but she might have been lucky and chosen characteristics not uncommon to white people of Irish descent, which I may have mentioned he was. I might have been less doubtful if she'd revealed a standout feature like a scar, a tattoo, or an unusual smile.

"You said you could hear him before, right?" Conall said.

Cadence nodded, her jaw jutting out as she crossed her hands over her chest and shifted her weight to one foot. "Yeah. I can hear him. I can't believe y'all can't."

"Ask him what his name is," Conall said.

Cadence watched the presence and raised her eyebrows to say, "Well?" Satisfied with whatever answer she was given, she gave a curt bob of her head. "He said his name is Ryan. Ryan Turner."

My foster parents' bodies stiffened as LaDonna's pine green eyes grew twice their normal, already considerable size, and Luke's knees visibly weakened.

Cadence was right.

Chapter 17

Conall's tarot reading forgotten, we gathered around the fire in my squishy patio chairs. Fresh logs added to the pit to heighten the warmth as the sun set, and we leaned in to talk over the flames.

"Why do you think she can see things we can't?" I asked. "I've always had a sense when someone was there before, and I haven't felt anything since—" *Since the day stuff started falling off the walls.*

"Was that you knocking stuff over the other day?" It felt silly directing my attention to the empty air since I couldn't tell where he stood. *He. My father? Ryan? What should I call him?*

It was eerie the way Cadence observed the words and motions of an entity more ethereal than a ghost.

"He said yes, it was," she relayed to us.

"Was there a significance to the deer?"

She listened again, her head tilted as if straining to hear, and said, "I can't say that." Cadence paused. "Say it one more time." Another pause. Waggled her head back and forth in frustration. Finally, she told us, "He said his middle name is Uhsheem? I don't know. It's not—I can't—"

"Oisin," LaDonna confirmed, giving it the proper Irish lilt, making it sound like *ush-EEN*. "That's what Nora used to call him. She said Ryan was too common for someone so uncommon."

"What does that have to do with the deer?" I asked.

"Oisin means faun or little deer," Luke explained. My Irish Gaelic was almost nonexistent, and I'd always wished my foster family had upheld the tradition and had taught me the language, even if it was dying. It's so beautiful, and it always sounded more like singing than talking to my untrained American ear.

"He said he doesn't understand why you can't see him," Cadence added. "He knows you can see ghosts."

"Maybe he's not a typical ghost? Maybe he's something else."

Conall had a point. I had always suspected that between the realm of the dead and the eternal spirits were beings who were hard to pinpoint—ones that had either once been alive or had been other-than-spiritual, but never wholly corporeal. If my father was one of those beings, it would explain why I hadn't seen him and why I'd never sensed him.

"Has he been trying to reach me long?" I directed my question at Cadence, because where else would I look?

Her head swiveled to the space between LaDonna and me and then pivoted back. "No. He said he must have been someplace else for several years because the last time he received a picture of you, you were only maybe eight? And your mother was alive. And he went… where he was not long after that."

I knew my mother had stayed in touch with him, but she never told me she'd sent him pictures. Why hadn't she told me? What was the big secret that kept him from my life?

Feeling both a bit touched and creeped out, I swallowed a hard lump in my throat. If I was eight, that would have been right around when my father died of a brain tumor, if my estimation was correct, and about two years before I lost my mother.

"Why are you here now, Ryan?" I asked. "Do you know?"

We stayed quiet while Ryan Turner briefly explained his story to Cadence. He was unloading a lot of information if the way Cadence's eyes followed his invisible hands and body language was any sign—whatever he was doing, it was adamant. Finally, Cadence held up a hand to stop him.

"Hold on, hold on, let me tell them that part before you keep going on, or I'll mess it up." She sighed, gripped the metal arms of the chair, and sat up. "OK, Mama Murph. He says he doesn't know exactly when he arrived back on earth because it didn't happen all at once—it was gradual. He said a lot more about that part, but it was really confusing. Anyway, when he was finally able to think using language—that's how he said it—he had this really bad need to come here and help you."

"Is he here to help me deal with this streak of bad luck I've been dealing with? Am I in danger? Does he know why it's happening? Does his presence have anything to do with Betony? Does Ericka play a part in this?"

Betony, who until then did not suspect that I thought she might be the problem, sat back and eyed me with confusion and hurt.

"One question at a time! Jeez!" Cadence directed her eyes back at Ryan and waited for his response. After a moment, she motioned for him to stop so she could speak. "Yes, he knows what's happening. No, it doesn't have to do with Betony doing anything wrong. But… Goddamn, this is a lot. Hold on, let me get all of this straight in my head first. There's another coven, and they are a… dark coven? Does that make sense? And he's been spying on them."

The rest of us nodded, and she continued.

"They tried to make their own Summate the night they killed Murphy's parents. But that didn't work, so this dark coven wants the chaos witch to be superior to the Summate now."

"It's the coven that killed our mothers," Conall breathed, his deep voice a hoarse whisper. "Holy mother goddess. They're back."

"My parents were part of that coven," Betony said, her eyes glassy and regretful. I didn't blame her—she was only a newborn. Her parents were trying to instill Betony with power they planned to steal from the Lughaidh coven. From me. Betony carried the burden of knowing her parents were responsible for the death of Conall's, Hanna's, and my mother.

"I can't be superior to Murphy," Betony argued. "Murphy has the powers of every witch color. I only have one."

A slight pause as Cadence listened with an ear cocked. "He said gray witches are more powerful than almost all other witches because they can cause chaos in other witches' lives, including the Summate's."

"Is that true?" Betony directed her question at LaDonna and me.

"It would explain why the universe only allows them on the earth every few centuries and always puts them near a Summate. That way, they can balance one another," LaDonna said.

My eyebrows arched as she unraveled her theory. It made sense. The universe wouldn't want two superpowered witches on the planet simultaneously without them being able to counterbalance one another.

"Betony, I secluded myself for my entire life trying to avoid ricocheting the gray energy you unintentionally put into the world," I reminded her. "Yes, it's possible. I'd bet a trained gray could outmatch an untrained Summate."

It made me wonder if there was a more significant reason for Betony and me to be on the planet together. Surely living in tiny

Gryphon, Alabama, our whole lives wasn't all there was to our existence if all we did was save one another from sending the world into a tailspin? Did the Universe have a greater plan in mind for us?

Cadence cocked her head as she listened to the unheard voice once more. Her body went stock still at something he shared, and her hands covered her mouth, although her face had become a mask.

"He says the goal of the dark coven is to let chaos loose on the world. They know you're the Summate. Now, the only way the gray can become the most superior witch is if the Summate is—is killed."

Oh, great.

Chapter 18

Cadence's last comment met with dead silence. Her story had unraveled so quickly, I had failed to follow the line of logic to its foreseeable conclusion until the words were out. Now everything clicked into place. The events from last October were only the beginning. Discovering I was the Summate. Betony killing her hateful, child-molesting father and going to juvenile detention. Betony learning how to focus her gray energy positively by helping other juvenile offenders do shadow work. Now, this. It was all connected.

Is Betony's mother still involved with them? Does she resent her daughter for running off and joining the witches she and her husband tried to kill to empower their daughter?

I had so many questions my head hurt, and I turned a pained face to Conall, who looked ready to swath me in bubble wrap and stick me in a padded room.

"We're all going to face this together," I assured him. "No hiding or trying to muddle through life like every-thing's fine. We'll figure it out; we'll figure *them* out. And we'll fight back."

Cadence's hands clutched her head, and she swung it back and forth a few times, her eyes shut as if she shared the headache pulsing in my skull.

"What's wrong, Cadence?" Betony asked. She rose and moved to her friend's side, placing a concerned hand on her back as Cadence bowed at the waist and put her elbows on her knees, her head buried in her hands.

"Headache," Cadence said. "I've been getting them a lot lately."

"Since yesterday?" I ventured, and her head bobbed, but she didn't lift it from her hands. I shot an intense glance at Conall and stepped away from the group. "Excuse me. I'm going to make a quick phone call."

Maybe saving a teen from the side effects of a love spell wasn't the most critical thing in the world, given that I'd just learned a coven of dark witches was out to kill me and unleash global chaos.

I hated to see Cadence in pain, though. She was such a sweet kid. I didn't want to take drastic action if it was just a headache, so I needed to call Hanna and learn what Miriam had told her about that last ingredient. I'd have called Miriam, but I had wedding news to share.

Hanna answered after the second ring sounding like she'd run to the phone. "Murphy! Hey, I've been worried about you!"

Her heightened alarm confused me. "You have?"

"I've been trying to call you, but you haven't answered!" She sounded more than worried; she sounded almost panicked. "Are you alright? Is Cadence? What's going on?"

My plan to tell her about the wedding and the dark coven took a backseat for the moment. "Is there a reason Cadence wouldn't be OK? Did Miriam find out something bad about the Eros oil?"

"Murphy, it could be bad. Miriam said that if consumed in large enough quantities, it could have long-lasting mind-altering magical side effects."

I closed my eyes and dropped my head as my free hand flew to my temple. "Did she say how much was too much?"

"That's the bad part, Murphy. It doesn't take much."

Damn, damn, damn, damn, damn.

"I'll have to heal her, and she'll find out all about Jake's ploy to keep her," I whispered.

I felt Hanna's sympathy through the phone connection. "You would have to heal her anyway," she reminded me. "You couldn't leave her lovesick over Rene forever."

"I could have undone a charm with another charm," I said. "This is a physical healing plus the undoing of a spell from someone un-trained. Cadence will have to be aware of what I'm doing because I'll need to be in contact with her for it to be effective."

She and I stood silently at opposite ends of the call, both of us feeling saddened. We'd been rooting for Jake and Cadence to make it, to be that cute high school couple who beat the odds and had their happily ever after. How would it make her feel if Cadence found out that Jake tried to put a spell on her to keep her from ever leaving him? My guess was violated, and a little scared. And right-fully so.

Jake, why'd you have to go and be an idiot?

I blamed myself for taking any part in it. A tiny charm to

heighten what the two of them shared so Jake would be less inse-cure wouldn't have been too bad, but I should have encouraged him to talk to her instead of pushing him to practice his craft. In my zeal to influence him to become part of the Lughaidh coven, I'd given him a charm he'd contorted into a potent spell. Compounded with whatever was in the Eros oil, there was no telling what he'd done to her physically.

"Murphy, the only thing you can do now is try to soften the blow," Hanna suggested. "It's not like he wanted to hurt her."

"But he did. It's going to be a hard pill for Cadence to swallow."

We said our goodbyes without me telling her about my good news. It felt like an awful time to bring it up.

I rejoined the animated group around the fire, where they were engrossed in their conversation.

"Is everything alright?" LaDonna asked.

"Um, well, sort of. Cadence, I need to talk to you. Privately, if that's alright."

Cadence looked around as if she could see what I needed to speak to her about. Maybe she was searching for Ryan.

"Talk to me? What about?"

The creak of my gate hinges announced a newcomer, and my hands balled into frustrated fists. This time, it was two newcomers. Jake and Rene strode into my backyard with the awkward confi-dence so many teenage boys have. In a heartbeat, Cadence switched from concerned listener to lovestruck, swooning teen-ager.

Well, it's better if it comes from him, anyway.

)O(

LaDonna strolled into the kitchen and returned with ingredients for s'mores, paper plates, and a set of long metal skewers. As Ca-dence remained captivated by Rene, who seemed oblivious to her infatuation because of Betony's constant presence, I pulled Jake aside.

"I need you to come clean with Cadence so I can heal her. I was going to do it before y'all got here, but I think it'd be better if she hears the whole story from you."

He took a step back, his eyes wide. "Now?" His eyes shot

around after he said it. He must have spoken louder than he meant to.

I nodded. "Now. I have to heal Cadence, Jake. Hanna said one of those ingredients in the Eros oil could set off some mind-altering effects." My brow furrowed as I it occurred to me that the side effects of the oil, not the spell, might be why Cadence was seeing my father.

He chewed on his lower lip and wrung his hands before crossing his arms over his chest. He pulled in a deep lungful of the smoky night air and exhaled slowly.

"Well, I'd have to tell her eventually," he admitted.

I reached out and put a consoling hand on his arm. "You've got this, bud. It's always best to be honest."

"I know," he said, his head hanging low and his dirty-blond hair two long, straight curtains on either side of his face. He kicked at a pebble on the concrete and set it skipping into my rock garden. "I wish I could take it all back."

"Tell her that, not me," I said, grabbing his elbow to steer him in Cadence's direction.

Chapter 19

Once LaDonna and Luke notified everyone about the encroaching dark coven and their objectives, everyone assembled posthaste. By nine o'clock, the Lughaidh coven had convened before the crackling fireplace in LaDonna's great room. Moonlight filtered through the bare winter branches via the ceiling-tall hexagon of custom cathedral-like windows.

Cadence was also there, and Rene was allowed to sit in on the proceedings since he was already in on the whole "witches are real" thing. Flanked by Betony and Cadence, he and the other teens took seats in the back of the room on giant blue pillows the high priestess kept handy for occasions like this. Jake sat to Cadence's left, all but unnoticed, his face long and his eyes cast down to the tile floor. He'd shoot the occasional glance Cadence's way, but it never lasted longer than it took for him to see he was unimportant to her with Rene around. I wondered how their conversation had gone with the handsome new kid sitting in the next room. Had she heard a word of Jake's confession?

"Girl, why didn't you *tell* me about this when you called?" Hanna scolded as she arrived. She accosted me with an enormous hug around the shoulders, her long, bronzed arms dressed in a pastel pink sweater that set off her beautiful complexion. "If someone wants to kill my best friend, I need to know!"

I returned her hug. "I feel like we haven't talked in days. So much has happened."

Her eyes flicked to the ring on my left hand, and her mouth opened. She stopped as LaDonna clapped her hands to halt conversation and asked for everyone's attention.

All nine coven members sat in a circle around the room. It was one of Betony's first meetings as an official coven member, and I was glad to see her taking her role seriously.

The high priestess requested that I join her at the head of the room. Together she and I cobbled the story of the past few days—from Ericka's arrival at LaDonna's greenhouse business asking about the local coven, to Cadence's ability to see my dead father even though he wasn't a conventional ghost. Jaws never stopped dropping as the tale unraveled, and when we recounted the story of the car crash, a wave of horror washed over Hanna's expression. At the conclusion, the room sat in utter silence.

"Ryan has something to say," Cadence interjected, breaking the quiet. "He said if you cure me, I won't be able to see or hear him anymore. Does that make sense?"

Her little spellbound ears didn't hear a word of Jake's confession or the story I just told. Well, crap. And Ryan's spying for us won't do a damn bit of good if Cadence can't relay what he's found out. How long before Cadence is permanently broken? We can't risk that.

"I have an idea," Jake piped up. His deep voice carried across the room. "Let Murphy or Miriam heal Cadence. I'll find a way to sneak into the dark coven and find out what's going down."

They met this idea with an outbreak of discussion around the room. Jake had won the hearts of the coven members on Halloween night when he'd felt drawn back to Witch's Brew at the height of the turmoil. He'd found himself in the middle of a ritual to save Betony from her father's evil spirit. No one liked the idea of him putting himself on the line.

"They know who all of you are," he argued. "They've been low-key spying on the coven through Ericka—maybe there have been more we don't know about. Murphy can't even go astrally since they're after her specifically. They've already been able to hurt her physically, and we can't risk them messing with her spiritually."

"I can go with him," Conall offered.

"They've seen you," I argued.

He smiled. "They've never seen Rolf. I could be Jake's dog. His familiar."

My mouth twisted. "I don't like this at all."

"I don't like it, either, but it makes sense, Murphy," LaDonna said. "This way, you can heal Cadence before she gets any worse."

"I can go to the prison and talk to my mother," Betony offered. "I can see if she's willing to help. If she's lying, I'll be able to tell, which might help me figure out the truth."

"How can you tell if she's lying?" Jake asked.

Betony grinned and tossed her fire-engine red hair over her

shoulder. She made a sassy snap with her hand and said, "Gray witch skills, baby."

"That makes my idea even better," Jake said. "If the dark coven has someone who can detect lies the way Betony can, I can honestly say I'm not part of a coven," Jake added.

"I don't like it," I repeated. "And they won't have a gray witch."

"They could have an indigo witch," Luke countered. "Never doubt an indigo witch's intuition."

Conall frowned. "You can't come with us physically; we can't risk that. But there may be a way for you to come with us."

This man was going to give me worry wrinkles. "How?"

"You could hitch a ride."

I cocked my head at him, much like his doggy form was apt to do. Twice, while astral projecting, I had unintentionally leaped into Conall's body. One of those times, he was the dog. It wasn't the least bit sexy coexisting inside my boyfriend's body—it was downright weird. Even weirder when he was on four legs and fuzzy.

"I've never done that on purpose before."

He cocked his head right back. "You've never tried before. I imagine it's the spiritual equivalent of taking a running jump into a swimming pool."

"Your aura mixed with Conall's should throw them off enough that they won't be able to detect you," LaDonna added. "It's up to you."

If my lips pressed together more, they'd be thin as a thread. I was not too fond of the idea, but couldn't come up with a better one.

"So, it's settled?" LaDonna said. "Ryan give Jake ideas on how to approach the dark coven, so they take him in without suspecting anything. Rolf will go along as Jake's familiar with Murphy riding shotgun. We can learn about their plans to destroy Murphy. Then we'll either fight them on their territory or tell the police of their intentions if it's something that doesn't involve a spell."

Heads around the room concurred, some reluctantly, and they negated the idea of putting a protection spell on us for fear the dark coven would detect it. I nearly ground my teeth at the thought of Jake going in unprotected, but they had a point.

Miriam pulled a pad of light green paper and a silver pen out of her Coach purse so Cadence could take notes on Ryan's intelligence. Cadence's eyes flicked to Rene every few seconds as she wrote; she had no clue about the depth of the sacrifice Jake had offered to make for her. It felt odd recognizing that we were getting this information from Ryan, only for me to heal Cadence and not be able to talk to him again. I had a million questions for my father, but nothing was worth sacrificing Cadence's physical or mental health.

"Before we go, I'd like to add one more thing," Conall declared. He wrapped his hand around mine. I knew what was coming, and my cheeks colored. "As many of you know, Murphy and I have been seeing each other for a while now."

"I think you've seen *her* for a lot longer than she let herself see you," Terry joked. "It's about time she caught on." The rest of the room laughed politely.

"True, Terry, true. But it was worth the wait. And after all this talk of dark covens and spying and spells gone wrong, I'd like to share a spot of hope. Murphy has agreed to marry me."

The room burst into joyous cries. Luke, who undoubtedly saw this coming, headed to the kitchen with LaDonna. They returned moments later with a tray covered in flutes of cold champagne and sparkling cider for everyone.

"A toast!" Luke said, raising his glass. "To Murphy and Conall. May love and laughter light your days and warm your heart and home. May good and faithful friends be yours wherever you may roam. May peace and plenty bless your world with joy that long endures. May all life's passing seasons bring the best to you and yours. *Sláinte*."

The words of the traditional toast brought tears to my eyes and a lump to my throat. I raised my glass with the rest of the room, who toasted to our health. They clinked glasses, we shared hugs, and more than one person asked to see the ring, which we gave Luke full credit for designing.

Hanna dragged her feet and was one of the last people to approach. Her enormous brown eyes reflected so much pain as she regarded us that my heart broke.

"I leave you alone for two days, and you almost die and then you get engaged, and that's just part of the adventures you've been through. I didn't hear about any of it except for the candy part until just now,"

She was right. I hadn't deliberately cut her out, and neither had Conall. Still, now that he and I relied so profoundly on each other, telling Hanna our predicaments had taken a backseat to supporting one another until we got through the madness.

"You're right," I said. Conall took my hand, and we faced Hanna together in our admission. "That was shitty of us."

"It was *really* shitty of you. You could've at least texted." Her words were nearly inaudible, and she wiped tears from her eyes with the back of her hand.

"We should have," Conall agreed.

Hanna's dam broke, and she started crying and laughing and hugging us, and there I was, crying and laughing and hugging her back.

"Congratulations, assholes," she said. "It's about fucking time."

Chapter 20

"You're sure you want to do this?"

Monday morning, Hanna met with LaDonna at her greenhouse to go over the pages of details Ryan had shared with Cadence. Betony and I, meanwhile, took a trip to the Leland County Jail. After parking in the gravel lot, we sat together quietly in my Corolla as the engine ticked and cooled. Betony needed to summon her courage before confronting her incarcerated mother.

The last time Betony had spoken to her was Halloween morning the previous year—the same morning she had killed her father. Once Betony sat down with the police and confessed what she'd done and why, the cops hauled her mother in. Virginia Yarborough admitted guilt to a multitude of sins, one of which involved being aware about her daughter's abuse and doing nothing to prevent it. None of her confession, however, involved killing anyone.

Remember how I said some folks deserved to be hexed? Virginia was one of those people. And yes, of course, I hexed her. I hexed the *crap* out of her. I have no doubt her life behind bars was even worse than… well, whatever everyday life behind bars was like.

"Yes, I'm sure I want to do this," Betony said. "I can't believe you're spending part of your Valentine's Day with me instead of spending the whole day with Conall. Y'all just got engaged! I could have come with Hanna." Betony had tied her hair down her back in a long French braid that made her appear older than her eighteen years. She'd toned down her usual gothic style today and wore a plain white t-shirt with a black cardigan thrown over it and a short skirt the same bright red as her hair. Her shoes were black Mary Janes, which I found adorable, and her stockings were white.

"No way," I said. "I'm not sending you in there with anything less than a fully loaded cannon. If the two of us face her together, she's a lot less likely to try to pull some shit."

"She better not," Betony said, her jaw jutting. Her face grew taut and her eyes narrowed; mine did, too. It's not every day a young woman has to face her abusive mother in jail.

"I'm not going to full-on gray witch her," Betony said softly. "I mean, I'll use my power to know if she's lying or not, but I'm not going to try to help her with her shadow self. Do you think that makes me a bad person?"

I put my arm around her shoulders and gave her a quick side hug, which she allowed. Betony wasn't keen on human contact. After years of physical abuse, I understood why and used it sparingly.

"I think it means you've done your shadow work successfully and set your boundaries well. I also think some people don't deserve forgiveness. You can't help that she is your biological mother, or that Everett was your father. That doesn't mean you owe her anything or have to love her."

"I know," she whispered, her voice reflecting her gratitude that I supported her. She didn't sound so sure that she believed it herself.

To my surprise, she took my hand as we strolled up the sidewalk like she was a little girl. Maybe coming to see her mom was stirring negative memories, or perhaps she needed the extra strength my presence added; whatever the reason, I gave it a gentle squeeze and held on.

We entered the facility together, and Betony released my hand and let out a pent-up breath.

"This place smells like juvie," she observed. She was right. The air was thick with bleach and pine cleaner that struggled to cover the scents of body odor and institutional despair.

We let the guard behind the counter know we were there, provided our identification, and added our names to the visitor's roster. Having done the necessary check-in, we stood in place rather than sit down in the uncomfortable-looking chairs. There weren't many available seats to choose from. Apparently, Valentine's Day was a popular day for visitors. I had the random curious thought of what gifts the women behind bars were allowed. Money for the commissary, maybe?

After almost an hour's wait, most of it spent avoiding eye contact with the other visitors, the guard called Betony and me back. We were patted down and had to leave our purses with one of the guards on duty.

"Cell phone?" the stern-faced guard asked. She was squat, strong, and no-nonsense, but her demeanor was amiable, and she smelled like sweet peas. I'd put my phone in my purse before we'd headed back, but Betony removed hers from a pocket hidden in the folds of her skirt and added it to her purse. I hadn't known until today that she owned a purse. Betony always carried everything in her black backpack with the colorful pinned-on buttons, iron-on patches, and a stuffie dangling from one of the shoulder straps.

For some reason, I'd always imagined prisons to be like movies, and expected to see a thick glass partition with phones on either side of a long counter. Instead, they brought us into a room that reminded me more of the one I'd seen when Jake, Lorina, and I had visited Betony in the juvenile detention center: a portable laminated table with attached stools on either side. The table was bolted to the floor.

Virginia Yarborough might have been a pretty woman once. Unlike her full-figured round-faced daughter, she was extremely petite, with an oval face. Her shoulder-length hair, which was a golden chestnut once upon a time, hung in dirty, lank brown tendrils. Her face was wrinkled deeply and profusely, her eyes deep-set hollows in a gaunt face, and her crooked brown teeth reflected a lifetime of smoking. She sat at the table, massaging her yellowed cuticles with a twitching thumb, her body as rigid and tense as a tightly wound watch.

"What do you want?" she growled before we sat down. Her raspy voice also pinned her as a lifelong smoker.

I remained standing, but Betony sat across from her mother, her spine straight and her face proud but not haughty. It was like she'd been taking lessons on bearing from LaDonna.

"I was hoping you could answer some questions for me."

Virginia scoffed, which turned into a barking cough. "Damn lungs. I been coughing like crazy ever since I been in here."

If she expected sympathy from us, she didn't get it. We waited for her to catch her breath, eyeing her like a bug on a pin.

"What sorta questions?" Virginia's eyes darkened.

Betony readjusted herself in the seat and met her mother's gaze. The older woman cast her attention elsewhere, finding something more interesting on the cinderblock wall over my shoulder.

"Are you still a part of the dark coven that tried to kill Murphy?"

Her mother laughed and turned to me. "Murphy? Your name is Murphy? What the hell kinda name is that?"

"Irish," I replied without an ounce of humor.

"Are you?" Betony pressed, leaning forward, her voice raised in irritation.

Virginia threw her hands up and then slapped her palms on the table. "Fuck, why you askin' me that, kid? You ever seen me doing any cunnin' shit in our house? I raised you inna church."

And look how great you turned out. You married a man you allowed to sexually abuse your daughter for years. That she'd dodged the question like a seasoned politician didn't escape me.

"You were part of a coven that killed Murphy's mother and the mothers of two of her friends," Betony bit off. "They're my friends now, my *coven*, and we have reason to believe your old coven is up to something again. I think it still exists, and I want to do something about it."

I agreed. Betony had played her cards well. She told her mother who I was and informed her we were aware of the dark coven, but she didn't explain why we were seeking them out. If her mother still spoke with the dark witches, they'd learn we were coming after them, but they'd know nothing about our plans to infiltrate them.

Her mother's nostrils flared, and her lips pursed, a mass of smoker's wrinkles turning her mouth into an odd-looking sphincter. The woman was not amused that her daughter had joined the coven she and her husband had tried to slaughter on her behalf.

"You don't wanna find them, Bet," her mother rasped. "That thing you called a dark coven will turn you inside out. You and the rest of—whassername—Murphy's stupid coven."

"Maybe. Or maybe we'll do the same to them."

Her mother crossed her arms, leaned back, and seemed to see Betony for the first time. She evaluated her daughter from the crown of her braided red hair to her staunch bearing and fresh new clothes, courtesy of LaDonna. Did she notice the new soft ring of gray around the pupil of Betony's hazel eyes?

"Ya might," she conceded. "But there's a lot more of them than there are of y'all."

"Are you sure?" Betony arched a single eyebrow. Dang, I wished I could do that. Both the eyebrow and the coy tone that revealed nothing.

Well played Bet. Make her wonder. And if she is still communicating with them, make them wonder if we have cards we haven't played. We'd been on the defense; they did not know what our offense might look like. Then again, I didn't, either. Not yet.

Uncrossing her arms, Virginia scratched her cheek with brown fingernails and leaned in. She resembled a mean, skinny gargoyle with unkempt hair and crooked teeth.

"Betony, if you got the sense god gave a billy goat, you'd leave those losers for the Stygian. They're so much bigger, and they got *power*. Unlike *them*," she motioned to me with a dismissive hand flip. "And they play dirty." She snorted derisively and sat back with a smirk. "And if them lame-asses decide to fight, I guaran-god-damn-tee you, *they'll lose*."

Betony set her jaw, stood up, and motioned to me to follow her. "She's not any help at all. She's as useless now as she ever was. We're done here."

I followed Betony as she stalked from the room, neither of us giving Virginia a backward glance as we strode the institutional halls out of the building. We subjected ourselves to an exit pat-down, gathered our personal effects, and nearly made it to the building's exit before Betony took my hand again and cried.

Chapter 21

Monday afternoon, after everyone got off from work, we reconvened at LaDonna's house. This time, Lorina, who'd escaped one of her many groundings for the day, joined us.

"The Stygian, huh?" Conall asked. "I wonder what it means?"

"Stygian means having to do with the River Styx or Hades," Betony explained. "I Googled it on our way back from the jail."

"The gray bar motel," Lorina joked, hunched over her drum box. She gave it a couple of raps with her hands in a complicated but gentle rhythm. Jake took up space in a nearby chair, plucking a mellow tune on his acoustic guitar. It started as a slow version of "Jailhouse Rock," but within moments, the song had morphed until the two of them had a gentle but unfamiliar tune playing. I'd wager they were making it up on the spot.

"Whatever," Betony retorted. "Aren't you supposed to be grounded?"

"My mom made an exception for Valentine's Day," Lorina said. "She felt sorry for my date, knowing I couldn't hang out for the holiday."

"You don't have a date," Jake pointed out, looking up from his frets. His tall frame had sunk into one of LaDonna's shorter, cushier chairs, giving him the illusion of being swallowed by pillows.

"Shhhh," Lorina said with a finger to her lips. "She doesn't know that."

"Is she cool with you being gay now?" Jake asked.

"I told her I was going out with Sam," Lorina said. "She doesn't know that Sam is Samantha and not Samuel."

"How did she hear about Sam, anyway?"

"She's got an app with a list of trigger words that sends her all of my texts and emails with those words in them."

Lorina bent back over her drum box and tapped the sides again in a new rhythm, one more in keeping with the new tune Jake had started playing. They took up a melody together, another one I'd never heard before, but knowing them, it was a spur-of-the-moment song I may never hear again. They did that a lot—complemented each other seamlessly in their music. I envied them. If Jake became part of the coven, I'd have to show him how music charms and spells worked. He'd be remarkable at music magic.

What color is that type of magic? Blue? I can't remember. We haven't had a music witch in the coven since I was a young kid. However, part of me sensed the flow and workings of it whenever I heard Jake and Lorina play.

I had taken a small break after returning from the jailhouse to allow my energy to stabilize. Betony had held my hand the entire ride back to LaDonna's house, and together we worked to control her chaos energy. The exercise involved using the thrum of the tires on the road, the wind blowing by the car, and the steady pumping of the engine as sources of earth, air, and fire energy to tame the wild flares of gray power Betony threw off like sun flares as I drove. I may or may not have swerved onto the shoulder once or twice. Maybe three times. I was focused on Betony, but in doing so, the Universe provided me with an awareness of how the two of us fit into the weave of our environment. It was both humbling and borderline overwhelming, but it also showed me how to not die.

Having found solace within the warded walls of LaDonna's home, Betony and I regained our composure. The time had come to help Cadence heal. She'd stayed up late the night before, relaying message after message from Ryan. Now that we had recorded everything he needed to relay, there was no need to keep her in danger. She'd insisted she felt fine enough to wait until after school today, since she was in a rush to make curfew, but I made Jake swear he'd keep an extra close eye on her.

As much as I wanted to sit down and talk with Ryan for hours and learn everything about him, Cadence's health was more important. I suppose having placed my father in a "People I'll Know Nothing About" box in my mind for years made it easier. Not effortless, but easier. He'd only been in my life for a little over two days, and I already had to close that door. It didn't seem fair, but after believing I was a gray witch for years, I was used to disappointment.

"Where's Cadence?" I asked.

"With LaDonna in the kitchen," Betony said with a pointed finger. I questioned why Cadence was absent, but then I noticed that

Betony and Rene's hands entwined on his thigh.

Well, that answers that question.

"Y'all excuse me for a minute," I said, heading for LaDonna's kitchen and the lovesick teen.

Jake slapped a hand over his guitar strings to silence them.

"Should I come?" he asked.

"It might be a good idea," I said. "I don't think Cadence remembers the talk you two had, so she may need to hear it again."

Jake leaned his guitar against the wall and stood to follow, trailing behind me. Lorina's drumbeats softened in the absence of Jake's accompaniment.

In the kitchen, Cadence sat crumpled in a hoodie and jeans on the tile floor, her back pressed against the white cabinets, designed to resemble tiny carriage doors. Her forehead rested against her arms, which she'd slung over the tops of her knees, and her frizzy blonde curls fell all around her. The blubbers and snivels she uttered in her sorrow showed no signs of letting up, and I wondered how long she'd been crying to still be going at it so hard. LaDonna shot me an expression of pity, her hands occupied with washing the dishes. I recognized the distracted way she cleaned; LaDonna had a habit of tidying up when she felt helpless and wished she had the power to fix things.

"Cadence?" I knelt by her side and heard her sniffle loudly. Behind me, Jake hovered in silence, his hands hung by his sides, thumbs hooked in his black Levi's pockets, his broad shoulders slumped.

Cadence shuffled her feet and wiped her nose gracelessly on the sleeve of her shirt. "What?" Her voice was thick with dejection.

I sat cross-legged on the floor nearby. "May I touch you? I'd love to hug you right now."

To my surprise, shy Cadence needed no further invitation but dove straight into my arms with deep sobs that broke my heart.

"I—I thought Betony was—I thought—Rene—" She shot Jake a guilty glance and stopped, her breath coming in gulps and sobs. Her eyes turned to the air by Jake's side, and she paused. A prickly feeling crept over my skin.

"Ryan's here," she said, and hiccupped.

I turned to where her eyes were fixed, but saw nothing. I hadn't expected to, but I had to try.

"He—he says—he says he's going to try to—to find a—a way to let you see him before—before he goes back." The poor kid could hardly speak for her sobs.

"I would like that," I said.

I pulled her gently to me again, and she allowed it. My hands caressed her bushy curls, and I shushed and cooed, holding her close to me as she wept. I used that connection with her to send energy into her body, allowing the universe to flow through me and locate all of the broken spots and heal them. She was a Libra, an air sign, so I concentrated on the air we breathed, the heated air flowing through LaDonna's home, and the chilly winter wind blowing through the trees in the cold garden beyond the French doors. I envisioned that air blowing through her and removing the impurities that the oil she'd consumed had set in her mind.

Mighty Goddess Hygeia, Maiden Astraea, Goddess Aphrodite, please heal the heart of this sweet child. Remind her what true love feels like, and remove this chemical and spell-induced infatuation that is breaking her heart and clouding her mind.

My hands turned ice cold and throbbed as if each palm housed a pulsating heart, and I was grateful for the insulation the hoody offered between Cadence and me. With each pulse, a wave of power moved from the universal energy field through me and into her. Her hiccups and sobbing subsided in less than a minute, and she drew away, studying me with puffy, red eyes.

"What did you do?"

"The feelings you were having… the ones that hurt? They weren't you, Cadence," I explained.

Jake crouched down and studied the top of his black canvas sneakers. "It was me, Cadence. The candy I gave you… it was my fault. I have no clue what happened. It was like my brain glitched or something." He fell onto his ass with a *thump* that sounded like a felled tree, and he crumpled into a ball. "No. That's weak. It was my fault. It was all my fault."

As Jake rocked back and forth, I took the time to explain to Cadence what Jake had done and why. Jake didn't cry as loudly as Cadence had, but he buried his sniffles and sobs in his arms. He couldn't even look at us as he rocked back and forth, clutching his knees. I finished the story with how Jake had volunteered to spy on the dark coven so I could heal Cadence, because that way, we wouldn't need to rely on her to communicate with Ryan.

Cadence took it all in, her face a mask. In less than five minutes, she'd gone from obsessed with Rene to being magically healed. Now she understood that her intense and painful emotions had been nothing more than manipulation brought about by her boyfriend's insecurity. The same boyfriend who'd felt so ashamed for his actions, he was now risking *his* life for *her* mental health.

Cadence leaned against the cabinets, staring blankly at the ceiling, her blonde hair pouring behind her like a curly waterfall.

"I don't know how to feel right now," she said, her voice flat.

"I understand," I told her.

"Jake, I—how could you?"

"I was *scared*," he said to his knees, his voice thick. "I was so scared." He started crying again like he'd never stop. "I'll never forgive myself, and I understand if you don't either. I do. I'm so, so sorry."

She leveled her chin and took in Jake's crumpled form and red face with a deflated attitude of her own. I saw a thousand thoughts whirl in her head through her flickering gray-blue eyes, and her expression reflected hundreds, possibly thousands, of memories she had of the two of them together.

"I'm really pissed at you," she said.

"I know," Jake croaked.

"Like, really, *really* pissed,"

"I know," Jake howled, his voice trailing into tears.

"You're a real fuckhead sometimes, Jacob Dean DePaulo." Her tone increased in frustration with every sentence, and Jake's head sank lower than I thought possible.

Jake sniffed. "I *know*."

"I'm not sure I've completely forgiven you for this," she added, her fingers drumming on the tile floor. "I don't know if I can."

He sniffed again. "I know."

"Damn it, Jake! Say something else!"

He pulled in a shuddering breath. "I love you, Cadence Hemingford. And even if you decide not to take me back, I will spend the rest of my life making this up to you somehow." His muffled voice came from somewhere near his knees. His legs are like tree trunks. It was hard to tell.

Cadence snorted. "Take you back? Did we break up?"

The hope in Jake's open-mouthed face when he lifted his head hurt my heart. They both wore splotchy red faces and red-ringed eyes from crying.

"You're not breaking up with me?"

A weary smile crossed her face, which radiated love despite her anger. "Not today."

Jake took a shaky breath and scrambled across the floor to her, pulling her slender frame into his brawny arms. He covered her face in kisses, and Cadence let out one of her throaty giggles I loved but heard so infrequently. LaDonna and I shared a glance of silent understanding and left the two of them to make up in private.

Chapter 22

The visit to the prison, followed by the ride to LaDonna's, where I spent my time stabilizing Betony's chaotic energy as she cried, and then healing Cadence, left me utterly exhausted. The car wreck and premonition that jerked me awake the day before didn't help. But it was my first Valentine's Day with Conall, and dammit, I had a gift to give him. I wouldn't let a little fatigue mess up my day. Yes, we had to plan our infiltration of the Stygian, but I postponed our preparations so Conall and I could dine together, and I could give him his gift.

God love LaDonna and Luke. They let us borrow LaDonna's antique green Mercedes for our date to have some time together. When they heard I was stopping by my place first, they insisted on following us in their SUV to make sure I made it in and out of my home safely. After my premonition, we all felt a little wary about Blackwell Manor. I tried explaining that my trip inside involved little more than Conall's quick one yesterday, but they wouldn't hear it.

"Murphy, we did *not* spend years sheltering and protecting you, only to have you do something without our protection now," LaDonna argued.

She was right. The walls of my warded house had been breached, first by Betony's chaotic gray energy, then by the Stygian. I never wanted to feel this vulnerable again. I should be the one protecting the people I loved—not the other way around. I promised myself I'd focus on mastering my unique gifts if I survived my current problems.

The evening drive down the Appalachian foothills from the Whelen's home to my house outside the village was uneventful, and I drowsed in the passenger seat as Conall cruised through the familiar streets. The Mercedes smelled pleasantly of leather cleaner and engine oil. The rocking of the car as Conall drove, mixed in with his shower-fresh smell, calmed me. Before I knew it, he'd parked in the lot nearest the veranda and killed the engine. I stretched and exited the car, Conall following close behind with a loud squeak of the shutting door.

"Murphy!"

He climbed the steps, and I turned, braced to tell him he didn't need to protect me, but he seized my hand and squeezed it. His large brown eyes reflected worry and the longing to protect me, but what came out of his mouth was, "Be careful."

I tugged the hem of my t-shirt to a more comfortable level from where it had ridden up when I'd stretched. Conall's concern, coupled with his acceptance of my decision, only made me appreciate him more.

"I'll be careful."

"You'd better be."

My key slid into the lock the like thousands of times before. The door opened on smooth hinges, the bells overhead jingled their merry chime, and I crossed the threshold and turned on my phone's flashlight. The air inside, filled with the scent of incense and coffee, felt almost as cold as the February winds outside, and I shivered.

It should have felt like home. It always felt like home. It was my home. But it wasn't. The physical building was the same, but the atmosphere was *not*. It was more than the absence of electricity. As I panned the light around the room, the place I stood was an alien construct of Blackwell Manor, a poor artist's rendering of what the Manor meant to them. It felt like a façade, as if I could take down the objects near me and see how the gems were glass, the shelves a cheap plastic, the essential oils mere water with food coloring. And the *air*… it was like breathing in a sauna, despite the chill: thick, cloying, and unnatural. Cold air should be crisp and invigorating, not make me feel I might drown with my next breath.

I reached for the Source, and my nerve endings snapped like a wire whose connection was sparking but not making contact.

I have to get out of here. I have to hurry.

My overzealous need to have one moment in my life go right pulled rank on my common sense. I moved as quickly as my feet would allow, reaching for the Source with every step like a blind woman searching for the walls in a vast cavern and not finding them. The smells of coffee and herbs overwhelmed me now, nauseating me. I forced down the urge to gag.

I all but ran the distance from the door to behind the counter, where I'd stashed Conall's gift in a velvet bag behind the register. As I reversed direction to head to the door, the world tilted like a see-saw. My free hand shot out to the counter to steady myself, and I pulled in another lungful of nauseating air tainted with the odors of muddy water and decomposition. The world spun, and amidst the dizziness and the putrid smell, bile rose in my throat, driving me to my knees. There, I retrieved a trash can and emptied the contents of my stomach into it.

The front door bells tinkled, the sound distorted and distant in my ears.

"Murphy!"

The counter hid me from Conall's eyeshot. I retched again, giving him all the direction he needed. I heard him say, "Holy fuck, what is that?" His steady steps advanced, sounding to me as if they came from underwater.

"Conall, don't—"

He appeared at the open end of the counter, looming over me like a skyscraper. Bending down, he scooped me into his arms and lifted me like a doll.

"Hold your breath, baby girl. I'm getting you out of here."

If he said anything after that, I didn't hear it.

Chapter 23

When I opened my eyes, LaDonna, Luke, and Conall surrounded me. I shivered with cold, the velvet bag with Conall's gift still clutched in my hands. My backside was freezing from lying on the wooden planks. How long had I laid there unconscious? La-Donna's voice responded to someone I couldn't hear, and for a crazy half-second, I believed she was talking to my invisible father. I realized she was on the phone when her earthy voice responded to a tinny one coming through a speaker.

"She's coming to, Miriam," she said into the phone, lowering a hand to caress my hair and brush it from my face. "Yes, her eyes are clear. Murphy?"

I waved my hand, but the motion was weak, and the bag with Conall's gift slipped a bit in my grasp. I fumbled to grab it and caught the drawstring with my fingers, but only by accident.

"I'll be fine," I insisted, but my voice sounded groggy. I tried to sit up, but the world spun again, and my stomach heaved. I laid back down, my head hitting the plank under me with a thump. *Ouch.*

"She seems dizzy."

"I'm *fine*," I declared, pressing an elbow into the wood to prop myself up. Conall dropped to my side and gave me a hand so I could rise to a sitting position, where I wavered like a sapling in a breeze. He put a hand on my spine to stabilize me, his hand warm on my chilly back.

"You're not fine," he said, his melodious voice assuring even as his words irritated the crap out of me. "But thank the gods, you seem to be doing better."

"I'll be *fine*," I said for the third time, which I imagine did nothing to convince those around me.

LaDonna put a hand over her phone speaker and turned to Luke and Conall. "Do you think she needs Miriam to come out?"

Did I need the coven healer? How bad had I been? I remembered how my store seemed real-not-real, the horrible smells, and how

I'd gotten severely dizzy. Had I thrown up? I recalled grabbing my trash can and being overwhelmed by a nasty, nauseating stench. My stomach lurched and my throat burned.

"I don't need Miriam," I insisted. Ugh. This was like having a horrible hangover without the fun the night before.

Luke agreed with my parents, though, and LaDonna arranged with Miriam to meet us at her house in a few minutes. Guess they outvoted me.

I let out a frustrated growl and glared halfheartedly at them all. Conall rubbed my back, and I wavered spinelessly under his touch, so he stopped.

"Wouldn't hurt for Miriam to come to look at you," Conall said.

I kind of wanted to hit him again.

"Oh, for fuck's sake," I said, struggling to put my feet under me. "I don't need to be coddled."

From a distance, I heard my phone ringing. Conall reached into his back pocket and then handed it to me. I flapped a weak hand at him.

"Just get it, please."

He unlocked it—I'd added his thumbprint ages ago to simplify things—and put an ear to the phone. Another tinny voice, this one robotic, came through. In a minute, Conall thumbed the screen to hang up. "Gryphon Utilities will be out first thing tomorrow morning to fix the weatherhead," he told me.

I nodded. It was good news, sort of. My house would have power again, and my business could open if someone could run it for me. Miriam might want to help—she was still searching for work, and an extra couple of dollars would probably be helpful. Until we figured out why I'd reacted the way I had when I was inside, I didn't want to step another foot in the building. Something positive might come from having to be babied by the coven's rose witch.

Why hadn't the house affected Conall the way it had me?

I slumped and pulled my purse to me like a security blanket as the events of the past few minutes sank in. My home, my warded haven, was now unsafe until we solved the mystery of the dark coven—who they were, how to ingratiate ourselves within them, and most importantly, how to stop them.

☽☾

I clung to Conall's gift while slumped in the passenger seat of the Whelen's Mercedes. There had been talk about me staying with them for a few days until I recovered, but I had no urge to feel mothered by my foster parents again. I made a few calls and texts and finagled a deal for Betony and Hanna to stay with Conall and me at his apartment instead. The coven would perform a warding to add to the fairly skimpy one Conall had in place. Betony would help Conall keep a close watch on me tonight, and she'd continue in the morning when he left for work. She'd report to LaDonna and Luke if anything suspicious or unusual occurred. This was all contingent on Miriam giving me the all-clear after her evaluation.

So much for our fancy Huntsville Valentine's Day dinner reservations.

The village of Gryphon sped by, and Conall took a call from the car rental agency. He turned down their offer to pick up a rental car to replace his broken Camaro and said he'd notify his insurance company he wouldn't be using their service. I was glad. Rentals might have that new-car smell, but the old Mercedes was comfortable and familiar.

Miriam's blue Subaru was parked at the curb outside of Conall's apartment when we arrived, and she emerged wrapped in a beautifully fringed cashmere shawl and wool slacks. Every nuance of the woman screamed class, and it was crushing her spirit to live for so long without a job; her previous one as an accountant had paid her generously. Her finances were taking a big hit. My mind flicked back to Ericka and her yellow witch power. A yellow witch would have made an excellent addition to the coven. Too bad Ericka was trouble.

Conall put the Mercedes in park, and my hand moved toward the door pull.

"Wait," he ordered.

"For *what*?" I barked. "Are you going to carry me inside, too?"

His stern expression said volumes. "If I have to, yes."

I huffed and crossed my arms, and Conall leaned across the car and kissed me on the cheek.

"It's just a precaution."

I huffed again as he exited the car. My cheeks colored, and I focused on the woodgrain dashboard and how the hazy February light made the lock to the glovebox shine.

Conall opened my door for me and stood nearby, prepared to help if necessary. I put two feet out to stand, supporting myself on the car's doorframe instead of my usual one-leg lift. I reached standing and gave him a smirk.

"See? Just fi—"

The world sloped, and he grabbed my elbow to steady me. Once I regained my balance, I saw Miriam watching us with concern.

"Let's get her inside," she said. "Let her lie down."

My knee-jerk reaction was to argue. As someone who rarely fell ill or sought assistance in my shop, it was unfamiliar and painful to have to rely on others just to remain on my feet. My nostrils flared in frustration, but I allowed it without dispute when Conall slung an arm below mine to guide me into his apartment. We walked—well, Conall walked, I tottered—inside, where he steered me to the couch. The odd swirling pattern in the artwork hanging overhead gave me vertigo, and I closed my eyes.

I heard the pop of middle-aged knees and Miriam's gentle voice. "Murphy?"

"Sorry to drag you out on a chilly day like this," I said, facing her. Her pale green eyes, light as lambs ear and slightly wrinkled at the corners, reflected concern and love.

She laughed softly. "Nonsense. I can't have the Summate not feeling at her peak." She giggled. "I'm sorry, it's probably not a great time for a dad joke, is it?"

Laughing despite myself, I said, "It's a great time for a dad joke, Miriam. And thanks for coming. Before you start, though, can I ask you a favor? I might need someone to take care of the store for a couple of days—"

Miriam waved me off. "Say no more. I'd be happy to. It'll give me a good excuse to see what sorts of new goodies you're carrying."

I pulled a sofa pillow under my head with shaky arms and laid back, noticing the sound of the front door opening and closing as the Whelens arrived. Conall pulled an armchair over so Miriam had a place to sit. She perched on the edge of the chair and closed her eyes. I felt a slight charge in the air as Miriam held her hands over my center. She stacked her hands flat and slowly moved them, scanning my body for impurities.

Other than the occasional shifting of clothes as someone moved and the humming of the heater, the apartment was silent. I closed my eyes and allowed Miriam to work in silence. We all did.

Miriam positioned her hand on my sternum, and I twitched a little when she touched my body. Her hands were like a dry sauna penetrating my chest, and the warmth and pressure eased the tension I'd been holding. My muscles relaxed, and my mind emptied as I focused on the healing compression of Miriam's hands. She changed positions, taking her hands to my shoulder, my temples, the hipbones, and the tops of my thighs. In time, I found myself relaxed and dozing under the influence of her comforting touch.

Miriam sat up, and I lay there enjoying the twilight slumber as she slowly stood to join the others.

"Is she going to be OK?" Conall whispered.

"I think so," Miriam said. "Whatever got inside her was the spiritual equivalent of poison, and she got a heavy-duty dose, but I can't sense much of it now. I think she'll be fine by tomorrow—maybe tomorrow night at the latest."

"What could do something like that?" LaDonna wanted to know.

"Whatever it was, either it targeted her specifically or got in there today," Conall said. "I walked in and out of the shop yesterday without a problem, and she barely made it behind the counter before she keeled over. Scared me half to death."

"I suspect it might be a hex placed inside her home," Miriam said. "Something that would be effective even after it's been put into place—perhaps growing stronger with time. If you can find whatever set her off, remove it, and then cleanse and ward the home again, it will help."

"Give me the keys to her house," LaDonna ordered Conall. "Luke and I will go there now. We'll tear that place apart if we have to. And put it back together nicely, of course."

"I'll go, too," Miriam offered.

"I'll call my dad," Conall added. "He'll want to help."

My heart soared with love for my coven, and I drifted to sleep.

Chapter 24

The elder coven members were gone when I woke, but Hanna and Betony had arrived along with Jake. They were quietly sitting at the dining room table, leafing through several sheets of light green paper with silver writing.

Ryan's notes! My sense of equilibrium rebelled at the sudden shift in direction as I sat up and gripped my head with my hands. It felt like a spiritual and physical hangover combined.

"Good morning, Sunshine!" Hanna chirped. "Feeling better?"

"More like I got hit by a bus," I admitted. My mouth felt like cotton wool, and I wrinkled my nose. I needed a toothbrush something awful.

"Conall! She's up!" Jake hollered. His deep voice rang in my head, and I flinched at the sound and covered my ears.

"Not so loud, please."

"Sorry."

Conall hurried into the room, his plaid pajama pants topped with a t-shirt emblazoned with a local craft brewer logo. "How are you doing?"

I slumped. "I honestly can't recall feeling much worse."

"Can I get you anything?"

"Do you have orange juice? I'd kill for some orange juice."

He grinned. "One orange juice, coming up."

As he headed to the dining room a few steps away, I asked, "Any luck on the search for whatever sent me into this tailspin?"

"You heard that part, huh?" He found the OJ and poured me a tall glass. "Not yet. They'll find it, I'm sure."

"Is Joey helping them?" I asked. Joey would be best suited to locating and breaking any lingering hex magic as the coven's black witch.

Conall chuckled. "Murphy, *everyone's* helping them. Except us. We're taking care of you."

Betony held up a handful of pages. "And going over the information on the Stygian that your father gave us."

"What time is it?" I accepted the tall glass of orange juice Conall offered. It tasted like a fresh slice of heaven.

"A little after eleven," Jake replied.

"After eleven? Shouldn't you be at home in bed, Jake? Y'all have school tomorrow."

"I'll be heading out soon, now that I know you're OK. My mom said I could stay late tonight because I was taking care of a friend. I got to watch the coven ward Conall's place—that was pretty cool. Besides, we needed the time to go over the plan to get into the Stygian coven."

"And LaDonna said I'm better off with you for now," Betony added. "Homeschool has its advantages."

"Well, if you have your plan figured out, go on and head home," I told Jake. "I have these three to look after me. They can fill me in, and I don't want you falling asleep in class."

Jake laughed. "That's what third block is for."

"What's your third block?" Betony asked.

Jake shrugged. "Art. I used class time to design an album cover, but I already had the concept down, so I'm way ahead. Mrs. Murray doesn't mind if I fall asleep as long as I finish my work on time."

"Yeah, I've heard Mrs. Murray's cool," Betony agreed. "She lets Lorina sleep in class sometimes when she needs to."

I stood, and the world only tilted slightly, an improvement I was unexpectedly grateful for. Conall held his arms around me, but at a distance, ready to pounce if I so much as wavered. Taking one slow, shaky step after another, I shuffled to the dining room with my glass of orange juice. I set the glass down, pulled out the remaining chair at the table, and sat—well, not so much sat as allowed my legs to give out from under me.

"What's the plan so far?" I inquired.

Hanna picked up a piece of paper the color of luna moths. She'd written over the silver text in a black felt-tip pen to make it easier to read. She pulled her tigers-eye hair away from her forehead and tied it into a knot behind her neck with a yellow pencil. I always envied people who could do that—my hair is far too thick for a pencil to conquer.

"Ryan said the coven meets every full and new moon. The full moon is Wednesday, um, the day after tomorrow, so we thought that'd be a good time to try and get in."

"Did he say how?"

"According to Ryan, the majority of their meetings are held in a trailer at the cotton gin just outside of town—you know, that place on Reignier Road? The guy who owns it is a coven member."

"Must not be a huge coven if they can meet comfortably inside a trailer," I observed. "Virginia—Betony's mom—made it sound like there were quite a few of them."

Jake stood to gather his things, and Conall took his abandoned chair and sat beside me. "Big coven or not, they've been able to make some powerful spells," he said. "Big enough to incapacitate even you. We can't underestimate them."

Hanna motioned to Conall with her pen, and the billowing sleeves of her oversized sweater flowed with her. "He's right, Murphy. Any coven with enough skill to target one person and with enough strength to disable you isn't one we need to take lightly."

Jake gathered his backpack, hugged me, said his goodbyes, and closed the door lightly behind him.

Betony's phone buzzed, and she checked the message. "Aw, it's Rene," her voice sang. "He wanted to check in and make sure you were doing alright. He is so sweet!" She clicked a few buttons in response with a huge grin on her pretty face. Betony had a habit of going through love interests pretty quickly. I hoped if Rene made her this delighted, it would last more than a month or two.

"This plan is only going to happen if you're feeling one hundred percent by then," Conall said, tipping his chair back to two legs. "If we have to, we'll find a way for you to dodge them for another couple of weeks until the next new moon."

I wanted to devise a different plan: *I'll be fine, we're doing this*, or *Jake and Conall can go without me; I'll stay back and recover*. No matter what, the Lughaidh coven would not sit back while the dark Stygian witches played with my life and the lives of those I loved. The idea of waiting two more weeks and facing whatever punishments they unleashed in their attempt to kill me was terrifying. Without the strength to fight back, I didn't see that I had a choice.

)O(

The past few days' events had worn me down to a nub, and I pleaded off any further planning that night, trusting that any developments were in the capable hands of my friends. As much as I hated to admit it, I needed to rest.

Someone had brought me a change of clothes and pajamas; I found them folded in a pile on Conall's bed when I used his restroom to brush my teeth. I changed into the pjs and wished everyone a good night. It wasn't until I lay down that I noticed the drawstring bag with Conall's Valentine's Day gift on the nightstand on my side of the bed.

I have a side of the bed at Conall's place. The thought made me smile.

I was so exhausted that I didn't even crawl out of bed to call Conall to open his gift; I texted him, feeling ridiculous for my laziness, and summoned him to the bedroom. He was at the door in seconds.

"Did you need something?"

I giggled. "Yeah, I want to give you your Valentine's Day gift before the day ends. That is, unless you opened it already?"

He shook his head. "Not yet. I thought you'd want to be conscious when I did."

He entered the room, shutting the door behind him, and I handed him the bag. I was thankful for the transition to dimmer lighting; the light shining from the rest of the apartment hurt my eyeballs.

He tugged on the strings, and first pulled out the dowsing board. It was a piece of black, round carved wood, about eight inches across, with a plethora of options for a pendulum to choose from—anything from yes and no to astrological signs, months, numbers, days of the week, and the alphabet, all written in silver.

"Whoa, this is beautiful!" he said. He turned it over, probably not expecting anything, but on the back, I'd had the artist add a note.

"What does *Is tú mo ghrá*, mean?"

"You are my love."

"You are my…" he chuckled and caressed the imprinted letters. "I love it, Murphy."

"There's more in the bag."

He raised his eyebrows and reached a hand inside and withdrew the opalite dowsing pendulum. The silver filigree detailed cap and pearlescent opalite were like points of light in the dim room.

"They're beautiful. I love them." He carefully placed his gifts on his nightstand and then leaned in my direction, placing a hand behind my head to pull me in for a kiss.

"I couldn't let our first Valentine's Day go by without giving you your gift," I said.

"That's right! I haven't given you your gift today." His gaze smoldered, and he didn't let go of my head. He kissed my chin, my cheek, below my ear.

"Conall, you already gave me an engagement ring. I don't need anything else."

He came closer, encouraging me to recline as he hovered over me, his taut body supported by his solid arms. "I can think of one more thing I can give you."

I giggled. "Hanna and Betony are right outside. They might know what we're up to in here."

Conall peppered my neck with kisses, and he started lifting my shirt. His hands found my breasts, and I pulled in a shaky breath.

"Oh, I have no doubt they know exactly what we're up to in here." He let out a low growl and climbed on top of me, and I could feel through the thin material of his flannel pants that he was hard. I fumbled for his drawstring, and he lifted his pelvis so I could pull it loose and ease his pants over his hips.

"Are you too tired?" he asked.

"Never for this," I breathed.

"Let's be safe," he said, pulling my shirt over my head. "How about you let me do all the work this time?"

I pulled in a shuddering breath as his hands roamed my upper body and then set to work on the fastener of my pants. *Damn, his hands are as magical as the rest of him.*

"If you insist."

Chapter 25

Tuesday morning dawned, and for a moment after I opened my eyes, I forgot where I was. Our sleepovers had always involved Conall staying with me. It made more sense with my business downstairs and his job closer to my home than his apartment. Then, the soft, beige color of his walls, the blue and white stripes of his bedding, and his arm slung across my body softly clicked. I was safe in Conall's apartment. My fingers caressed the tattoo on his arm, and his eyes fluttered open.

"What time is it?" His voice was thick and sleepy.

I rolled over to read the bright red numbers of his digital clock. "Six-thirty."

Conall hustled over and gave me a quick kiss. "Shit. Gotta go. I'm running late." He rolled over, threw off his comforter, hopped out of bed, and rushed to the bathroom in nothing but his fleece pants. I watched him go, admiring his broad shoulders and the muscles along his spine as he shut the door behind him. The sound of the shower started along with Conall's cheerful humming as he performed his morning ritual.

Stretching out languidly, I rolled out of bed and tousled my hair into something resembling order. I found my socks and slid them on my feet before shuffling into the kitchen. This morning called for coffee, but then, what morning doesn't? There's a reason my business is called *Witch's Brew*.

Betony lay on the couch in the living room. Her long, berry-red hair tumbled over her face as she slept. I opened the blinds in the room just enough to shed a hint of light, but not enough to wake her, I hoped. The gently increasing glow of the rising sun would be easier for her than switching on an overhead light.

After I did a bleary-eyed early-morning fumble through Conall's cabinets to prep his coffeemaker, I grabbed my phone to text

Miriam. Knowing her, she'd already completed a circuit of her neighborhood, showered, and was starting on her first cup of tea.

Good morning! Have you finished your morning run?

Miriam:
Just out of the shower and enjoying my tea. What's up?

Did LaDonna give you my key?

Miriam:
Yes. Don't worry about a thing today. I'll be at your house whenever the electricians get there. If they finish early, I'd be happy to open your shop. The coven found those hex pouches, did you know?

When she relayed the details, it sounded like Ericka had placed them in locations she had traversed during her visit for hexing supplies. Despite trailing her, I hadn't seen a thing. She must have suspected that I'd be watching.

Realistically, all Miriam would probably have to do that day would be to let in the electricians. But if they finished quicker than expected, it would be great to have the doors to the shop open again. When I asked her where they'd found them,

Conall bustled out of his room dressed in blue jeans with a flannel layered over a thermal shirt, gave me a swift kiss on the cheek, and grabbed a thermos from his cabinet.

"They found the hex bags," I told him.

"Good," he said. Out of habit, he flicked on the overhead light, and Betony complained with a sleepy moan from the next room and threw her arm over her eyes.

"Sorry, Bet," he apologized and turned the light off.

"Hmph," Bet grunted.

Conall gave me an exaggerated *Oops* face and poured himself a generous helping of coffee from the pot into his thermos.

"How are you feeling today?" he asked me. I stretched, and his eyes raked my body as he reached into the refrigerator for creamer.

"A lot better," I said. "I think sleep helped."

"Good," he said. After finishing with the coffee creamer, he paused. "Maybe I should call in. Just in case."

"Go," Betony said, drawing the word out insistently. She sat up groggily. "I'm here. She's not alone. I'll keep my phone fully charged and close. I know CPR if it makes you feel better."

His mouth turned into a pensive frown, and he shifted his weight to one leg as he re-evaluated me.

"If I told you to spin around right now—"

I did a little dance move, crossing one leg over the other and spinning in place. I rocked a bit but recovered in less than an eye blink, confident I'd played it off without him noticing. I was wrong. When I came to a standstill, Conall had his arms crossed over his chest and his head cocked to the side.

"You wobbled."

Exasperated, I slouched. "Barely. My legs are still waking up."

He frowned and shifted his stance.

Betony stood up and strode in our direction, rubbing sleep from her eyes. "Conall, I got it. We're good. We can have a chill day here around the house. I won't let her out of sight. I'll even follow her into the bathroom if it makes you feel better."

The aggravated part of my brain waged an argument with the sensible part. If Conall had a dark coven set on killing him, and he was left alone with only a teenager to guard him—even a powerful one like Betony—I'd hate to leave him and head to the shop.

"Hanna said she'll be here as soon as she's done shopping. We'll be fine," Betony added. Hanna had a small catering business quickly growing into a full-time job. It was only a matter of time before she would need a storefront and employees, which was why she saved every nonessential nickel and dime. It was also why she still lived with her father at twenty-six.

Resigned, he pulled me in for a tight hug.

"You have my number, right?" he asked Betony over my shoulder. I heard her "Mm-hm" in response, and he let me go. "Please be careful," he said.

"I will."

He grabbed his thermos, gave me a kiss and an embrace full of anxious energy, and left. After he shut the door behind him and enough time had passed to ensure he wasn't coming back for something, Betony pivoted and gave me a wry look.

"You *are* going to be fine, right?"

I sank into one of the black dining room chairs and took a long sip of hot coffee. "I hope so."

My phone buzzed, and I picked it up. It was Gryphon Utilities informing me they were on their way.

It's only seven o'clock. They're on the ball today.

I messaged Miriam and told her to expect the electricians soon, and she sent back a smiley face and a thumbs-up. Maybe life was looking up. I might have my shop open after lunch, and Miriam was earning a few dollars. Then tonight, we could infiltrate the Stygian coven and learn how to stop them.

I wanted to believe it, but I didn't.

☽○☾

I felt well enough to make Betony and myself some scrambled eggs and toast and downed another cup of coffee while I watched the morning news. We were unusually quiet, but I was grateful for the silence—my soul needed it. Any other Tuesday, and I'd be mentally preparing myself to open the store. Lounging around Conall's living room while everyone I knew was working or in school felt weird. Everyone but Betony, that is. Her job was watching me today. And my job was recovering so I could hop aboard Conall's transfigured canine body and help him and Jake sneak in and observe the dark coven.

"This is boring," Betony said after about the third news story covering the president's visit to a foreign country. "We should do something."

"Like what?" Knowing Betony, "something" didn't narrow it down much.

"When was the last time you did any shadow work?"

I hesitated, taking a moment to turn off the television and set the remote on the coffee table. I considered how to answer Betony's question, since I was reluctant to tell her the truth.

"I guess I never have," I admitted. "I've had moments of reflection and prolonged introspection, but nothing I'd consider deep shadow work."

"Murphy!"

"I know, I know. Every witch worth her salt should take the time to dig into her shadow self and learn what triggers her. I just... I guess I always thought it was pointless because I was so isolated from everyone."

Betony crossed her arms and regarded me with an expression I couldn't read but didn't seem flattering. "Murphy. Did you ever think that diving into some shadow work could have helped you feel less alone?"

"I *like* being isolated."

"Why would anyone like being isolated?" Betony's life was enormously social. When she'd found out she was the gray, she was terrified it might mean closeting herself off from humanity the way I'd elected to. Fortunately, she'd found that shadow work with others helped her channel her gray chaos energy positively. During her time in juvenile detention, she'd learned that drawing out the stories behind those who'd acted out in pain and helping them work through their problems not only helped those inmates, but herself as well. The turmoil within their stories strengthened her chaos energy, which she, in turn, harnessed with her generous spirit and heart. Betony then returned it to them in the form of acceptance, love, and contentment.

"It was safer for me to be alone," I explained. "I didn't hurt people if I stayed inside my warded house."

"Yes, but did you like being isolated 'cause it kept you safe, or were you only safe 'cause you stayed in your own bubble?"

My brow knit, and I puzzled over her statement before asking, "What's the difference?"

"Were you like, intentionally isolating yourself to keep everyone else safe from you, or were you just protecting yourself from everyone by being on your own?"

Damn, she's good. I hadn't even been aware we'd started the shadow work, but here we were.

"Both, I think," I said after a moment's introspection. "I've never been outgoing. Not like you and Hanna."

"LaDonna's told me you used to be different as a kid," Betony countered. "Very happy and friendly."

I frowned. "She's told me that, too. I don't remember it."

"You don't? Not at all?"

I shrugged. "I don't remember a lot from before my mother died."

Betony's posture slumped in frustration. "Murphy, you probably need to do shadow work more than *anyone* then! Has anyone told you stories about times you don't remember? Stuff since your mother died?"

I shook my head, sat forward, and fiddled with the bent edges of a science magazine on Conall's coffee table. "Everything until the night she was murdered is spotty," I admitted. "Most of my memories from before then are about her. My memories seem to be pretty intact after that, though."

"How did LaDonna figure out that you could be the Summate?"

Whoa. Talk about a change of subject. Weird.

"She told me about her suspicions the night she came over when we were playing with the Mystic Spiral, remember? Lorina's grandmother had just popped onto the board, and then LaDonna and Hanna knocked on the door? With 'Rolf?' That was the night when she told me a sixteen-year-old gray witch might be disrupting my energy and that I might be the Summate."

Betony's excitement grew, though she did her best to suppress it. "So, the high priestess—her partner being an orange prophetic witch—randomly pops up with your two best friends the night after the wards on Witch's Brew got busted, without knowing about the dude who tried to jack you. And then she drops the bomb that there might be another gray witch in town, and you might be the Summate. Oh, and she also says how Conall can transform into Rolf to help you spy on the gray. But, did anything else even go down before that to give you a hint on why she was thinking all that?"

I shook my head. "No, nothing."

Betony snorted derisively. "Murphy, I can't believe you didn't see it."

"See what?"

"Luke must have told LaDonna it was time to tell you what they'd suspected *from the start*. You've always had power that a gray witch shouldn't have."

I shrugged. "Maybe they thought that part of being a chaos witch meant my power would be chaotic in more than one way. Maybe it jumped all over the spectrum because it couldn't settle." That was the story I'd told myself over the years to explain my ability to perform skills of varying types.

Betony sighed, her eyes reflecting maturity beyond her eighteen years. "Murphy, I think it's time for you to be really honest with yourself. Do you, like, think there's a chance you don't remember what went down before your mom passed 'cause you were scared you might misuse your powers?"

My hands flew to my temples. Betony was talking in circles. "What do you mean?"

"Think about it, Murph. You were a powerful, happy kid. Life was great—you had a sweet mom and a great family in your coven and were probably displaying all sorts of crazy talent in small ways. And then your mom and your two best friend's moms all die right in front of you."

My head swam as I considered the suggestion. I'd been able to kill the killer if I wanted to, but it was wrong. Had I become afraid of my power, of my feelings, and my anger? My hand slid to my forehead; it was cool in comparison, and it felt wonderful.

"You knew you were powerful, Murphy. You knew you had some major potential, maybe even a bit too much. So you would've ghosted and kept yourself away from the world to keep yourself and everyone else safe."

I let out a long breath as the idea tumbled around in my head.

"It's just one possibility," Betony admitted, "but, hey, it's worth thinking about, you know?"

"No, that's good, Betony. I never would've come up with that on my own."

My phone buzzed, and I picked it up. It was Miriam.

"Hey, Miriam! What's—?"

"Murphy! Where is your power box?"

"It's in the pantry. Is everything—?"

"Do you have a fire extinguisher?"

"For an electrical fire? Yeah, I have—it's in the pantry, too. Miriam, what's—?"

"There's a fire. The roof. I'll call you back as soon as I can!"

Chapter 26

I hung up in a daze. *A fire on the roof*? It must have started somehow during the electrician's work on the weatherhead. And here I was at Conall's, helpless to do anything but tell Miriam where to locate the fire extinguisher.

Then again, I was the Summate. And across from me was the chaos witch whose power was so strong that during the years I reflected her power, I thought *I* was a gray witch.

"Murphy, what's wrong?"

Gathering a storm wouldn't work. The sky was too cloudless. Too many elements would need to be involved too quickly, and the environmental repercussions could be disastrous. Besides, water and electricity are a dangerous mix—what if Miriam didn't get the power switched off?

"Murphy!"

"There's a fire. My roof—it's on fire. Betony, I need your help."

Her eyes grew large. "Anything. What can I do?"

I crept to her side and gripped her forearms firmly with my hands; she held my arms likewise.

"Picture the roof. Can you see it? Gray shingles? The little turret part?"

"Yeah, I can see it."

"OK, now imagine us—you and me, right now—encasing the roof. Better yet, the whole second story. All of it inside of an enchanted barrier where all the oxygen in the air is disappearing. Better yet, all the air. Just all of it—gone. Like a vacuum. But—but any human there won't be affected. They are sheltered. I don't know how, but the Universe will protect them."

"No air, no fire," she concluded, and I liked its sound, so I repeated it.

"No air, no fire." More words came to me, and I added them, turning them into a chant. "It goes no higher. No air. No fire. It goes no higher."

Together, we gripped each other's hands and focused. Usually, when I conduct a spell, I typically turn my attention inward, blocking any stimulus from the world around me the best I can. But the intensity of Betony's gaze, as she peered into my eyes, assured me of her strength, which assured me of my own. I felt like a Gemini twin, with Betony as my other half. One half of me clinging to Betony in Conall's apartment, the other detached and floating above my home.

"It goes no higher. No air, no fire. It goes no higher. No air, no fire. It goes no higher. No air, no fire…"

Although I hadn't seen the fire in the physical world, I detected the intense heat in my connection with Blackwell Manor and the years of love linking me to my home. Flames shot from the tiny window in the short attic I hardly used except to store a couple of boxes of old decorations I never used. But it wasn't just the roof anymore—I could see straight through the damage to where the fire had descended into the upper story and was striving to destroy everything in its path. Smoke and fire filled my bedroom and living room, tongues of flame licking over the walls, consuming my books, curtains, a closet full of clothes, and my beautiful painting of Papa Legba. I heard the fire crackling in the walls and something that sounded like maybe sparks of electricity.

Oh my god, this is bad.

My eyes watered, and my vision blurred. It grew hard to breathe, almost as if I was physically present and pulling in lungs full of acrid smoke. I coughed, and Betony's grip on my arm held me tight, ensuring I didn't break our bond.

"It goes no higher. No air, no fire. It goes no higher. No air, no fire. It goes no higher. No air, no fire…"

I blinked, and twin tears broke free and raced down my cheeks. As I watched through the eye of my Gemini twin, the flames engulfing my home gradually dwindled, the air cut off by the power and the intent of our spell. Through the haze of thick smoke lingering through the dying flames, the wood beams of my upper story stood exposed like a blackened skeleton.

"It goes no higher. No air, no fire. It goes no higher…"

Betony's voice drew me back to the apartment, where she clenched my forearms in her grip. My arms clung to hers as well. Despite being surrounded by the bland, beige walls of Conall's apartment and facing Betony, I could still smell the smoky air of my burning house.

I gasped and tasted the tears I had shed while traveling.

☽◯☾

Knowing my home was still smoldering was killing me, but I couldn't leave straightaway. Betony didn't have a car, and my Corolla was back at my house. Would that be a casualty of the fire, too?

I grabbed my cell phone and pushed a familiar sequence on the screen. The phone rang for five agonizing rings before Conall picked up.

"Conall," my voice cracked, and I paused to collect myself.

"Murphy? What's wrong?" The tone in my voice had sent him into an instant panic.

"My house… there's been a fire."

"Holy shit." I heard soft sounds as Conall moved the phone away from his mouth. "Justin!" From a distance came a deep-voiced reply. "I gotta run. There's been an emergency." The deep voice said something that sounded affirmative but unintelligible from my end. "Alright." Another muffled sound came through the speaker, and Conall was back.

"Murphy, I'm on my way. Do you need me to do anything? Call anyone?"

A beeping tone alerted me to an incoming call. It was Miriam.

"No, Conall. I just need you. Just you. I've gotta run. Miriam's calling."

We signed off, and I switched to Miriam's severely distressed but still dulcet voice.

"Murphy, honey, I am so sorry to hang up on you so fast, but I had to run."

"I know," I assured her. "Fire travels quickly."

"Your house… honey, we tried, but it was so fast. The upper story—"

"I um… I saw."

"You—oh, you did? That might explain some things. The firefighters have been acting strangely. The worst of the damage seems to be over, though. Do you need someone to come and get you?"

"Conall's on his way. What happened?"

"The electrician accidentally started the fire on the roof while he was working on the weatherhead. With the dry weather, everything took off quickly as all get out."

"The Stygian couldn't find me, so they struck at my house again," I muttered. "Either that, or they're still toying with me."

Miriam was silent for a moment. "Yes, you're probably right. We're not gonna let this rest, though, honey. We're all here for you."

I thanked her, and we said our goodbyes. Then, I had nothing to do but anxiously wait for Conall to take me to my fire-ravaged home.

Chapter 27

Conall pulled up to the curb next to Blackwood Manor with experienced ease. Although my house's charred outline stood out against the clear blue dawn, my mind refused to accept the sight for several moments. This couldn't be Blackwell Manor. Surely this was a nightmare, and I'd wake up soon in Conall's bed with his arm around me and his quiet, even snoring soothing me.

I opened the creaking door as soon as we were in park. The air from the Oberon Street curb reeked of my burned house and charred belongings, and the overwhelming smell instantly made me sick to my stomach. The emergency vehicle lights still pulsed on the street, though the excitement had subsided, and the crew was returning their gear to the fire trucks. One of the emergency responders was roping my property with yellow caution tape. An ambulance stood behind the fire trucks. Nearby, a thin, shaggy-haired man in a Gryphon Utilities uniform strove to appear as innocuous as possible. I resented him from the moment I laid eyes on him, although he was likely an unwitting pawn of the Stygian. He caught my angry glare and looked away hastily. *Probably afraid I'll hex him.*

Miriam noticed our arrival and hurried over to greet us. She embraced me tightly, her hug exuding the scent of expensive perfume that almost masked the smell of smoke. She and I clung to each other for a long time, each soothing the other in the only way possible. When she let me go, she hugged Conall next, and he reassured her that neither of us found her to blame.

"I'm so sorry, Murphy. I tried—"

I embraced her tightly. "There wasn't anything more you could do, Miriam. It'll be fine. I've got good insurance. The most important thing is that you're OK. Have you seen Rex?"

"He ran into the pantry when I started panicking, but I haven't seen him since."

My heart tightened with concern as Miriam laid a hand on Betony's shoulder and gave it a friendly squeeze. They both appeared ready to cry. I wanted to cry with them, but it would have to wait. I needed to see what had happened.

I stepped to the curb and was halted by the arm of a firefighter still garbed in a yellow protective jacket, his helmet off. He had dark skin and dark eyes that had seen a lot of trouble in his lifetime; at the moment, those eyes reflected deep sympathy.

"Ma'am, is this your home?"

I nodded and swallowed hard, determined that this man wouldn't keep me from surveying the damage. Yes, this house had nearly killed me the last time I'd stepped foot in it, and now a size-able chunk of the upper story was a burned, ruined mess, but no matter what the Stygian did to it, Blackwell Manor was my *home*.

"I'm afraid I can't let you go in there yet. We haven't assessed its structural damage."

"The second-story floors weren't affected, correct?"

He blinked, flabbergasted. There was no way I could have made that calculation from where I stood, and we both knew it. I wasn't going to fuck around right now, though. If he deduced I was a witch from my supernatural deductive skills, so be it.

"Yes, but the heat—"

"And the back portion of the house, including the stairs, is still intact?"

"The fire may not be completely out. We think it is, yes, but it's still not safe."

"It is safe," I asserted. "And I need to get in."

"Ma'am, I'm afraid I can't let you do that yet."

From the curb, a familiar voice called, "It's alright, Charlie. Murphy can take care of herself." I turned and saw Officer Kenny Hendricks near his patrol car. Slim, dark-skinned, and kind-faced, Officer Hendricks was one of my favorite people in Gryphon. That he was a cop who'd often dealt with the chaos-causing version of me for years and did it without a complaint didn't hurt.

"Kenny, if she gets hurt, she could sue."

Kenny shook his head. "She won't."

"Won't what? Get hurt, or sue?"

"Either. Will you, Murph?"

I held up one hand and put the other over my heart. "I swear on my mother's grave."

Charlie's skeptical expression and tight mouth told me he was not convinced by my oath, but Kenny's solemn nod proved to him something my words had not.

"I'm coming with you," Charlie said. Pointing a finger at Conall, Miriam, and Betony, he barked, "You stay here."

Charlie insisted I follow him to the truck, where he pulled out his helmet and a secondary one, which he handed to me. "Don't take this off until we're back outside."

I agreed and donned the protective gear before following Charlie under the caution tape and around the back to the porch and the kitchen entrance. As he lumbered forward, I watched the letters GFD written in black on his yellow jacket above a strip of reflective fabric.

We reached the back door, and Charlie stopped so quickly I nearly collided with him. He faced me, his jaw set in his stern face as he ensured I was paying attention.

"You step where I step. You don't touch a damn thing unless I say you can. Got it?"

"Got it."

Charlie made a grumpy "hmph" sound and opened the door. I caught him grumpily mumbling something about Hendricks under his breath, but I didn't understand much else.

A haze lingered in the bottom story. Pale motes of dust and ash floated in the air as we entered the kitchen, my steps tracing Charlie's. I wasn't sure what else to call him. *Are firefighters officers, or is that just police?* I'd have felt more proper calling him by his rank if I had known what it was.

Jake and I had made candy for Cadence in this room only days before. It felt both familiar and eerily foreign, like the front of the store had when I entered before my weird attack—a weird real-not-real sensation, this time brought about by the trauma of the fire instead of the spell.

We climbed the stairs together, my footsteps continuing to mimic Charlie's, as directed. When we reached the top, the space looked much the same as it had when I'd seen it during my chant with Betony, only bigger. However, underneath the stench of burning wood and other items came the lingering stink of standing water and decay. My house did not smell of decay, and it was too soon for the water to have caused rot. The air was malodorous with the scent of curse residue. Any lingering reluctance I held in believing that the fire might not have been caused by the Stygian completely vanished.

I followed Charlie to my bedroom, where little remained that was distinguishable. My bed was half consumed; the metal frame scorched and tilted, the mattress a muddy pile of ash. All my clothes and shoes were trashed. The floors were intact, but the upper part of the frame and the roof stood exposed to the sky.

"Damndest thing," Charlie said. "Normally, when a building has a cockloft like yours, the whole upper story goes up in flames. Your fire stayed almost completely to the north." His voice had softened. Charlie either felt bad for me or appreciated that I'd followed his orders. Probably both.

He allowed me to trail him to what remained of my living room. The fire had reduced my novels to ashes, and my couch was a mess of wet charcoal and mushy cushion.

"Papa Legba?" Charlie asked. Sure enough, half of the face of the loa—a voodoo spiritual mediator between humankind and Bondye, the creator of the universe—lay on the ground. It was all that remained of my gorgeous painting.

I nodded. "I have a painting of another loa—Baron Samedi—in my office."

He tilted his head curiously. "You study voodoo?"

I shrugged, noting his tone was not condemning. "A little. I'm a witch, and I love my craft. Witchcraft is where my family and roots are. I have an affinity for them, though, and I respect and admire them, even though I don't use them in my practice."

Charlie tilted his head, his countenance curious, but said nothing. White voodoo aficionados are pretty uncommon, I imagine.

I was hoping for a salvageable token of my life before the fire from the hollowed-out rooms, but nothing was reclaimable. Recalling how Conall had taken pictures for his insurance company after the car crash, I pulled my phone from my back pocket and snapped a few pictures. I'd have to call my insurance company soon to get an appraiser out to the house. That could wait for now.

"Can we see the other rooms?" I asked. Compassion returned to his large brown eyes, and Charlie reluctantly allowed it.

He led the way across the hall to my Room of Power, which remained almost undisturbed, save for a pair of smoke trails on either side of the doorjamb. The guest bedroom and hall bathroom stood intact as well. I wondered how long the smell of smoke would stay after the house had aired out for a couple of days.

"What does the roof above these rooms look like?" I inquired.

"Amazingly good," Charlie said. "Like I said, the cockloft always spreads the fire throughout the upper story in any fire I've seen before. Your house is the only one where it's almost all contained to those two rooms."

"But it looks like those two rooms and the roof above them are where the worst damage was?"

He nodded. "As far as we know, yes, but it's still early and I can't say for sure. We better get out of here. I know Kenny vouched for you and all, but this is not how we do things."

I trailed behind Charlie, my gaze fixed on the swinging doors to my shop, attempting to peer inside and gauge the extent of the damage.

My mind reeled. *Has water from the firefighters' efforts damaged the shop? How much of my inventory is salvageable—or is it all trashed?* I anticipated most of the stock would be affected. Those hoses always packed one hell of a punch on TV shows. *How much remediation will my house need before repairs can start? How long will it take before I could move in and open back up?*

Only a short time ago, the four days I had to close because of the damaged weatherhead sounded like an incredibly long time. How long before things got back to normal now? Months, probably. Thank goodness for my savings account.

The anger I had directed towards the electrician when I first arrived paled compared to the rage I now felt towards the Stygian.

When I reached the ground level, Conall was standing at the curb with one of my favorite customers, Rita, a sweet woman in her late thirties or early forties with colorful hair and arms in matching hues. Rita had brought someone with her today I'd never seen, and they couldn't appear more different. Where curvy Rita had multiple bright tattoos and hair that transitioned from blue to magenta, her companion was trim, with long, white, spiraled curls. Rita's style was hippie-esque, a long-sleeved tie-dyed t-shirt and a rainbow-striped jacket over jeans and boots. Her companion dressed conservatively in slacks and a cardigan over a turtleneck.

"I didn't know you were closed," Rita said. She offered a hug, which I gladly took. "I brought my mother here so she could see your lovely shop. She's visiting from Salem. Conall's been telling me how rough things have been for you lately. Oh, Murphy, I'm so sorry."

Rita was a customer whose many purchases and conversations over the years had tipped me off she was a genuine practitioner, not a craft hobbyist. We'd chatted several times when the store was slow about aspects of the craft, and she was a woman I thought of not just as a customer, but as a friend. So it was with a certain comfort that I muttered, "Yeah, nothing like being the target of a dark coven to help you grasp how vulnerable you are."

"Dark coven?" Rita barked, her eyebrows shooting up. "Is it local? I hadn't heard of one around here."

I saw in my peripheral vision how one of the firefighter's ears had perked up at our discussion, so I motioned for Rita and her mother to step a few feet away with me. Rita quickly made introductions, and I shook hands with her mother, Madeleine. Then I resumed my story.

"I think it may have disbanded and then started over recently," I said. Soon, I was unspooling the story: our mother's deaths years ago, the recent revelation that I was the Summate and Betony the gray, the trouble that started last October, the current issue of Ericka trying to join our coven, and Betony's mother's story about the Stygian coven. I left out some of the more incredible parts, like Conall's ability to transform into a dog, but I kept all the critical details in.

"They could break through your wards?" Rita said, flabbergasted. "It sounds like your coven could use a hand."

"We probably could," I admitted.

"You're in luck," Rita said. "Guess who is the leader of the largest cyber coven in the Southeast?"

Cyber coven? I'd never heard of such a thing, but of course, there had to be. There was no reason that the power of electronics couldn't be harnessed like other energy to fuel spells.

"You?" I ventured.

Rita beamed. "Yep. We're on all the popular social media platforms. I started our website, and we host spiritual social events and online ceremonies. Quite a few local members shop at your store—they all appreciate the positive energy there. I could put the word out that you need help, and you'll have hundreds of witches across the globe who can lend you a hand."

I pulled out my phone and logged on. "What's your coven's name?"

Rita beamed. "The Worldwide Witches Web." Not terribly unique, maybe, but I loved it.

Over the next few minutes, we exchanged information, and Rita and her mother both promised they would be waiting for a text or call from us.

When we settled into the car to head back to Conall's apartment, I felt optimistic for the first time in days. A global network of witches cooperating with the gray and the Summate. The Stygian didn't have a chance.

I hoped.

Chapter 28

I made the necessary calls to the insurance company, and Conall and I contacted LaDonna and Luke to catch them up on what happened. The rest of the afternoon was a flurry of worried phone calls, texts, and emails between the people I loved and the people I was required to deal with. The appraiser would be out Monday to assess at the damage to the house. I used Conall's computer to announce the bad news on the Witch's Brew social media sites. Maybe the flurry of activity should have worn me down, but my anger fueled me beyond what might otherwise have been possible.

When school let out, Jake and Lorina joined in the exchanges. Eventually, Jake, Lorina, Cadence, Conall, and I drove to the Whelen's to meet with the rest of the coven and Rita to discuss the plan to infiltrate the Stygian meeting. Rita had spent a chunk of her afternoon arranging a mutual coven meeting between the Worldwide Witches and the Lughaidh.

When the four of us arrived, a new presence stood in LaDonna's meeting room: a laptop, camera, and microphone equipment. The shiny, modern equipment starkly contrasted LaDonna's earthy treehouse décor.

Rita had been cautious and spent some time earlier that afternoon enhancing the cyber coven's tight security. We couldn't risk any dark covens intruding on our plans. Rita explained the precautions they took to keep their transmission private, but other than the word "encryption," the terminology went right over my head. Ultimately, I had faith that our communication would be impenetrable by anyone who wasn't an exceptional hacker.

Welcome to witchcraft in the twenty-first century. I'd always been a bit old-fashioned. Hanna had been bugging me for years to update my register to a model that tracked inventory. I'd stashed my microwave and television inside cabinets to give my Victorian home the illusion of being suspended in time. Maybe

Rita's participation might drag us, however reluctantly, into the modern world of witchcraft.

"Lorina, you get out more often than any grounded person has a right," Betony joked.

Lorina shrugged and stretched her lanky body. "I'm with a youth group," she said.

"A youth—" Betony snorted. "Well, technically, you're not wrong. We're a group of youths." She pointed to the four of them.

"Exactly," Lorina said with a sly grin.

"I'm never having kids," I joked, rolling my eyes.

"Come on, you love us," Lorina cajoled.

"I do. I'm still never having kids."

Terry and Miriam entered with heavily laden arms. Terry had brought bags of clothes she said she never wore anymore—we were roughly the same size and shared a similar style. Miriam had a basketful of hand-crafted personal care items to pamper myself with—bath bombs, body butter, and soaps she'd made. The woman was nothing if not crafty.

"They're all specially made to help your spiritual healing," she said. "Gardenia, right?"

My favorite fragrance. I gave the two women enormous hugs. They had arrived together and had undoubtedly spent the day contemplating ways they could help me feel more like myself again.

We didn't have much time to iron out the last details of our plan to sneak into the Stygian meeting. It started in the cotton gin office at 8:00 in the evening, and the Lughaidh coven was set to meet two hours before. Rita started her broadcast, and then LaDonna took a few moments to provide everyone with an abridged version of how the Worldwide Witches coven joined the Lughaidh in our battle.

"There's one part that's unclear to me," Rita said. "You keep saying Jake's going to be the one they interact with, but Conall's going, too. What's his role?"

"Familiar," Jake said, his eyes sparkling.

"Familiar? How's that? I've never heard of a human familiar."

"It's probably easier if I show you," Conall said, then

directed his attention to the camera. "To all of you—excuse me. Give me just a second."

I waved to catch Rita's attention and mouthed, "Grab the phone," while pantomiming the action. Rita gave me a swift bob of her head, hastened to the tripod, and detached the phone. She trotted after Conall, who ducked into the small water closet off the Whelen's kitchen. Moments later, a scratching sound came from about knee height on the door, and I obliged him and opened it.

Out trotted Conall in "Rolf" form, an adorable pup who resembled a squat German shepherd mixed with a miniature wolf.

"Rita… Worldwide Witches… meet Rolf," I said.

Rita hurried to the door of the tiny room Conall had just left. On the floor lay his clothes in a messy pile from where he'd quickly shed them.

"Hold on," Rita said, her voice disbelieving. "Are you telling me *that's* Conall?" She panned her phone inside the tiny room, allowing the viewers to see what she'd figured out—there were no secret passages, seams in the painted walls, no places for Conall to hide.

"Mm-hm," I said. Rolf came to my side, and I picked him up and cuddled him, marveling at his weight. Even as a dog, Conall was muscular as hell; the stocky pup was way heavier than he looked.

"Holy shit. That's sweet. May I?" She extended a hand in the dog's direction, and Rolf opened his doggy mouth and smiled at her, panting adorably. She gave him a couple of head scratches, marveling at the magic she'd witnessed. "That is amazing."

"I'll be joining Jake via astral travel by way of Con—er, Rolf, here," I added. "Hitching a ride in him will allow Conall and I to communicate silently. If Conall and Jake run into any trouble, I can jump out of his form, head back, and alert the rest of the coven. *Covens*," I corrected, eyeing Rita's phone. *This web-witching thing is going to take some getting used to.*

"Excellent," Rita said. She hit a button to reverse the camera's perspective back to her face. "Y'all, is that amazing, or what? I'd give up every phone upgrade for the next ten *years* to do something like that!"

She hit the reverse button again and aimed the phone at us. Rolf gave a disturbingly human salute with his doggy paw, and I set him back down on all fours.

"Damn," she said as Rolf trotted off to join the coven. Many felt the need to pat him on the head and give him back scratches, even though it was Conall. Ever the good sport, he ate it up.

"Now it's my turn, I guess," I said. I headed into the neighboring room—what Luke called the study—where my foster father waited in a chair next to a chaise brought down from an upstairs bedroom. I flashed back to the last Halloween, when Luke had guided me through the most challenging night of my life. I had a moment of panic. What if the Stygian figured out I was there and knew how to trap me inside Conall's doggy body? How much of a risk were Conall and Jake taking? What if we got away with spying on them only to learn we had no way to combat their plan?

I took a deep breath, counted to five, and let it out slowly.

One step at a time. Standing around and waiting for the Stygian to figure out how to kill me isn't the best plan.

"It'll be OK, Murphy," Luke said, and even though he couldn't be positive, hearing those words from a prophetic witch helped.

Rita entered the room with her phone pointed in our direction. "Will it bother you if I'm standing here and sharing this with everyone? I don't want you to feel self-conscious."

I'll feel self-conscious alright, but I reckon you need to do it, anyway. What came out was, "It's fine."

Once my eyes were closed and I turned inward, focusing on Luke's voice alone, the presence of a camera wouldn't matter. Seeing the phone's lens pointed at me, all I could think about was how many people might watch us conduct our meeting. I trusted Rita's talent, but still felt vulnerable.

Don't think about them. Think about Luke, tonight's plans, and stopping the Stygian.

Luke waited patiently—which was typical of him. The man had more patience than anyone I knew, except for maybe Conall. Maybe it was an orange witch thing. Ten years ago, poor Luke volunteered to be the one to teach me how to drive a stick shift. I'll never forget how we had to wait through six red lights before I figured out how to swap the brake and clutch pedals for the gas when our car was stopped on a hill. Maybe being aware of what the future holds makes it that much easier to wait for it.

I crossed the room and sat down on the chaise, kicking my shoes off onto the tile and tucking them underneath before I reclined with my feet up. I fussed with the pillows until I found a position I could keep for a long time without discomfort, laid my hands across my stomach with my fingers interlaced, and closed my eyes.

"Ready?" Luke asked.

Not trusting myself to speak, I nodded.

Word must have gotten out that we were starting because the noise in the background in the next room grew to a low buzz.

Luke's voice began its steady cadence in the reassuring, sedate, low tones he used when guiding others on an astral journey.

"Murphy, allow yourself to hear only my voice, and your own internal spirit. Remember, you can return to yourself whenever you like, and that your travels will be safe. Feel the sofa below you, the velvet fabric, the soft cushions…"

Within moments, my limp body, seemingly devoid of muscles, had sunk deeply into the cushions below me, and my respiration was steady.

"Allow yourself to see your body, to detach from your physical form and elevate your consciousness into the spiritual plane."

With Luke's assistance, separating my spirit from my corporeal form was as easy as stripping off an outfit. Only this time, I had a specific destination in mind. Floating free of my body, I pivoted around and saw Conall's furry form waiting for me at the foot of the chaise.

Let's see if it really is like taking a running jump into a swimming pool.

My astral form took a swan dive at Rolf. Given my speed, it seemed odd not to hear the wind rushing by my ears. I was glad I had no physical body when I collided with him and ricocheted off, my spirit hovering low enough to peer into Rolf's eyes. He blinked, and I wondered if, in his dog form, he saw me or saw through me.

OK. That didn't work.

The question was, *why* didn't it work? I'd rushed at Conall just as I had before, but this time, I encountered a spiritual barrier. Why? What made my attempt so different this time?

It occurred to me I'd never merged with Conall—spiritually speaking—on purpose before. A sense of urgency had always brought it about. Perhaps it wasn't a problem of inertia so much as need. Spirits didn't experience speed or time the way physical beings did, but they did *feel*.

It didn't take much to stir up my motivation to unite with Conall. Recalling the events of the past few days was enough: the car crash, the blackout, the vision of my home's charred rooms, Betony's mother's threat, the Stygian, my father's message that they wanted to kill me to start a wave of chaos, the Cadence and Jake's botched spell…

I didn't just want to ride along inside Conall to hear what they said at the meeting that night; I *needed* to know what these evil jackasses were planning. Were they a local coven? Did they have a global network the way Rita did? There was only one way to learn to save my life and keep the town of Gryphon safe—and whatever other places the Stygian intended to overcome.

And that was through Rolf.

Infuriated, frustrated, and determined, I rushed the short little dog again, this time willing myself into that home within him, my comforting soulmate who would travel with me to uncover a solution, no matter how hard or what the cost.

We blinked. The world had changed color, and I balanced my weight on four furry feet. This time, I was oddly aware of the absence of an opposable thumb and the presence of a tail.

Welcome aboard, Murphy.

Thanks, Conall. Man, this never stops feeling odd.

Chapter 29

Poor Jake was emitting stress in such intense waves that Rolf and I picked it up with our enhanced canine sense of smell. Never mind that he was a black belt wearing steel-toed boots—Jake was never one to seek confrontation. His presence tonight, parked outside of the cotton gin in his sporty Mitsubishi fixer-upper, spoke volumes about his love for Cadence.

He'd chosen a smart parking place near the road that would allow for an easy exit if we needed to leave in a hurry. Several sun-bleached, blue metal outbuildings stood around a gravel lot, almost three-quarters full of cars. A couple of short silver silos and a port-a-potty had been placed near a tall building on metal legs with three huge funnels on the bottom—for dispensing cotton, I assumed. Though the cotton processing season was long since over, a few balls of raw, dirty white material lingered in the tall grass at the edges of the property.

"OK guys, I guess this is it," he said, barely higher than a whisper. He studied the pale trailer office door. His hand reached over and ruffled us on the head. "We can do this, right?"

Rolf and I huffed our agreement. I checked the clock; it was seven fifty-six. We were right on time.

Jake got out of the driver's side, and we strode down the gravel road behind him. The air was bitter cold, and the sky was clear and full of stars. Together, we walked past a handful of people hanging around outside the only building with lights on. The glow from cigarettes explained why some of them had braved the cold rather than heading into the meeting. The potent odor of cigarette smoke hit our nostrils, and we sneezed.

"Bless you," Jake murmured. We huffed our thanks.

Jake avoided eye contact with the people outside as we proceeded to the office door and took the cinderblock steps. Jake knocked three times on a cheap metal door. The door swung open, and a man with a dad bod, dirty jeans, and a long-sleeve t-shirt greeted us, along with a blast of heat from inside the building.

"Hey," Dadbod said, and offered nothing else.

"Hey," Jake replied. "Um… can I come in? I was told this is where the meeting was."

"Dog stays out," Dadbod ordered with a motion to the gravel parking lot with his chin. His eyes were flinty and stern, as if he was used to playing bouncer for a rowdy dive bar.

Jake shrank a bit. "Can he please come? He's my familiar, and I'm nervous. It's my first meeting. And it's really cold outside—he'd freeze in the car."

From where we stood with our paws on the top step, we could see the room beyond was filled with milling people from across the human spectrum. The interior smelled like sweat, raw cotton, dust, and sweet tea. Some folks sat in folding chairs waiting for the meeting to begin, but others stood in groups chatting.

"Amos!" the man who greeted us hollered over his shoulder. "This guy's got a dog. Says it's his familiar. That a problem?"

We looked up at Jake's bearded face and sturdy frame. It hadn't occurred to me until then, but seventeen-year-old Jake could easily pass for someone in his mid-twenties. That might work in his favor tonight, since folks might be inclined to accept a responsible adult with a dog when they'd have reservations about a teen.

The people standing in our way blocked Amos's reply, but it must have been in the affirmative. The greeter opened the door a hair wider and waved us inside.

"Just keep an eye on it. And if it shits on the floor, you're both leaving. After you clean it up, of course."

"Not a problem," Jake mumbled. He turned to us and asked, "Up?"

Probably a good idea. We don't want to get stepped on.

It's a lot more crowded here than I expected, I added. We crouched down, bracing to show Jake we agreed, and he bent down and scooped us up. It wasn't until he had us held to his chest that I appreciated how tall he was to a creature who stood only eighteen inches high.

God, I hope he doesn't drop us.

I sensed Conall would have laughed if he could.

"If everyone could take a seat, please," a female voice called from one end of the room. Jake milled around until he found a vacant chair. Like many meetings, the seats toward the back were taken first, leaving us only a spot in the third row if Jake didn't want to walk in front of many people. Thankfully, he got a chair near the end of the row, once again planning a quick exit if necessary.

Conall and I bobbed and weaved our head, trying to get a glimpse of the speaker at the head of the room. The voice sounded familiar, but I was having difficulty placing it until I saw a pair of turquoise eyes topped with close-cropped, platinum-blonde hair.

Ericka.

It was no surprise she was present. She must be in the upper echelons of the Stygian coven if she was opening the meeting. I wondered if she would lead the entire gathering or introduce someone else who would take charge.

"Thank you all so much for coming out tonight. As most of you know, my name is Ericka Moore, and I am also the high priestess of the Stygian coven."

High priestess?

Damn, I figured she was up there, but high priestess? Shit.

"I know several of you have traveled pretty far for this meeting," Ericka continued. "Some of you, like myself, have even tried to integrate yourself into the Gryphon community recently. I know it was a genuine sacrifice moving here from Atlanta, but I swear by the river Styx that in the end, achieving our goal of getting rid of the Summate witch and supplanting her with the gray will be incredibly worth it."

The crowd erupted into a disturbingly enthusiastic round of applause. Rather than join in, Jake chose that moment to pet us, which soothed all three of us. As the clapping continued, I heard the door behind us open and close a few times. Apparently, the smokers had been sucking on cigarettes until they heard the meeting start. Sure enough, a wave of cigarette smoke hit us, and we sneezed again. We tried to keep it quiet, but some folks gave Jake and us a dirty look. We might have sprayed them a little. It's not as if we could put our nose in the crook of our furry elbow.

"Sorry," Jake whispered to the woman in front of him. She grunted her response over her shoulder.

"I've been speaking with Virginia Yarborough. Her daughter Betony, the gray, visited her the other day. I have visited with Ginny several times in jail—clergy has that privilege. As most of you know, Ginny's daughter is the gray, and she's already shown some great potential. It's unfortunate the first person she killed was her father, but if murder doesn't show chaos potential, what does?"

Another round of applause followed, and I fought the urge to shake my head. This was like some sicko political rally.

"We are days away from harnessing the power of the Sovereign Darkness and using it to eliminate the Summate. Once she is gone, its chaos can sweep across our country and the world, wiping it down to its foundations, where we can rebuild a stronger world with our Sovereign's help. Its lieutenants have already begun their work, and Miss Blackwell's confidence in her power is undoubtedly shaken. Once it is thoroughly corrupted, we will strike.

"My son has *finally* joined me from Atlanta. He's agreed to spy on the Lughaidh coven to help fulfill the dark power's purpose. I will let him tell you what he's uncovered. Together, we will discuss how the coven will work to kill Miss Blackwell. Son, would you come forward?"

It was disturbing how blasé she was about my death. Jake continued to stroke Rolf, and his hand smoothing our fur was the only thing keeping me from trembling. I'm not sure if it was from rage, fear, or both.

There was a stirring from the back of the room, and Ericka's son stepped forward and joined her. Short, dark hair, broody brown eyes, stubble-covered, solid jaw, fit.

Rene Basilio.

Chapter 30

Jake's grip on us tightened as he fought the urge to bolt for the trailer door, but it's hard to leave subtly when you're a tall, long-haired man gripping a sturdily built dog. Rene's eyes barely widened as they noted Jake's presence in the crowd, but Conall and I both saw it. Rene's jaw jutted forward, and his eyes narrowed slightly, but other than that, he showed no sign that he registered our presence. He placed his hands on his hips and addressed the crowd, his confidence mimicking his mother's, but not wholly reflecting her self-assurance.

He must wonder if Jake is defecting. Why else wouldn't he expose us as Lughaidh traitors?

"I've, um, I've become close with the gray, Betony Yarborough. She has started thinking of me as her boyfriend, which is good. Murphy is pretty shaken up about her house catching fire. And the car wreck, of course. That scared them."

So, the deer was their fault. I sensed Conall's gloom as he recalled how fond he was of his wrecked car. Perhaps the deer had not been real; maybe it was a glamour conjured to cause the wreck.

A few titters broke out around the room, and Rene waited for them to stop before continuing.

"They have an idea that the disruption to Murphy's life has originated somewhere."

Oh, shit. Here we go. Rene's going to blow our cover. He's been in all of our recent meetings, and he's been talking with Betony. He knows what we've been planning, and he's going to tell them. We're sunk. Jake expected it, too; his legs tensed under us, prepared to bolt.

"But they haven't figured out where yet."

What?

What?

Rene's coffee-colored eyes flicked our way momentarily in an unspoken warning. Jake's hold on us loosened a tad, but he maintained enough grip to heave us into his arms and dash out if he felt we were threatened.

"I think they're narrowing it down, though," Rene added. "It's probably only a matter of time before Betony talks her mom into spilling the truth."

From the way he glanced at Ericka, he wasn't sure if his mother was aware that her buddy, Ginny, had already told us about the Stygian coven.

"I think if we're going to take action, we should do it soon," he added. "We don't want them getting organized like we are."

A nasal female voice from the middle of the room asked, "What have they figured out so far?"

"They, um… they found the hex bags."

"But the house went up in flames!" a masculine voice protested with a thick Alabama accent.

Rene cleared his throat, and I saw him weighing out whether he should tell them the bags were found before the fire. "It didn't burn down all the way," he said, weighing his words' effect on the crowd. "They um… Betony and Murphy contained the fire somehow. It took out a couple of rooms of the upper story, but it didn't burn down the house."

A heavy rumbling around the room expressed everything from disgust at their failed attempt to destroy my home and business to concern over the power Betony and I possessed when working together.

Ericka gave an approving head bob at her son's words and stepped forward, dismissing him as the meeting's speaker. Relieved to no longer be the center of attention, Rene stepped to the side of the room but remained standing. It worked for me—this way, Conall and I could observe him.

"Thanks, Rene. Good work. Yes, it's disturbing that she and Betony could stop the fire, but you've got to remember it was the Summate and the gray working together. If we pull Betony away from her, keep them from working together to create an earthly balance, the Summate will be crippled."

She kept calling me "she" and "the Summate," effectively removing any hint of humanity from how they thought of me. And did she really believe my power would be all but thwarted without Betony's participation? I threw a freaking car the other day! Not that she knew about that.

Calm down, Murph.

Our little doggie body needed to pant to let out some of the heat and stress, and the cranky woman in the row in front of us turned to sneer at us again.

I hope she's allergic to dogs. I sensed a lightness in Conall's spirit that revealed his amusement at my snarky thought.

"It's time to learn the coven's decision on who will bear the power of the Sovereign Darkness, as we channel it into a human body for the global polarity spell that destroys the Summate. To be clear, even if you are not selected, none of us has an insignificant role. We will contribute our energy to the spell's power, joining forces with our fellow coven members in a global network. Once the Summate has been eliminated, all of us will benefit from the anarchy that flows in her absence, from earth washed free of human incompetence. We'll all undoubtedly share in the power released by her removal.

"We've had the voting up on our coven page for two weeks now in anticipation of tonight's meeting, and coven members around the world have cast their votes. Of course, as high priestess, I reserve the right to veto the coven's decision if I feel the elected person isn't prepared to handle the duties required of them."

Someone from the front row handed Ericka an electronic tablet, and she deftly pressed a few buttons on the screen to reveal the results.

"And the result is…." Her eyes lit up with joy. "Rene!"

Rene, whose attention had been distracted by the faces in the crowd, blinked and jerked in astonishment. He swiveled his body in his mother's direction to see her beaming with pride that the coven had chosen him.

"Me? They chose me?"

Ericka, who had eyes only for her son, distractedly handed the tablet back to her assistant. After reviewing the results, the assistant nodded to verify the election had indeed chosen Ericka's son as the host for their evil leader. Rene would spearhead the Stygian's global scheme, initiating a chain of events that would ultimately lead to my demise and plunge the world into chaos.

"Rene, isn't that wonderful?" she gushed, sounding much more like the Ericka I remembered from my shop. I'd never realized dogs could flinch.

Rene blinked, his face flushed and challenging to read. He ran a hand through his hair and swallowed hard. In that moment, I wished for the ability to read his mind as effortlessly as I could read Conall's. He and I were both struck dumb with panic while our thoughts tumbled over worriedly.

"That's… um… wow. Uh, thank you." He took a shaky step toward his mother, who crossed the short distance and hugged her son fiercely. The surrounding crowd broke into applause. It sounded like Rene was a coven favorite. He pulled away and waved at the group seated around us, a weak smile on his handsome face.

Jake, Conall, and I sat still as Rene took in the attention of everyone in the crowd but us. The trembling I'd held back earlier took over, and I shook as if I'd been left outside in the winter cold.

It was odd thinking that I sat there facing the young man destined to try to kill me. The young man to whom Betony, the chaos witch, had grown quite attached.

Chapter 31

The Stygian coven discussed possibilities for a time and a date for the ritual, and it registered on some level, but my head was still reeling. Erika said she'd weigh the proposed choices with the rest of the global leaders as soon as the meeting was over, and the meeting let out shortly after that.

Jake scooped us tightly into his arms and scarpered for the door as soon as it was socially acceptable. He didn't bother with post-meeting pleasantries other than to offer a couple of unobtrusive head nods as we stole to the door. He didn't run to the car, but his long legs made fast work of the distance.

We had nearly escaped without interacting with any of the Stygian. Jake set us down on the ground to dig his car keys from his pocket when Rene's voice called across the parking lot.

"Jake! Hold on a sec!"

"Should we run?" Jake asked, doing his best ventriloquist impression to keep his lips from moving.

I wanted to say yes, but Conall took control of our muscles, and shook our head. If he'd gotten a premonition, it'd slipped by me, but I trusted Conall's instinct. Years of being an orange witch had given him an almost frightening insight into the future.

Jake lingered to see what Rene had to say, but he took a moment to unlock his car as we waited. Jake swallowed, and the muscles in his jaw tightened as he watched Rene jog across the parking lot, his breath emerging in large plumes as he moved.

Once at our side, Rene stopped momentarily, seeking the words he needed.

"Hey, um. Hey, are you… Are you…?"

"Am I what?" Jake said, his irritated tone barely hidden behind a veneer of false patience.

Careful, Jake. He couldn't hear me, but the words crossed my mind, anyway. We have been on the outskirts of the crowd at the moment, but it was only a matter of seconds before the people leaving the trailer office made their way to their cars and were within earshot.

Rene rolled his eyes and let out an exasperated sound. "It's not... I'm not..."

"The son of the high priestess of the coven who wants to kill Murphy? The guy who just got appointed to be the host of the force that's supposed to do it?"

A loud sports car raced by on Reignier Road, its muffler and souped-up engine deafening us temporarily. The tailpipe backfired a couple of times, and the three of us jerked a little.

I pawed at Jake's leg worriedly, and when he peered down at us, I directed my muzzle to the dispersing crowd heading our way.

"I liked you, Rene," Jake said, his deep voice sincere. "And I'm grateful you didn't say anything too dangerous in there. But if you thought I was defecting, you're wrong. My loyalty to the Lughaidh and my friends hasn't changed. You've got to decide."

Rene registered the nearing coven members, and his mouth tightened in frustration. His hands moved from his hips to across his chest, and he stepped back and let us get into the car.

Jake held his composure well as he loaded us into the passenger seat, crossed to the driver's side, and bent to get in, but his hands trembled as he put the keys into the ignition. He refused to give Rene a second look. I put our paws on the back of the passenger seat and saw a forlorn expression on Rene's handsome face as he watched us drive away.

)O(

"And they said they wanted to perform the ritual when?"

We convened in LaDonna's meeting room, Conall and I restored to our usual human forms. Rita and LaDonna had worked together to close a protection circle around us to prohibit our conversation from prying ears. Rita told her coven she'd update them with further details once we'd gone over the events of the evening.

Jake shifted, picking up a corner of the table cover and playing with it. "Before the worm moon and the spring equinox. I know the equinox is next month, but what the hell is the worm moon?"

"It's the March full moon," I said. "Nearly a month away."

"I can't see them waiting that long," Luke said. "Not when they know we're narrowing our search for the cause of Murphy's troubles. Not to mention that the spring equinox is about balance and new life, which is what they're trying to stop."

"I can't believe Rene is part of the Stygian coven," Betony reflected, her face downcast and her body slumped in disappointment. She'd barely taken part in the discussion, instead staring at her phone and scrolling through distracting apps and websites. La-Donna placed a gentle hand between her shoulder blades and gave her back a motherly caress.

"How will we know when they set a date for this ritual?" I asked. "I tried getting onto their website, but you have to have a password."

Rita snorted. "That's easy to get around," she said. "Give me a few minutes with my laptop; I'll bet I can crack it. How soon do you need it?"

Thank you, Mother Goddess and Father God, for bringing this tech-savvy witch into our world.

"Today?" I said. "Now would be great if you can. No sense waiting."

Rita patted the table with a sturdy hand. "I'm on it." She left for a moment and returned with her laptop. She logged into her system with expert swiftness and made her way onto the Stygian coven's website. Her fingers danced between the keys and her mouse adroitly. She stared at her screen, a slight crease forming between her eyebrows as her eyes panned the screen.

"March second," she said. "There's a conjunction of Mercury and Saturn in the Capricornus constellation, and they think that's a good time."

"Why is that a good time?" Jake asked.

"Hmm," Rita leaned in as she adjusted her horn-rimmed glasses on the bridge of her nose. "Ah… it doesn't say."

"Mercury is the god of thieves and tricksters," Lorina explained. "He'd totally vibe with their coven's beliefs, you know?" She had found LaDonna's small wooden riding horse toy made for toddlers and had perched on it. She rolled back and forth, her skinny knees jutting higher than her elbows.

"What about Saturn?" Cadence asked.

"God of harvest," Lorina explained. "If they think of him as a harvester of the world as we know it, it checks out. I mean, he *was* ruler of the universe."

"I thought he was a god of peace," I countered.

Lorena scoffed. "You can make beliefs from anything. Just look at what the Bible has been used to justify."

"And Capricorn?"

Lorina shrugged. "That's not really my thing."

Luke picked up the thread. "Capricorn is associated with the god, Pan. Depending on how far this group will go to cause global chaos, it might mean they plan to turn the world back to its natural, untamed state."

"He's one of the oldest Greek gods," I added. "He might even have existed before the Greek pantheon as we know it. He didn't follow the traditional rules of other gods—he didn't have temples built in his honor. Most of his places of worship were in nature."

"The word panic comes from his name," Luke continued. "According to the stories, he could throw an army into fear, down to the last man, and they'd scatter."

Silence fell as we digested this.

"OK, so when will we strike against them?" I asked, trying to get the conversation and brainstorming rolling again.

LaDonna picked up her phone and pulled up a calendar. "How about the twentieth?"

"This coming Sunday?" Rita queried after pulling up a calendar on her monitor. "Any reason for that day?"

"It's a Sunday. Most people have the day off, and we'll be able to get the most participation."

"February twentieth is Kurt Cobain's birthday," Jake observed.

"Awesome. They've got Mercury, Saturn, and the god of panic, and we've got Saint Cobain of the Fender Mustang." Lorina let out a snort of laughter.

I hated to agree with Lorina, but she had a point. The Stygian was organized, spanned the globe, and had been planning an attack for who knew how long. We were on the offensive, and our odds didn't seem too promising, even with Rita's Worldwide Witches on our side.

"Jupiter is the king of the gods," Lorina said, still rocking. "He beat Saturn. Made him puke up all the kids he ate, and then he and his brothers and sisters took down Saturn. Jupiter became king after defeating his dad."

"Ew," Betony said, wrinkling her nose. "Saturn ate his kids?"

"Yep," Lorina said with a shrug. "Mythology's weird."

We had a plan. A shaky one, but a plan nonetheless. We knew when the Stygian would strike, and we would take preemptive measures to keep it from succeeding. Maybe there was a little hope after all.

Chapter 32

The next three days passed at a crawl. On day one, Betony returned to my house with Jake and Lorina, and together they located Rex sunbathing in his favorite hiding place on a top store shelf. They coaxed him into the carrier to bring him to LaDonna's and grabbed some cat food, litter, and toys for Rex on their way back. I appreciated their efforts tremendously. No doubt my house still smelled something awful. It touched me that the high schoolers generously spent a little of their hard-earned dollars to help me and my familiar be safe and together. He was extremely glad to be with me again instead of inside our stinky house, and trailed me everywhere until he noticed the birds on the branches outside. After that, he spent his time gazing out the windows.

At the coven's insistence, I stayed holed up at LaDonna's house under their protection, sleeping every night in my old bedroom next door to Betony so there would always be someone to watch over me. I would have preferred Conall's, but it made more sense to stay with my foster parents. Their house was simpler to ward than an apartment complex.

It was odd to have the walls of my old bedroom around me and the view of the tranquil mountain slope outside my window. The walls were the same golden yellow as black-eyed Susans—my favorite flower the year we'd painted it. I think I was twelve at the time.

LaDonna displayed my treasured books on the maple wood bookshelf opposite the bed. The bed itself was thrifted, adorned with gauzy butter pecan curtains cascading from a cleverly built ceiling frame, and a constellation tapestry replaced the absent headboard. LaDonna's eclectic throw pillows added a bohemian touch to the room, evoking a cozy charm I hadn't felt since childhood.

To my relief, Hanna and Conall took time off from their jobs to join me as I hid at the Whelen's. If the Stygian had been studying my life as we suspected, they would be aware of my ties to them, and they were in danger as well. The Stygian coven played dirty. No doubt they'd kill someone to weaken my spirit and hinder my ability to defend myself when they attacked. Anything to let their Sovereign Darkness loose on the planet.

We celebrated Hanna's birthday with a low-key celebration with the coven at the Whelen's. The dining room table was pulled out to its ridiculously long size, and we all gathered around and toasted her long life over her favorite meal—eggplant parmesan and a huge Mediterranean salad.

Conversation over dessert inevitably gravitated to our spelling plans. After a lengthy debate, it was decided that our goal was to change Ericka's heart or to give Rene the strength to walk away from the clan or both.

To prepare for the Lughaidh gathering on Sunday, a constant rotation of coven members moved in and out of the Whelen's home. Everyone lent a hand in designing their best spells. I provided Miriam with a list, and she headed to my place, gathering any undamaged the tools and supplies she could find from the shelves. I instructed Miriam to allow any member of the Lughaidh into Witch's Brew to pick up anything they desired for their personal spell-making to enhance the energy of Sunday's event—no questions asked, just please maintain a record of the items removed.

We gathered in LaDonna's kitchen, putting everything on the counters. Our tasks began: smoky quartz for negative energy removal, clear quartz for amplifying positivity, and blended salts for purification—combining black lava sea salt to symbolize the Stygian darkness, traditional white salt for the Lughaidh, and pink Himalayan salt for love, bridging their animosity. We bound herbs for smoke purification—sage for protection, basil for love, and bay for banishing negativity. Rex, ever playful, batted at the tied flowered heads as they were tied together.

We rolled beeswax candles by hand and added ingredients to increase potency and strengthen our chance for our desired victory. We ground herbs and oils, salts, and spices and mixed them into tinctures, powders, and philters. Countless protection and banishing spells took shape, along with incense infused with these elements. Each witch created a scent imbued with their intent to banish negativity and safeguard the world from the impending harm of the Darkness.

Jake showed up every day after school, and I was thrilled to see how seamlessly he fit into our coven. With Ericka out of the picture, I believed his chances of joining our ranks were excellent. When he wasn't grinding salts and binding herbs, he strummed his guitar, filling the room with music and weaving melodies. Lorina and Cadence, their homework and strict parents permitting, joined us whenever possible. The infusion of youthful exuberance raised the energy levels of the adults tenfold. One night, Jake's guitar and Lorina's drum box played familiar tunes while the coven sang along. The positive atmosphere was just what we all needed.

I watched how Jake took in the group's flow, noticed what songs brought out the most singers and the most toe-tapping, and how he drew from that to determine which song came next.

I may not need to teach him music magic—the kid's a natural. The universal joy and musical power flowed from his soul to his fingers, through his guitar, and into our hearts. It brought a lightness to our spirits, making the work fly by.

Although I was a member of the Lughaidh, the Worldwide Witches coven was open to anyone, so I signed up to track the communications. Rita periodically texted her online group to announce times she would go live, and about every twelve hours, she'd update her global coven. The support and love in Rita's community blew me away.

"We don't keep negative Nellies around," Rita explained when I mentioned this. "It disrupts the coven's energy."

Saturday night, the entire coven, including Rita, gathered at the Whelen's, prepared to commence the ritual at dawn. The traffic on the Worldwide Witches website skyrocketed. From the sound of it, hundreds—perhaps thousands—of witches from across the globe planned to join us. Hanna issued a special message to red witches, urging them to amplify their love magic at dawn Central Time. Joey called upon black witches to provide protection, while white witches were implored to tap into their power to purge negative energy. When they were done, Rita ensured her recording equipment was ready on LaDonna's patio so the Worldwide Witches could take part in the morning's ritual in real time.

I slept fitfully, aggravated by everything from the sound of scraping branches outside to the way my fitted sheet chose that night to start peeling from one corner of my mattress. When La-Donna stirred around four to mix the mulled wine, I crept out from under my thick down blanket, careful not to disturb Conall. I crossed through the front room where Miriam and Terry were either spending a very late night or a super early morning doing some last-minute candle rolling, sprinkling some herbs into each beeswax fold.

By the time I reached the kitchen, LaDonna was halfway through preparing the morning pot of coffee. I leaned against the counter sleepily and waited. The drip of the electric coffeepot mesmerized my sleep-addled brain, and I jumped a little when La-Donna spoke.

"You ready?" she asked, her gravelly voice extra low with sleep. I wasn't sure if she was genuinely curious or just making conversation, but the answer was the same either way.

"As I'm gonna be."

She gave me a weak smile, which I returned.

Luke trudged into the kitchen and waited with us for the pot to stop brewing. He stirred together a cup of cream-laden coffee before dragging his sleepy body outside to start a fire in the deep firepit at the center of their patio. He fumbled in the woodpile for some logs and sticks and seemed to take a moment before remembering where the rest of his fire-making paraphernalia was.

"Is he going to be alright?" I asked.

LaDonna laughed and blew on the top of her coffee before taking a sip from the thick ceramic mug. Her eyes sparkled with love as she watched Luke stumble through starting a fire.

"He'll be fine. He could do this in his sleep."

"Which is good, because I think he is."

LaDonna pulled two bottles of Merlot from a countertop wine rack and poured the contents into a large ceramic pot. Together, we chopped apples and sliced oranges for luck and love, added nutmeg to heighten our spiritual connection, and topped it with allspice to increase the power of the concoction. LaDonna stirred it all together in the pot with a heavy wooden spoon—clockwise, of course—and set it to low.

We grabbed a second cup of coffee, bundled up in hats and coats, and headed outside to check on Luke's progress with the fire.

By the time dawn rolled around on Sunday, LaDonna's study

had grown into a miniature version of Witch's Brew and smelled almost as heavenly as my store. I was drained from restless nights and anxious days broken up by short nightmare-filled naps. It might have been the only thing keeping me going, but dammit, I'd made it through the week.

Now, the genuine test awaited—to see if our coven would prevail in its counterspell against the Stygian.

Chapter 33

Luke had a substantial fire built with flames licking waist high. The mulled wine was warmed and ready to drink when the others woke. LaDonna often used wine to help lower inhibitions when the coven tapped into large amounts of energy. The conversation I had with Betony earlier that week came back to me.

You knew you were powerful, Murphy. You knew you had some major potential, maybe even a bit too much.

Just how much power did I have the potential to wield? Enough that an entire dark coven felt the need to take me out before releasing their Big Bad onto the planet, apparently. Enough to throw a Camaro flying several feet overhead in a moment of panic. Enough to heal my boyfriend—*fiancé, dangit*—within seconds after a fence picket had impaled him last Halloween.

Maybe I was afraid of the extent of my power. To hell with coffee. That morning, I needed wine.

I downed two glasses of the delicious brew probably quicker than I should have. I was a bit tipsy and leaning against the kitchen counter, my body relaxed and warm. I was about to grab a third mug when Conall came into the kitchen, still rubbing his eyes. He yawned, reached into the cabinet for a cup, dipped it into the mulled wine, wiped the drips from the edge of the mug, and peered through the windows overlooking the patio where most of the coven had congregated. Rita was doing some last-minute broadcasting to prepare for the ritual, a tiny black microphone in her hand as she stared intently into the eye of her phone's camera.

I sidled up to him, and he slung an arm around my middle. I tipped forward at the waist and helped myself to another mug of wine.

His brows lifted and creased. "How many have you had?"

"This is my third," I admitted.

"Careful," he said. "You want your inhibitions lowered, not gone."

"I'm sipping this one," I replied somewhat defensively, picking a clove off the top of my cup, and flicking it at the garbage disposal.

"You're our anchor in this," he reminded me. "We can't have you… unmoored."

I laughed. "Unmoored, huh?" I pivoted to face him, taking in the dark morning stubble on his chin. Running a hand over it with my thumb, the corners of my mouth turned up, and I leaned in for a kiss. He pulled me in with one arm, cautious about the hot drinks we both held. We kissed deeply, and I knew the wine had taken hold when I swooned more than usual.

"Is LaDonna leading the ritual today, or are you?"

I blinked, surprised he posed the question. "LaDonna, of course."

He shrugged. "I thought maybe she would let you take the lead today."

I shook my head. "Too much at stake. I'm the one they want to kill. We don't want the group's focal point disturbed if anything happens in the middle of the spell."

His brow furrowed. He hadn't considered this, and the idea clearly disturbed him.

"I'll be fine," I said, hoping it was true. Grasping Conall's hand, I tugged him toward the French doors. "Come on. Let's go. We need to get started."

)O(

The sky had evolved to the gray-blue tones of a cloudy dawn. We set our coffee and wine mugs on the wooden patio ledge and lit incense in containers ranging from miniature cauldrons to brass censers, backburners, and stick holders before taking our positions around the firepit. Fragrances designed to muster our desires for peace, love, and protection tickled my nose, and the smoke trails danced in the freezing morning air.

Rita stood near the circle but slightly behind, willing to join but unwilling to insert herself into the coven. I knew how she felt. Not too long ago, I would have gladly stood where she did, on the outskirts, watching but unwilling to insert myself. Today, I stood between Conall and Hanna and waited for the nervous butterflies to stop dancing in my stomach.

This was the moment. We were ready to make our stand. Yet,

deep down, a sense of unease lingered. Why did I harbor the lingering feeling that something was amiss?

LaDonna stood in her ceremonial green robe with a hand raised at the north end of the circle. Luke, dressed in amber-colored robes, stood to the south. LaDonna held back no punches today and brought out her wand to help her focus her energy to a point. It was light wood, made from an ash tree and engraved with sigils she'd designed and burned into the wood herself.

"Goddess Diana of the hunt, we turn to you...."

Diana of the hunt? Smart call. She's bringing the fight to them today.

"...and Hecate, goddess of all magic and spells...."

Yep. Definitely not holding back.

LaDonna progressed with a ceremony unique in design, but which held many of our traditions. The circle of salt that she trailed to surround and protect us was white, unlike the salt used in our spells to end the Stygian coven's hostility. As she wove her magic words and implored the universe for help, she paced the circle and lit our hand-rolled candles. We joined her when cued and directed our hearts and minds to unleash maximum power into the ritual.

As things progressed, I got increasing numbers of curious glances from the coven. There was no question in my mind about why. In recent months, the coven has considered me the witch with the magical rainbow toolbox and the ability to tap into the universe at a whim. They all wondered why was I holding back when so much was on the line?

I wasn't holding back, though. When I reached for the Source, it was like trying to coax a flame from a lighter with no fluid. The spark was there, but not the gas. I sensed the Source all around me but couldn't touch it.

Don't get frustrated. Focus on what you can do, and let the Universe do what it needs to. Don't focus on what you can't do—it will only make it worse.

I willed my frustration to ease and concentrated on LaDonna's melodic, smoky voice as she finished her summons of the gods and goddesses. She took her place at the north end once more and lifted her arms with us. The wide fabric on her moss-colored sleeves dropped to her elbows, and she turned her face to the sky, which had grown blue and bruised with low-hanging clouds.

I fought the urge to fidget the way I had when Conall, Hanna, and I used to when we made faces at one another as the adults handled critical parts of the ceremony. I hadn't felt this unimportant since I was a small child and knew what magic was, but couldn't wield more than a spark.

I'd felt like a sheltered kid this week, and staying at LaDonna's had increased that impression. Sleeping in my old double bed with Conall had felt like I'd snuck my boyfriend through my window in the middle of the night. *Maybe that's my problem. I need to remember who I am.*

What made me who I am? Still a maiden in the eyes of the coven, but not a child. Who was grown Murphy? I'd transformed Blackwell Manor from a sizeable house to my home and business. I'd spent years paying my way, running my shop, and hiding from the world to protect them from the gray energy I projected. Later, when I discovered I was the Summate, that weighty position came with certain responsibilities. I was still figuring it out. I'd used my power to strengthen the coven and had taught them how to use the Source. I'd discovered I was capable of love and willing to accept a lifetime of love from a wonderful man.

I wiggled my left hand and rubbed my pinkie and middle finger against the now-familiar feeling of the Welsh gold engagement ring on my third finger.

There. Right there.

The thought of Conall and our engagement had kindled a bit more than a spark. That flicker of encouragement brought to mind the way Conall looked at me. My heart swelled. I grasped his hand, and his deep eyes found mine, reflecting a hint of curiosity at the thoughts he knew were flying around in my head. I held his gaze. I stretched my right hand over to take Hanna's, and her cool fingers wrapped around mine.

Love. As much love as we can summon.

Conall and Hanna seemed to read my mind, as they often do. Hanna gripped her dad's hand with her left, then Conall took his father's on the opposite side. The chain grew until it nearly drew to a close. I raised my eyebrows at Rita and tilted my chin, indicating she should join us. She beamed with joy before jumping in as our last link.

Love. Love.

LaDonna and Luke, who'd raised me. Miriam, the coven healer who was helping me with my shop and my health. Joey, who'd so recently found the hex bags that had made me feel ill. Betony, our sweet, gray chaos witch, who had finally found a home and the true meaning of family. Paul and Rafael, my friends' fathers, whom I loved so much. Terry, whose generous heart and humor bound the coven together when times were tense.

The Source LaDonna summoned flowed. Just a trickle, but it was a start. I imagined the flow to be like the pinprick hole in a dam that worked away at the dam's fortitude until the whole reservoir came flooding through. My fingers tingled as the current grew, and my heart lifted with hope. The current swelled until it arched across my body from fingertip to fingertip, and I fueled it with the endearing thoughts I held of each member of the Lughaidh. The power traveled from witch to witch, an electric current, steady and unbroken, a hum felt in the veins, synapses, and hearts. The sensation was enchanting, uplifting, and lightened my spirits until my chest filled to bursting. The love within the coven flowed and swelled in it, solidifying our bond.

The wind rose and stirred flames, a sign of an oncoming squall. I pulled in a lungful of pre-storm air and incense smoke full of black cohosh and cornflower, allowing the essences of these energies to enhance my connection. It was nowhere near the power level I'd grown accustomed to, but it helped.

The sun rose in the sky, and still, we stood, hands joined, force rolling through the circle over and again. In time, the swell subsided and ceased.

"We thank you, Mother Goddess and Father God," LaDonna said. "For the gifts of this coven and our guest, Rita, and for the love traveling the globe this morning. May you and the beings who dwell on this earth feel a sense of peace and harmony. May we remain united in our desire to see all humankind treating one another with love and kindness. So mote it be."

"So mote it be," we echoed.

Chapter 34

The coven unclasped hands and released a collective breath. La-Donna traveled counterclockwise around us, extinguishing the candles and uncasting the circle. I closed my eyes and drew in more humid air, now tinged with the scent of candle smoke and incense, holding it for a few seconds before letting it out in a rush.

It didn't work. Well, that wasn't totally accurate. Despite the heightened positive global energy, I intuited that my safety was still at risk, Ericka was still hell-bent on killing me, and the unfinished Stygian plan was still a go. I don't know what we were thinking. The Stygian would not respond to an enormous uptick in global harmony. And while our protection spells were strong, Betony's mother was right; the Stygian was formidable. Nothing short of a direct confrontation would stop them from their goal.

Without a word, I turned from the group and picked up my mug from the collection on the patio ledge. A couple of floating flies had decided wine would make a tasty breakfast and consequently wouldn't live to see lunch. Before heading inside, I tossed the remaining drink over the ledge into the wooded drop-off beyond the railing.

The air in the kitchen felt stuffy and still after the chilly, breezy air outdoors. I took off my jacket and tossed it onto a chair. I rinsed and washed the cup, dipped it back into the wine, and took a long pull. It was cooling, and many of the spices had sunk to the bottom, but it was still delicious. I checked out the time on the microwave above the oven. It was eight thirty-four.

"Feels later, doesn't it?" Hanna commented. She'd entered as I'd refilled my mug and tossed her coat on top of mine. The rest of the coven was outside milling around the fire, which Luke was stoking back to life with a long metal poker.

I nodded and swallowed hard. My heart was tight in my chest, and words wouldn't come.

"Do I need to ask how you think things went?"

I sighed. "It…" I put the mug down on the counter, and wine

sloshed onto my hand as my shoulders drooped. I didn't want to
say. Putting it into words made it real. But it had to be said.

"It hasn't changed what's coming."

Her brown eyes became sorrowful and concerned. Hanna pulled
me in, and we hugged tightly. Hot tears sprang into my eyes, and
then they were pouring down my cheeks. Maybe it was a side-effect of the two glasses—almost three—of wine, but that didn't
change my life was still in danger.

We pulled apart, and her eyes were glazed with tears as well.
"Do you want to tell them?"

I pulled in a shuddery breath. "In a few minutes. Let them bask
in the afterglow. It was a nice ceremony."

"It was," she agreed before helping herself to a sip of my wine.

)O(

Food always follows rituals. Energy stores are low, and blood
sugar needs to be raised, and that morning was no different. I
sneaked down the hall and stayed hidden in my old bedroom,
avoiding contact with the group until I was prepared to tell everyone what they may have sensed. I needed to think about what words
to use. *"Good effort, everyone, but I'm probably still gonna die.
Oh, and the world as you know it may end soon,"* didn't seem suitable.

I ran my hands along the gauzy curtain surrounding the bed and
the edge of a bookshelf. An assembly of some of my favorite old
stuffed toys stood bunched in a small net in the corner. I picked the
largest one from the center—a frog with googly eyes and long,
floppy legs nearly the size of Rolf—and hugged him tightly to my
chest. Some girls had teddy bears. I'd had Filip, the frog.

"What am I going to tell them, Filip?" I asked. Filip, of course,
stayed silent. Stoic little froggy.

Rex crept from his hiding place under my bed and wound himself around my ankles before batting playfully at Filip's hind flip-
pers.

A soft rap came from the door, and it swung open a crack on
quiet hinges. Conall poked his head into the gap in the door.

"You OK?"

Glad it was Conall, who already knew about my long and

abiding love for Filip and Rex, I nodded, my speech skills on par with my amphibious stuffie.

His face full of compassion, he pushed the door open enough to slip in and shut it behind him. He leaned on it, reluctant to approach.

"Anything I can do?"

I frowned and buried my chin onto the top of Filip's head, depressing the gap between his bulbous, wiggling eyes.

"Come here," he said. I set Filip on the edge of the bed and allowed his arms to envelop me in the center of the room. It's funny how much smaller the space felt now compared to when I lived here. Conall was warm and smelled of wine, fire, and incense. He rested his chin on my head, much like I'd done with my frog. The thought made me giggle.

He pulled back a bit to take in my expression, puzzled at my swift emotional shift. "What?"

"You—I—" I pointed at his stubbly chin, then at the frog, as I tried to dig for the words in the empty space my mind had become and failed. I lost my composure again in another fit of giggles. Jeez, what was wrong with me?

He waited for an answer, but since I failed to come up with a decent explanation, I said the first thing that came to mind. "I'm your Filip."

My words meant nothing to him, but they made him chuckle, and I giggled at the jocular tone of his voice.

"Well, you have lovely long legs like your friend over here," he said, taking one of Filip's webbed feet and wiggling it.

"And big-ass feet," I added. I was tittering so much that it was getting hard to breathe. "Mother goddess, I'm insane." I plopped onto my bed when I caught my wind. "I'm marked for death by an evil global coven, and I'm here laughing at my resemblance to a stuffed frog."

Conall sat next to me and rubbed my leg. Then he rubbed Filip's.

"Nope. Yours feel better," he joked. I shot him a wry look. "Seriously, though, try not to worry too much right now. This was our first try. We've still got time."

"But for what? I can't think of anything we didn't already try, can you?"

The hand on my leg grew taut under his fingers. "Not yet."

)O(

Brunch was a quick assortment of sliced cheeses, crackers, meats, and fruit, positioned buffet-style along the kitchen counter alongside coffee, water, and various juices and sweet tea. Easy, heavy on carbs, and tasty—just what the doctor ordered. I picked out a dessert-plate-sized portion of my favorites—apples, cheese, and crackers—and grabbed a water bottle from the drinks stashed on ice in the large cooler next to the counter. I sat silently at the long dining table, munching on my food and giving everyone an "I'm OK" look when they sent inquiring glances my way. Conall placed a hand between my shoulder blades before taking a seat on my left. When Hanna arrived with only a glass of tea, she sat on my other side, tossed her hair over her shoulder, and leaned in conspiratorially.

"How are you doing?" Her voice was quiet, but not enough to make it sound like she was trying to hide our conversation.

I gave her the tiniest of head wags to show her my answer wasn't a good one.

The worry in her expression doubled. "I had a feeling."

My appetite gone, I did a quick headcount, discovered that everyone was present, and cleared my throat for attention. Conversation ceased. Maybe I should have stood up, but I didn't trust my legs. They felt about as sturdy as Filip the stuffed frog's.

"I um…" My eyes shot around the room to my coven family's patient faces. None of them struck me as hopeful. I didn't want to drag it out; subtlety has never been my strong suit. "I can't thank everyone enough for all the work you've put in this week. This morning was beautiful. It was a fantastic ceremony, but it wasn't enough."

"You're sure?" LaDonna asked.

"I'm sure my ability to touch Source power wasn't as full during the ceremony as it normally is, but even without it, I can tell. It's like, of all the things I can tap into, the sense of imminent danger is there."

Everyone processed this for a few beats, and Luke said, "We'll try again."

I turned my attention to Rita before I replied to him. "Rita, have you reviewed the comments from Worldwide Witches since the ceremony?"

She let out what sounded like a gallows laugh. "There's so much I haven't read it all, but I've seen maybe half?"

"Did anyone offer their thoughts on things we hadn't tried? Things they meant to do but didn't have the equipment or would have done if they'd had more time?"

She frowned a little, and the movement looked unpracticed on her. "Not really. Some said they didn't have time to prepare, given the relatively short notice; some witches would have preferred to be able to use a different phase of the moon than was available these past few days. But other than that…." She let her sentence trail off, and I faced the table again.

"There's no way to stop evil everywhere," I said. "The Stygian coven is too widespread. There are too many unknowns to stop it all. And doing a spell to change Ericka's heart was… nice… but it wasn't effective. It was like shooting buckshot at a bullseye by when we need a silver bullet."

"What do you think is effective?" Joey asked. Ever the inquisitive one.

"A counterspell," I said. "Fighting their coven's energy with ours when it has a real focal point we can defend against. They want to bring this Sovereign Darkness of theirs onto the planet. Let them try. When it tries to merge with someone here on earth, we'll have a target."

"You mean Rene," Betony pointed out, her voice trembling with fear.

I hesitated, but honesty was always the best. "Possibly…. Probably."

"Will he die?"

I thought of the handsome soccer player and how he'd made my sweet young friend so cheerful for the first time in such a long time.

"I hope not."

It was the best I could do.

Chapter 35

Torn between wanting a nap and the urge to pace the floor like a caged animal, I settled on cleaning to burn off my stress-induced energy—something I'd picked up from years of living with La-Donna. First, I scrubbed and mopped the hall bathroom. Then, I tidied up my room, sorted laundry, and started a load in the wash. I grabbed a broom from the pantry, swept leaves and ashes off the patio, and wiped wine residue from the wooden banister to discourage ants. The movement made me feel productive and gave me a pleasant feeling of accomplishment.

Rita had packed her electronic equipment into her Subaru beside the garage. I found her taking a few extra minutes attached to the Whelen's Wi-Fi to scroll through the Worldwide Witches forums. The now-familiar black, purple, and green banner at the top caught my eye.

"How's it going?" I inquired as I placed a hand on the chair back next to hers.

Her eyes didn't leave the screen, but she said, "Just checking the forums for ideas that might give us something to do before the Stygian ritual. Some of the coven is offering to try spells to change Ericka's heart or give Rene the strength to tell them he won't be the host—if he really doesn't want to, that is."

I wanted to tell her not to bother, that it was a waste of their energy, but I decided it wasn't my place. Besides, what if there was another host of the Source on the earth somewhere, and that person could pull off a miracle? Who was I to believe I was the only one who could stop them?

"It's worth a shot," I said.

"A lot could happen in ten days," she added.

Goddess bless, is it really ten days? Ten days until we fought their spells with our own and found out who prevailed. If my tension level was any sign, I might have LaDonna and Luke's place sparkling like a new-cut diamond when the second of March rolled around.

I loosened my grip on the back of the chair; my fingertips had gone white.

"Ten days is a long time," I said. "Can you tell the people on your forum that I said thank you?"

Rita inclined her two-tone head to the keyboard once more and typed my response into the chat.

$$\supset\!\!\bigcirc\!\!\subset$$

The wise course of action would be to stay at the Whelen's house as much as possible, but life had to be dealt with. Keeping myself busy was the only way to keep from screaming with frustration. Having people trail me everywhere was a marginally bearable frustration, as I needed to be sure my house was on track to return to a livable state. I might have to wait until after the Stygian coven's plan was beaten before hiring any contractors—if I valued their lives, it was prudent to do so—but damned if I couldn't get the paperwork started and the plans made.

I guess shit would get canceled if I died, but I wasn't dead yet.

On Monday, I received the fire report. Joey, Hanna, and Hanna's father, Rafael, accompanied me to my house to speak with an adjuster to determine the extent of the damage to Blackwell Manor. The adjuster had been out there earlier last week and had found a few things he needed to discuss with me.

Pulling into my driveway felt surreal. I once again experienced the "was-not-was" sense that the building before me looked like my home, but also had evolved into a horror movie set or a trap waiting to be sprung. I circled the house, noting what I could tell from the outside as I waited for the adjuster. The roof's charred upper stories had been sealed to prevent further damage from the elements, and the first-floor windows had been boarded up to discourage looting. The second-floor windows—the ones that remained—had been left open to allow the house to air out. I heard the distant hum fans and questioned where they were getting the power to feed them. They must have brought generators.

The adjuster pulled a well-maintained pickup truck in next to Rafael's Chrysler. The man who stepped out was a grizzled good old boy dressed in well-worn khakis and a polo shirt stretched tight across an ample gut. He introduced himself as Frank and shook my hand before shaking those of my friends. We exchanged pleasant-ries only a moment before heading up the veranda steps.

"Do you have an inventory of your expensive household items anywhere?" he asked as we entered the front door. "List of things around the house that might need to be counted when we calculate the reimbursement?"

We cleared the threshold, and I coughed, stopping myself as my hand automatically moved to the useless light switch. The air was pungent with the smell of lingering smoke.

"Pictures?" he added. "That would help."

"I do have some pictures," I offered. "I didn't have fancy jew-elry or expensive works of art, though." I thought of my ruined Papa Legba painting and frowned.

We took out our flashlights and aimed the beams around the darkened room. Frank took in the salvaged furniture I used to fur-nish the shop and spotted the cabinet in the corner, where I held some of my spelling supplies and tarot cards.

"Antiques?" he asked. "Some of 'em can be pricey and hard to replace."

"Yeah, I have some up—" I caught myself. "Upstairs. Had some upstairs. My bedroom was all antiques. There were a couple in the living room, too. Oh, crap. Yeah. The cabinet. God, that thing was huge." *Shit. This is going to be more challenging than I thought.*

The wardrobe had held all my games, some of which had been passed down for generations. My entire wardrobe and my bedroom furniture were ruined, for sure.

Noting my sorrowful expression, Frank said, "Well, let's head upstairs and see how things look."

We took the stairs, and things appeared much as I remembered, only darker and dryer. Large fans rumbled noisily. Although the restoration workers had done a great job removing the standing wa-ter, the damage from the fire and water remained. Remarkably, the fire had stopped at the front portion of my house. The guest bed-room, bathroom, and study—my Room of Power, which held my spell books, spelling equipment, and altar—were relatively un-touched.

"Were the doors to them two rooms closed?" Frank motioned with a thick, hairy finger to indicate the front of the house where my bedroom and the living room had been. All that was left was the blackened skeleton of some studs that once framed the house. In the wreckage, I saw what used to be part of my bed—an old Victorian-style wood-framed one—tilting in the ashy remains of what had once been my nightstand. All I could identify was a chunk of the headboard. The rest was unrecognizable.

"I—um—I don't know. I wasn't staying here. My friend Miriam was here taking care of things while I stayed at my foster parents' place for a couple of days. Maybe she was trying to keep the cat from getting into things."

"Looks like they musta been shut. Closed doors can save a room in a fire." The way he said the last word sounded like "faar."

Thank goodness. That must have been a Miriam thing—I never close the doors in my house. My pantry door, the changing room in my bedroom, and the doors leading to the rooms upstairs all stayed open most of the time. Between the closed-off rooms and Betony and me working to contain the damage, my house had come out remarkably well.

"The firemen musta got here quick," Frank added. "They stationed close to here?"

"They're on this side of town, but they're volunteers."

"Huh. They musta been there washing the trucks or something."

"Musta been," I echoed.

)O(

Once I returned to the Whelen house, I shared with LaDonna and Luke the strange off-putting sensation that haunted me when I arrived at my home that morning. LaDonna made a few phone calls, and the following day, the coven and I traveled to Blackwell Manor to reestablish the wards protecting the house. Although it would be days before contractors did any work, we didn't want to wait and leave the house exposed to more potential mischief. We certainly didn't want any misfortune to befall folks handling the repairs.

Before we left, everyone under the Whelen's roof applied all the protection measures we knew—sachets of herbs, oils, jewelry, sigils, you name it, we inscribed it, packed it in our pockets, and put in our cars to keep us safe. The odds were good the Stygian coven had taken steps to curse my home and anyone who attempted to defend it. We were not willing to take any risks.

One by one, cars arrived, and we greeted one another with determination and a sense of lighthearted optimism. I gave everyone a firm hug and thanked them for being there. Every hug knocked my ear warmer out of place, and I would barely have it situated when another member arrived and knocked it askew again with a fierce hug.

"Want me to put your ear thingy in my pocket?" Conall offered.

"No!" I said, "It's freaking cold! Brr!" I slapped my mittens together and rubbed them to warm my stiff hands.

"Alright," LaDonna said with a clap of her hands when we'd all gathered around at the front of my house. "Y'all ready to protect Murphy's place and put the whammy on those buggers who think they can hurt our girl?"

To my delight, everyone cheered with enthusiasm.

"Alright! Let's do this!" she announced.

My heart warmed with their eagerness. I think we all viewed replacing the wards on my home as a symbolic buttressing of our coven's defense against the Stygian, an emblematic thumbing of our nose at them and their plans for us and the rest of the world.

We spaced out equidistantly around the house, each standing within easy eyeshot and earshot of one another. The cold, still air of the late February morning made sounds more evident, and LaDonna had little need to project as she called out to the deities.

"Goddess Hestia of the hearth, hear us. Goddess Brighid, protector of homes, hear our call...."

The words carried on, calls to the north, south, east, and west, to fire, earth, air, and water, and to the ancestors to ask for their guidance, protection, and help.

As LaDonna addressed the deities, the air around the Manor shimmered as if dusted with tiny stars, and the fabric of space wavered and rippled. A pencil-thin circle, the exact brightness and color as starlight, formed at the base of my home. It burst from the earth before creeping to a peak in the sky above my chimney. The air smelled of an odd combination of moss, cypress, ozone, and snow, although no flakes fell from the clouds. My spirit grew heartened, lightened with the joy of casting a spell of such positivity and magnitude.

The charge moving from witch to witch in our circle grew

electric, and the stars shimmering in the hazy fabric around my home sparked and snapped, the sound popping like distant fire-crackers and popcorn. Lost as I was in conducting the spell, I didn't hear what words LaDonna used to stretch the ward to the street and over my yard, but it was impossible to miss how the glimmering air covered the road in a swath of magical drapery.

The ward was complete in less than fifteen minutes, the air in-visible again, my heart light as the winter air. I circled the house and reveled in the sensation of the unseen walls protecting Black-well Manor. I found Terry in the back, leaving offerings for the Seelie fairies, who would hopefully continue blessing my home with their benevolence. I'd never seen one—the Seelie are more of a Scottish tradition than Irish—but Terry worked with them often, and I appreciated her effort. I'd take all the help I could get. I hoped she'd be there to help me keep them happy if they came around. I didn't need bored and mischievous fae capering around my back-yard.

Strolling back toward Oberon Street, I couldn't help myself; I extended a hand to caress the unseen fabric of protection surround-ing my home. It wasn't until I opened my third eye and grasped a trickle of Source energy that I felt its presence at my fingertips. Lenient but prickly, like caressing a soft-spined cactus that would stab if manipulated in the wrong direction or with excessive force.

"This one feels stronger than before," I told LaDonna as she strode from the backyard to join me near the street. Her heavy skirt, the color of asphalt, swished around her leather boots and settled.

"I may have added a little extra oomph this time," she admitted with an adorable nose wrinkle.

"I think we all did," added Conall's father, Paul. "Our major concern used to be protecting you from humans and the occasional troublesome spirit before we got wind about the Stygian's plans for you."

"Yeah," Betony agreed, throwing her long hair over her shoul-ders. The strands fell over the adorable straps of the overalls she'd layered on top of a thick sweater, and her ears and cheeks were beautifully pink. "It wasn't anything you couldn't handle alone be-fore. I mean, you could've handled it before. You just didn't know, you know? Oh, never mind."

"Also," Paul said, "I'm going to have an alarm system added to your home as part of the rebuild."

"Dad, don't—" I started, but he cut me off.

"I know I don't have to, but I want to. You mean the world to us. And to my son." He gave Conall, who had just arrived, a loving side-hug, which Conall returned, tipping his father, who stood a whole head lower, onto one leg. "I'm guessing you two will live here after the wedding?"

My mouth gaped. Conall and I hadn't had that discussion yet. "Well… um… I suppose so. It'd make sense, don't you think?"

Conall scoffed. "Yeah, of course. I'd never ask you to leave your home."

"Then consider it an early wedding gift," Paul said. "For your protection, and Conall's, too."

Paul Barry, owner of the construction company that Conall worked for, would undoubtedly pay for whatever top-of-the-line system was available. While I understood his desire to do everything in his power to defend us, I also hated him spending that much money on me. For Conall's sake, however, I acquiesced.

"You'll probably never need it," Paul said. "The wards, they are much stronger than before, and I imagine we'll all work to keep them that way. But if life has shown us anything these past few days, it's how unpredictable it can be."

I couldn't argue with him there.

☽○☾

It was time to take Rex to the vet to have him examined. I was reasonably sure he was fine—the little imp has a supernatural ability to not be wherever the trouble is, and I didn't sense anything weird—but I took him as a precaution. He always climbed into the pet carrier without a fuss, but getting him out of the thing once he was on the vet's table involved loads of hissing and usually a pair of protective gloves. The little bugger fought fiercely, but in vain, only for the vet to assure me he was fine. Once released, the loveable little demon scarpered right back into the box, glaring at his caregivers malevolently.

The folks in charge of further water mitigation showed up for work on Tuesday afternoon, and the dumpster rental driver dropped off the bin I'd requested at the curb. When I received the text telling me it had arrived, I trooped back to Blackwell Manor with Hanna and Miriam to sort the damaged items from the undamaged ones. Due to limited daylight because of the time of year, our work was constrained to a few hours during the day, and even that was challenging. We carried lanterns and flashlights to help us deal with the dim light in the mornings, and they cast spooky shadows on the soot-stained walls.

The three of us swept, bagged, toted, and sorted through the upstairs rooms, depositing bag after bag of ruined items into the bin at the curb. Wearing face masks, work gloves, and, in some cases, hard hats & safety goggles, we sifted through the mess for two days. Medicines and personal hygiene items we tossed straight into the trash, even though the bathroom appeared untouched—who knew what unseen damage the heat might have caused? The same for makeup. The contents of my closet had been reduced to ash and unidentifiable melted fabrics, plastics, metals, and rubber. A handful of books in my sitting room were salvageable, but most were goners.

As we neared the end of the second day, the sound of the dehumidifiers and non-stop fans blowing was driving me crazy. I made a list of tasks that remained to be done on my phone to keep my mind off the noise. Once the second story was rebuilt, I'd need to have all the walls repainted and the curtains and downstairs furniture washed. Windows & window screens needed to be cleaned or replaced. All remaining solid surfaces upstairs needed to be washed, preferably with something Miriam concocted to help eliminate the smoky smell. I'd have to change the air filters and have all the ducts cleaned. My insurance would cover most of it, probably, but I guessed a chunk would come out of my pocket.

The rooms that had closed doors still displayed trails of soot around the cracks that led up to the ceiling, where the paths of smoke continued. The door edges were also stained with oily soot. The gunk seemed to spread everywhere as I tried to remove it with wet cleaning rags. The stuff smeared the doors and walls with gray-black stripes and covered my work clothes and gloves with stinky chemical-smelling ash. I'd gone to the home improvement store to buy a cleaner recommended by a fire restoration guy on YouTube, but it didn't work for me the way it did for him.

This is terrible. I frowned at the streak of black and gray that tracked along the edge of my once-white door and wished I could magic it away.

Well… why not? We'd done plenty of physical work getting the place into shape. I could see the floors in my bedroom and living room now. It wasn't as if the outside world—who only suspected that I was a witch and only had an inkling of what that might mean—could see anything I did inside. Unless they'd peeked outside during our warding spell yesterday.

What elements would that entail? Fire, of course, but expended fire. Water to clean, maybe? And earth? Air to carry it away…

I extended my hand and touched the door. Instead of encountering a sooty, damaged piece of my house, I peered through it, glimpsing the essence of the wood that composed it. I could sense the craftsmanship and strength embedded within, envisioning the hands and tools that had shaped, painted, transported, and installed it. Memories flooded back of its previous appearance, worn from years of hanging as it led to my living room, which had once upon a time been someone's bedroom.

The soot doesn't belong here. It's not part of my door. It's part of an unfortunate event that had no business happening here.

The more I remembered how my door once was, the more my heart grew light with my Source connection. The wood under my fingers tingled, charged with a vibrant current as it metamorphosed into what it is. Old, imperfect, but beautiful in its well-loved way. The smeary stain lifted as if transported by an invisible hand and vanished.

No sense stopping there. I cast my eyes around my home and saw in my mind the way it had once been—dry, with clean walls and shiny floors scratched from generations of wear from cat claws and child's play. The smoke had infiltrated to the molecular level, and extracting the smells and sights that didn't belong demanded tremendous effort. The blood at my temples pounded, and my eyes felt too large for my skull, but watching the results appear as my gaze cast about the room was worth the pain. As I panned my attention from one corner to another with aching eyes, the streaks of soot and smoke damage faded and vanished under an unseen power until it was as if they had never been.

Now to do something about that smell. I thought about one of my favorite fragrances in the world—the enchanting blend of hay, fog, and heather that wafted whenever my ancestor, Aislinn Black-well, made her presence felt through the different methods employed by our coven, such as a channeling board or a summoning circle. I drew that smell through the air and willed it to replace the stagnant, charred, lingering odor. The blue tarps atop the house billowed like a hot-air balloon filling. I pulled the freshened air along the ductwork and envisioned them cleaned and purified. Every trace of fire and smoke damage evaporated. I blew the fragrant air back and forth through the window screens and left nothing behind but clean, country air.

Not satisfied with cleaning the second story, I strode downstairs feeling like a queen returning to reclaim a castle ruined by an invading army. I could practically feel the sensation of a royal cape and train following me as I descended the stairs, my spine erect, my stride confident as I understood at a universal level what needed to be done. I paced the rooms and waved my hand as I pulled the damage from each chair cushion, erased the ash from each tabletop, countertop, and display case, banishing it beyond the walls of my home as if it had never been.

Satisfied and exhausted, I lowered my hands and allowed the warm sensation flowing from my heart through my home to lessen and rest. My heartbeat raced as if I'd performed an Olympian effort, and it took several seconds before the pulse in my chest and throat eased back to normal.

"That was *really* cool."

Hanna's voice made me jump so high I could have hit the ceiling. When my heart settled back into place, I faced my friend, who flushed to the tips of her hair. She laid a hand on her chest and moved toward me slowly as if afraid to startle me again.

"Sorry." she apologized, "But wow. I love watching you work like that!"

"I wish I could use it to fix everything," I said with a slight pout as I sank into a newly cleaned chair. "I'd love to move back in tomorrow."

"Yeah, but people couldn't handle seeing magic at that level. And it'd be hard to explain to the insurance company. We're already going to have to come up with something to tell the repair folks." She tested the air, wrinkling her nose as she sniffed. "That smells familiar."

"Mother Aislinn," I reminded her.

"Oh my gosh! That's it! Wow, you've nailed it."

I heard Miriam trooping across the veranda, probably from one of her many trips to the dumpster. When she opened the door, she froze with the knob in her hand. The smell of fresh air must have been a bit of a shock after a morning of smoky residue.

"Murphy? What in the name of great Odin's ravens—"

"Murphy did it!" Hanna exclaimed. "Isn't it wonderful?"

Miriam stepped inside, her head swiveling to and fro as she noted the absence of ashes and soot and wet. She stepped through the vestibule and peered around the walls to the rooms on either side of the entry. "It's remarkable."

"It's the same upstairs, only better!" Hanna gushed. "Murphy did it all, and it only took her a couple of minutes."

"I stopped short of any noticeable construction repairs," I added. "But the air ducts are clean, the house is free of soot and ash, and if there was any water remaining, it's gone. I might have done a touch to fix the floors from water damage," I admitted.

"The neighbors have seen us doing some work these past two days sorting through the damaged and so forth," Miriam said. "That should satisfy their curiosity, I would think, if they've been watching for us to put in some effort." She gave me a proud smile and pulled me in for a hug. "Nicely done, Murphy."

Nicely done, sure, but now that I'd eliminated the distracting labor I'd planned, I had six uneventful days to worry about the upcoming ceremony.

At least, I hoped they'd be uneventful. I never did figure out who Ericka was planning to hex.

Chapter 36

Feeling like a conqueror after my success with magically cleaning my house, I strode into the Whelen's house with a grin and a pep in my step. Evening light streamed through the tree branches outside, casting spidery webs of shadow on the glossy hardwood floors. Hanna and I found Conall with Luke and Betony in the kitchen, preparing dinner. Jazz music streamed from a Bluetooth speaker linked to Luke's phone. Betony was chopping broccoli and cauliflower on a wooden cutting board on the counter while Luke seared a delicious-smelling piece of meat in a cast-iron skillet on the stove.

"Looks like *some*body had a good day," Conall said, his expression brightening when he saw mine.

"You should see her house!" Hanna exclaimed, her wide brown eyes impossibly huge. "It's spotless. All they need to do is put on the walls and roof, and she'll be ready to move back in!"

"How'd you manage that?" Conall said with an arched brow, the corners of his eyes wrinkling as he smiled.

Hanna gave Betony a bump on the hip with her own, cautious of the chopping knife, before reaching over and snatching a piece of raw broccoli. "A better question would be, 'How'd she *magic* that?'" She popped the broccoli crown into her mouth and wiggled her shiny fingertips at him.

Conall turned to watch me drag one of the wooden dining room chairs into the kitchen. "You magicked it clean?"

I slid into the chair and wrapped my arms around myself. Despite all the heat from the cooking stove, drafts still penetrated the old kitchen when the weather was its coldest. "Yep. And now I'm wiped out and need something new to keep my mind busy the next few days."

"You can start by making the garlic bread," Luke joked, pointing an elbow toward a long baguette and the softened butter on the counter. "After you pour yourself a glass of cabernet blanc, that is.

Unless you want a red, in which case, there's an open merlot on the dining room table."

The family spent the next few minutes in the companionable bustle of dinner making. Luke led LaDonna through an impromptu jazz dance in the middle of the kitchen. As Betony roasted the vegetables, Luke finished the steaks and LaDonna made Hanna's favorite dessert—white chocolate and macadamia nut cookies. When everything was nearly done, I set the halved loaf of buttered bread sprinkled with garlic under the broiler to brown.

Even now, when my life had gone to crap in so many ways, I had a lot to celebrate. We were all still alive. My best friend had celebrated her twenty-seventh birthday. My home was freshly warded. We had new friends around the globe with the Worldwide Witches. We had insight into the Stygian's plans, if not a sure way to beat them yet. My home had also survived, albeit a bit marred, and was only a couple rooms' worth of construction away from being as good as new. Or, in the case of my historic Victorian, as good as old but fabulous. Life might not be perfect, but I decided at the moment to take the intermission between crazy and even more crazy and love it for what it was.

Seated elbow to elbow around the dining room table, we dug into our feast. I'm not a big steak fan, but I *am* a huge fan of Luke's steaks. He's the only person who prepares them in a way I enjoy; incredibly flavorful, and they melt in my mouth. I swear the man has a hint of brown witch hiding in him somewhere—he's too much of a whizz in the kitchen not to be.

"Can I have a sip of your wine?" Betony asked me. Her hazel eyes, with their cloudy gray ring around the pupil, eyeballed my glass of merlot longingly.

"A *sip*," I said. "No more."

She snatched up the stemmed glass with such zeal the red liquid splashed dangerously close to the edge. "It's not like I'm *driving*," she drawled.

"It's not like you're an *adult*, either," I retorted. I swear she was becoming more and more like my little sister every day.

Betony sampled the liquid and returned the glass to the table. "Hmm. Not bad."

Something about the wine brought a pensive frown to Betony's face. She stared at the glass, watching the legs of wine seep down into the shallow pool at the bottom.

"What's the matter?" I asked.

"I was thinking about Lorina. And Jake. And Cadence. Do you think they're safe? From the Stygian?"

Dismissing for now how the wine might have brought her friends to mind, I recalled how Rene had chased Jake down to talk to him after the meeting in the trailer and of the forlorn look on Rene's face as we drove away. It was clear the young man valued Jake's opinion. Whether it meant he was on our side remained to be seen.

"I think Rene genuinely likes Jake," I assured her. "And if I'm right, Cadence and Lorina are safe by extension, since Rene won't do anything to piss Jake off." I refrained from mentioning Rene's behavior toward her, since I wasn't sure if it was genuine. His affection struck me as a ploy to infiltrate our coven, and Betony seemed to agree, at least for now.

"I wonder if he really thinks he can recruit them. Like, he kept trying to chat me up after Jake came back and told us about what went down," Betony said dolefully, her thumb caressing her phone out of habit. "I finally had to block him." This was the first I'd heard of Rene's attempt to contact one of us; until now, I thought he'd avoided us since the Stygian meeting.

"Does he bother any of the other kids at school?" Conall asked, wary.

She shook her head. She'd stopped poking at her phone and used her fork to prod her steak and broccoli. "He stopped coming," she muttered.

I suppose there isn't much point in attending school when you're going to be the leader of a global coven and the host of universal evil.

"It's just as well," LaDonna said as she spooned more vegetables onto her plate. "It wouldn't do to have a magical showdown in school. Think of all the ramifications."

Betony scoffed. "I don't know why we don't just come out of the broom closet. All of us."

"We don't want another Salem," Conall explained, his face downcast.

"Or Early Modern Europe," I added. "If people think of us as just another religion—one without the potential to prove our deities exist, like the others—then we're fine. If they discover we can manipulate matter, there'll be hangings, burnings, drownings, and torture again. Humans tend to be afraid of what they don't understand."

Manipulate matter. We could manipulate matter, predict events, read the stars, and heal the sick. What would it matter if people feared our ability to affect the world we lived in if the world we lived in didn't exist anymore? Would my life matter if the likes of the Stygian coven overran the world? The Stygian wanted to overthrow governments, create anarchy, ruin society as it existed, and replace it with one of their making. Would that be better than the world knowing we existed?

No, it wouldn't.

My eyes locked with Conall's bottomless, loving brown ones, and he said the words that I was thinking.

"It's pretty likely they're going to find out, anyway," he murmured. The words were soft and sorrowful and mirrored my heart's fears.

If we stayed in the broom closet, the only witches the world knew would be the Stygian. If we came out, it would change… well… everything.

)O(

We'd made a potentially world-altering decision over dinner: the world may learn that witches and magic were real within days. It was time for Conall and Luke to do what they did best—divine the consequences of our decision. Conall had never gotten around to giving me that reading he'd planned; we were probably overdue.

Using multiple witches to tap into their prophetic powers simultaneously was highly unusual. Trouble can arise when one witch gets a glimpse into a portion of the future that seems to contradict another. Frequently, the cause of this is individuals seeing the same event from two different perspectives or unique points in time. I've heard stories of covens that dissolved completely over what appeared to be a contradiction in their visions. Although the covens hadn't survived to record much after that, I would wager that the problem wasn't always the witches' powers of prophecy. It was more than likely the interpretation.

Another matter we needed to consider was that any prophecy they witnessed represented only one of many *potential* futures. It was the future that would play out if everything stayed its course. That's the beauty of having a prophetic witch—or, in our case, two—in the coven. It allowed us to alter the future before any unfortunate events occurred.

Hanna used smoke from a clary sage bundle to cleanse the handmade oak table where Luke preferred to perform his readings, and I carried a second bundle to purify the rest of the room. I fanned the curling plumes of smoke with a wide feather until it reached every corner, casting out any negative energies. Hanna and I set our smoking bundles in a stockpot-sized 3-legged cauldron in the corner. As the reading took place, the smoke could burn out safely while continuing to add purifying smoke to our environment.

After dimming the overhead lights, LaDonna brought in the cast iron candelabra stands and added tall, white tapers to illuminate the room. Igniting a wooden match, she touched the flame to each wick as the men shuffled their decks, their stances taut with worry. Betony waited a few feet from the table's edge as we finished our preparations, her curious gaze missing nothing.

Once they'd blended the cards to their satisfaction, each man offered their tarot cards to us one by one. Depending on how the Universe guided us, Hanna, LaDonna, Betony, and I rearranged the decks following our intuition. Conall's time-honored Rider-Waite deck was so symbolic of his personality—traditional, dependable. Luke's deck was another beautiful favorite—the colorful Tarot of Marseille.

Conall and Luke met in the center of the room and stood across the table, placing their decks face down before them. At six feet tall, Conall towered over Luke's five-foot-seven, but Luke was clearly in command. Conall nodded to Luke, indicating he felt ready to proceed, and Luke spoke the opening incantation. His succinct supplications always reminded me of what a Christian prayer might sound like.

"Blessed ancestors of the past and mighty guardians of the future, we petition you now. Guide us in our journey to see through the veil of mystery that would hide the coming events from our eyes. Blessed be."

"Blessed be," we all echoed.

Lukas and Conall eyed each other across the table somberly.

"Ready?" Luke asked. Conall assented.

They had already set an agreement to flip the cards over, inspect them, and scribble down their own take on what they saw before discussing it. By doing so, they prevented inadvertently affecting each other's translation.

Together, they each reached for the top card on their respective piles without saying another word. They flipped their cards onto the table.

Conall's was The Hermit. Luke's was *L'Hermite*.

I think we all blinked to see if what we saw was right or if maybe it was a trick of the smoke. Luke's head bobbed as if he'd half expected this.

"Alright," he said, "I guess we know that's supposed to be the first card."

We all tittered nervously as they prepared to turn card number two. Hanna interlaced her hand with mine, and we gripped each other tightly. Conall and Luke regarded one another somberly, like gunslingers facing off at high noon. With a flick of their wrists, two more cards lay face-up on the table. Conall's was The Wheel of Fortune. Luke's was *La Roue de Fortune*, the French equivalent.

"Damn," Betony exclaimed. "What are the odds against that?"

"Pretty high," I murmured.

Undeterred, Luke placed his hand on top of his deck once more. "Last time."

Conall didn't reply, but coordinated his turning of the final card to match Luke's. Conall's card was The Eight of Cups.

"*Huit De Coupe*." Luke tapped his finger on the eight golden chalices depicted on his card. Three for three matches—they even all faced upright to whoever dealt the card.

"Holy Mother Hecate," LaDonna breathed as we all beheld the cards where they lay across from one another like off-kilter reflections.

"Anyone know where we can Google the odds of that happening?" Conall asked.

"I can tell you, I think. Give me a few minutes," Betony said, grabbing a sheet of paper from a table behind us and searching for a writing tool. "I aced statistics."

Luke waved his hand at Conall. "You. Paper. Write your

thoughts down. Now, before you start thinking about it too much."

Conall grabbed his paper and pen and started scribbling furiously across from Luke, who did the same. After about five minutes, I wished I'd given him my laptop—it would've been quicker.

Luke finished first, and we all waited, shuffling our feet and quietly fidgeting while Conall wrapped up his thoughts. Once he did, he lifted his gaze from the notepad and plopped his pen down.

"The Hermit," Luke prompted. "What thoughts did you have?"

"I wrote that although we've been withdrawn, staying away from the Stygian, we've also used the time for contemplation and being productive. You?"

"I wrote 'Isolation from the world, self-preservation, inner scrutiny.' What'd you put for your Wheel of Fortune thoughts?"

Conall checked his notes. "Rapidly shifting events coming that will have a powerful impact on many lives."

"I wrote 'Upcoming drastic and quick shift in reality.' And for your Eight of Cups?"

"I said, 'If we don't decide soon, our inaction may lead to the shifting events predicted by the Wheel card to manifest negatively.'"

Luke read off his notepad. "'Confusion leads to negative events unless steps are taken to forestall them.'"

Betony breathed and stared at her paper, pulling all of our attention in her direction.

"You OK, Bet?" I asked.

Her head moved widely from side to side in amazement. "The odds against those three cards coming up in a row like that ... if my math is right… is over four hundred and fifty-six thousand."

It sounded damn hard to accomplish, alright.

No one spoke. I pressed my hands to my mouth. Betony sniffed. Conall tapped his pen on his notes until LaDonna shot him a stern look. Luke crossed one arm around his chest and pressed the other to his mouth before letting a long exhale out of his nose.

"Well," Luke said, "I guess there's no doubt Conall and I are seeing eye-to-eye on this thing."

Maybe it really is time to come out of the broom closet.

Chapter 37

It was no small decision. If we fought the Stygian in a magical showdown, we risked exposing the reality of magic to the rest of the world. Every witch across the globe would risk being outed by the steps we took in the next few days. Not everyone would be grateful for the opportunity to be recognized for what they were and what they could do. While the ability to touch and affect nature with our spirits came as naturally as breathing to us, to normal humans, it can appear dangerous and eerie.

"The Worldwide Witches will help us reach out to others and spread the message. We can caution that some of us will come forward. That'll give them a chance to do damage control or take any other precautions they want," Conall said.

"There's a reason the Universe put Rita into our path that day," I added. "If my house hadn't caught fire, we never would have had that conversation with her—the one that led to us finding out about her coven."

"Whoa," Betony said. "That's the shit. Like, the Universe used the Stygian coven's negative energy against them, and they didn't even realize it."

"The Universe does that when you try to fuck with her balance," LaDonna said. "She's all about homeostasis." Her uncommon use of an expletive surprised and amused me.

"We don't have to out anyone, though, right?" I said. "This whole thing might happen on the down-low if we keep things from getting out of control. They can't be planning to shove their evil spiritual leader into Rene's little body, and then—*poof*—the world instantly changes. We could keep everything a secret if we stop them first."

I didn't want this to happen. I didn't want to cause thousands of lives to alter forever. Damned Stygian. This was all because some stupid group of selfish asses who called themselves witches decided the world needed to be turned on its head because they weren't satisfied with how things were going. Yes, life can always be improved, but not by tearing it down to its foundation and leading it with darkness.

"We'll keep things as restricted and as concealed as possible," Luke assured me. "But we can't know for sure until the fight starts."

"The Stygian doesn't care if they unveil us all. Not anymore. It's their first step in causing worldwide chaos."

Sometimes I don't like to be touched when I am upset. I sat in a ball on the floor and put my hands on my knees. Betony joined me, sitting nearby with crossed legs. I felt her support, yet she gave me my space—what Hanna sometimes called my "grumpy space." Betony had a keen sense of empathy, being a gray who was also not big on physical affection, almost like an emotional vampire, but in a positive way. She pulled negative energy away from others and used it as fuel.

"We're gonna be OK," she assured me.

I rocked back and forth, clutching my knees with a frown on my lips and a crease between my eyebrows. "You can't know that."

"No," she agreed, "I can't. But fuck 'em if they don't like it. Fuck the world if they find out and can't decide what to do with us. And a big 'Fuck you' to the damn Stygian coven for putting us in this position."

I snorted, trying to suppress a laugh, which then made me laugh in earnest. Betony smiled, and her round face lit up.

"Seriously, Murphy, can't you see how everything's falling into place? My parents being part of that coven that killed all of your moms? You discovering you're the Summate, and me finding out I'm the gray? Jake totally screwing up that love spell, which brought us to Ryan, who was dying to warn you about what the Stygian was going to do? And then the whole house ordeal leading us to learn about Rita and the Worldwide Witches. It's like you've got this insane dose of lucky girl syndrome or something. Yeah, messed up stuff goes down, but somehow it always leads to something good."

She had a point. I stopped rocking and sat up tall.

"We need to find out where they're having the ritual," I said. "That way, we can use directional energy."

"Barring that, we can use physical energy," Conall half-joked. I didn't doubt for a second he'd tackle Rene if he thought it'd stop him from becoming the Big Bad that killed me.

"We can't astral project until they spill the details," I said. "It'd be a waste of energy, and not safe, besides."

"You could try a new skill," LaDonna suggested.

My eyebrows came together. "What's that?"

"The same gift your great-grandmother Aislinn had. The ability to see the future in still waters."

)O(

Whenever I use a gift for the first time, I feel like a bumbling idiot. I'm terrified something will go wrong, I'll botch everything up, and stuff will explode, melt, break, or catch fire. Exactly like it did when I reflected Betony's gray energy.

Conall and Luke filled the clan cauldron partway with water at a spigot in the garage created for this specific purpose. With care and a great deal of strength, they hauled the heavy iron pot to the center of LaDonna's living room, gently setting it on top of a thick quilt. With my typical sense of trepidation, I knelt before it, hesitant to peer inside. When I did, the water glimmered like sparkling black ink under the lights in LaDonna's ceiling fan. Confident now that nothing would jump out at me, I craned my neck over as if I expected a vision to materialize with no effort on my part. It didn't happen, of course.

Mother Aislinn, if you can hear me, I could really use your help right about now.

I edged up to the enormous cauldron and bent to caress it gently around the rim. My fingers came into contact with several water droplets, and I imagined the paths the water had taken in its lifetime. From rainclouds to rivers, lakes, oceans, and back to the earth. The ability to flow in powerful crashing ocean waves, and yet gentle enough to caress a newborn's skin. Wearing paths in rocks over centuries of following a path. Giving life to creatures in the sea and on land. It offered bountiful seafood and vast spaces to explore. Water was power.

The blanket below the cauldron was orange, and I allowed my eyes to close slightly until the colors blurred and almost appeared fire-like. *Fire warming the water. Heat. Energy.*

Below the fire conjured in my mind, the vast earth supported us all, grounded us in its sturdy embrace, fed us, its fertile soil providing us with plants and herbs for healing. It nurtured diverse ecosystems that sustained countless magnificent creatures. Earth provided us with minerals, wood, and divine inspiration that helped us form homes and communities.

I exhaled and watched the water's surface move under its influence. *Air that gives us breath.* Air that moved the clouds, bellowed sails, gifted us with oxygen, and cooled our skin during hot summers. Air that stirred the grasses and supported birds as they flew. Shimmering air that enveloped us with each breath, carrying the sweet melodies of birds.

Together, the elements of fire, earth, water, and air wove a universal tapestry that intertwined lives and bestowed upon us the profound gifts of nature and the power it held.

Easing into a seated position next to the cauldron, I embraced the iron pot, performing the same ritual Aislinn had performed to begin her cauldron prophecies. She preferred the circular stone well behind her home, but weather or extreme dry spells sometimes prevented her from doing so. At those times, she filled her pot inside her house and embraced it, thanking the water for its life-giving properties and releasing the knowledge of the future to her.

I let go of the thick iron pot and assumed a position that allowed me to gaze comfortably into its depths. The surface of the water trembled from my movement and stilled.

Thank you, fathers, Poseidon and Hydros, for this life-giving force, and to mother Phoebe for what you are about to reveal to me.

While orange witches can use their gift to see the future in the stars with astrology, it takes astronomy to nail down the exact time of an astronomical event. Our coven didn't have an astronomer, but Rita used her familiarity with astronomy websites to narrow down a window of time when it was most likely that the Stygian coven would gather. During this conjunction of Mercury and Saturn in Capricorn, their opportunity would be in a position—literally—and their spell-casting goals most likely to bestow success. We'd use the conjunction of Venus and Jupiter the day before in our preparations, those of us who used the deities in our practice petitioning those gods to aid us in our efforts.

Imagine it is March second. Send your vision forward. See the stars in their position in the night sky. Where is Ericka, and what is she doing as their plans unroll? Where is Rene? Drawing on my limited understanding of their strategy, I sent out psychic feelers to locate their energy signals like a missile tracking a heat signature. *Find the darkness. Find the Stygian.*

My first attempt to connect with the veins of universal information was scattershot across my neighborhood. Then, as I found distant chords that resonated with the correct key, I followed them through the town of Gryphon, then down the streets of Leland County. Hoping I'd recognize the precise answer I sought once I found it, I allowed my consciousness to widen and my mind to open until I lost all sense of my body and became the energy sweeping across the streets and fields.

I knew it when I saw it: a spiritual energy signature that didn't emit a colored aura like most souls do. Instead, a hazy shadow surrounded its physical form, and the body itself was hard to distinguish in my energetic state. The entire person appeared to be a shadow self.

OK, you've found one. Can you extract any information from them, like where the ceremony will be and when?

The idea of coming in contact with the phantomlike soul had about as much appeal as diving headfirst into a swimming pool filled with motor oil, but it had to be done. Keeping most of my energy intact and distant, I reached out with a single strand of power.

Spiritually touching the shadowy edge of the thing's aura was like allowing biting, stinging insects to crawl on my hand and arm—grotesque and wildly uncomfortable to the point of pain. Avoiding any thought that was not relevant, careful not to disclose my presence to the thing I touched, I searched the mind for the information I needed.

There. I saw the clearing, the odd circle of maple, hickory, and pine trees in lower Appalachia that I'd never, ever forget. Years later, the spot still held little growth, as if plants feared setting roots in the desecrated space. I could smell the leaves under my feet and the bitter cold in the air that promised snow, though stars still gazed down through the broken cloud cover. I heard the wind blowing through the bare branches overhead until they clacked and clattered like dry bones.

It was the spot where our mothers had been killed.

Chapter 38

I hadn't set foot in the clearing since childhood, but I'd know it anywhere. Nearly two decades of recurring nightmares kept the place clear in my mind. Despite the slight haze from arriving via the inky prophetic waters, my impression of physically standing there was unshakable. It couldn't have been clearer if I'd sunk into a hypnotic state or lucid dream. I saw the dead grasses and rocky ground under my feet and the crisscross of moonlight shining through the branches onto my arms.

Pitch-black black shadows emerged from the tree line. These weren't psychic shadows like the soul I'd contacted to enter this vision. No, these forms were human. Black robes cinched at the waist with gray cords, the edges hemmed in gray. Smoky tendrils entwined through the shimmering fabric in such a way that it appeared as if they'd arrived through the mists of the river Styx itself. Mists surrounded their feet and traversed the ground like ghostly minions feeding on their vileness, preparing the way. I hoped it was a side effect of the vision, but I dreaded the idea that they summoned the clouds as part of their ritual. Having that level of control over the elements implied the Stygian coven had reached a level of coordination of power the Lughaidh did not have.

A bitter, icy wind blew, and the smell of stagnant water and rotting plants hit me. I gagged on the stench, desperately wishing to block it, but the closer they came, the stronger it grew.

It's only a vision. It's only a vision!

My heart pounded so loudly that rushing blood and the drumbeat of my heart whooshed and thumped in my ears. If it was only a vision, why was I so cold? Why did I smell the air around me? How was I able to count the stars in the sky above me?

OK, I've seen where they'll be and some elements they'll be wielding. I can go now.

My spirit, however, disagreed. It was like one of those dreams where the Big Bad Villain is in pursuit, and no matter what I try or how much I will my feet to move, they refuse. This time, it felt like my body was encased in ice, frozen to the earth. And the Stygian was getting closer.

This isn't as bad as it seems. It's just a vision. Like a lucid dream. They can't see you. You just have to pull yourself out. But how?

It didn't matter if I strode right by one of the creepy coven members—this was a vision of the future, not the present—but the energy they emitted triggered my preservation instinct.

They were all around me, close enough now that no matter which direction I turned, there was no escaping them without coming into spiritual contact with them. I was disembodied, but I was loathed to touch them even with my soul essence as I remembered the painful, stinging, crawling, biting insect sensation that came over me when I came into contact with the first phantom soul I found.

Fly. FLY.

I flew. Despite my fearful panic, I tapped into a buried reserve of willpower and propelled myself into the sky, focusing on soaring back to my body. Was this astral projection? Or was this a new means for my spirit, my contact with the Source of all things, to allow me to move through the spiritual realm? No time to think about that; my only aim now was to reconnect my floating thoughts with my body. I could contemplate the complexities of spiritual travel later.

Propelling myself across the countryside, I eagerly sailed back to the Whelen home and into my body, which, oddly, still stared into the cauldron as if my spirit wasn't traipsing outside of it. I returned to myself and teetered off-balance until I plopped heavily onto my bottom.

"Shit!" I breathed, my hands helping me regain my balance as I waggled my head to clear it.

"Do you want to try again?" Conall asked. "Maybe it just takes practice—"

"Fuck no," I said. "That was enough. I'm wiped out."

"Are you OK?" Betony inquired, her hand on my shoulder to steady me. I nodded.

"You—you did it? You saw in the water?"

I nodded again and pushed my hair past my shoulders. Stars

danced in front of my eyes, but I didn't feel like I was going to faint anymore. "I saw them everywhere. And I learned a lot. I know—"

My mouth froze and my sentence stopped mid-stream. There, poking his head into the back window of LaDonna's home, his face lit by the recessed lights in the eves, was Rene Basilio.

☽O☾

None of us moved. None of us were eager to let Rene in the door. We stood there paralyzed in our indecision until, finally, Betony spoke.

"LaDonna? Luke? It's your house. What do you think?"

Quiet lingered for a few more heartbeats as we all contemplated. Sure, they warded the house as any good witch would. However, welcoming the enemy inside meant exposing ourselves to vulnerability and prying eyes. Or, more fittingly, *spying* eyes.

Or did our spell work? Is Rene not willing to play a part in their scheme anymore?

"It's our home," LaDonna said, "but it's your safety—*everyone's* safety. We've all seen how strong the Stygian are when they work together." I remembered the smell of my charred home and the overwhelming odor of rot whenever their coven came to mind and my nose wrinkled.

Betony's phone chirped with the sound of Disney birds. She withdrew it from the back pocket of her overalls, and her eyebrows raised in surprise.

"It's Rene. He said he needs to talk to us."

"Well, no shit," I said. "I didn't think he drove all the way out in the cold and the dark to stare at us through the windows."

"He said my mother—"

Her phone made another sound, one that reminded me of the Leland County tornado alerts. Her face drained of all color. We waited for her to speak, but she was frozen, her eyes large with fright.

"What is it, Betony?" LaDonna encouraged.

"It's an alert from the Alabama Department of Corrections. My mother's escaped."

Hanna made a small, frightened sound and brought her hands to her mouth. I bit my lip in thought. "Could be a ruse," I suggested.

"Maybe it's an elaborate glamour spell. They're trying to fool us and make us panic."

"Panic…" Betony's eyes lit up, her concern about her mother's escape momentarily dimmed in her excitement. "I've got it! I think I know how we can beat the Stygian." She laughed and almost danced in place. "They want chaos?" One of her beautiful dyed-red eyebrows cocked. "Oh, I'm going to give them chaos."

ᗘOᗡ

We risked it and let Rene inside to see what he had to say. He crossed the threshold into the Whelen's home with red-rimmed ears and purple fingers and stomped his feet, presumably to get his circulation moving again. He had not dressed for the cold, wearing only a t-shirt under a hoodie, a pair of jeans, and the same black leather athletic shoes he'd worn the first day I'd seen him. He blew warm air into his curled hands to warm them up, and when he looked up, he had eyes for no one but Betony.

"Did you get my message?"

She bobbed her head, her gaze locked on his. "I got an alert from the Department of Corrections, too." She paused. "Is it real?"

Grey witch skills, baby. She was testing him for his honesty using her gray gift as her own personal lie detector.

His mouth tightened, but his guise remained sincere. "It is. My mother helped orchestrate it."

That shouldn't have been a surprise, and yet it was—to me, at least. I hoped they'd hurt no one in the process.

"I want to change sides," Rene said.

"Change… sides?" Betony asked.

"Leave the Stygian. Join the Lughaidh. I've been wanting a way out my whole life, but I've never had a way to do it before. I've never met another coven before the Lughaidh. And now I've met Murphy and you, and…" his hands reached toward us as his voice faltered, and he stopped, unable to level his gaze with us. "I think my mom arranged it. Me being the 'chosen one' for the Sovereign Darkness. I don't want it. If I don't want it, how can it be me?"

"Do you want to leave because it's the right thing to do, or because you're scared to be the host?"

"Both," he admitted. "But honestly, my mom freaks me out. Her whole ideology scares the hell out of me. I mean, the last thing I want is for her to rule the world. And I'm pretty sure that's why she wants me as the host. She thinks having me as the vessel will give her some control over the Darkness. But honestly, I don't think she has a clue what she's getting herself into. She just likes the idea of being some Stygian royalty or something. It's all about power for her." His voice trailed off, lost in thought.

I was dubious. Rene was not only part of the Stygian, but he had to have a significant amount of magical talent if they expected him to host the ultimate Big Bad. He sounded sincere, but he'd sounded sincere all along. Ericka, and possibly her entire coven, had faith in Rene's ability to handle a tremendous amount of power. A teenager. He had to be more than the average teen for them to have that much trust in him. But what if Rene was being honest? What if the whole thing had been rigged or bought off because Ericka thought she could keep the reins on her son?

What if our spell had worked?

I wanted to trust him, hoped like hell that this was the sign we'd been waiting for, but it was too big a risk. I couldn't allow a soft spot for the boy who'd befriended my young friends and put anyone at risk—much less the world. And the Stygian wouldn't be content until they'd let chaos loose around the globe and burned it all down. We had to plan, which meant he had to go.

"Rene, you understand why I can't let you stay, right?" I stated, stepping into his line of vision. "I want to have faith in you. I really do. But there is way too much at risk."

"What can I do to prove myself to you?" His eyes were deep with concern and shone with what might have been tears. Betony appeared ready to run to his side to console him, but she refrained, and I was proud of her. The old Betony would have given everything up for someone's affections.

"Don't let it in, Rene," I said. "When the time comes, fight the… the…."

"Sovereign Darkness?"

"Yes, fight it. Refuse to let it in."

His chin trembled, but he fought to hold his composure together. Either his emotions were for real, or he was an Oscar-worthy actor.

"I don't… I don't know if I can."

Chapter 39

It was nearly midnight before Rene left, but none of us were in any mind to sleep. Besides, I needed to know what Betony was talking about before we'd permitted Rene to enter LaDonna and Luke's house. Her enthusiasm for giving the Stygian chaos struck me as a tad concerning.

LaDonna and I made cups of tea on the stovetop, and I warmed my cold hands near the gas burner. Luke prepared himself a cup of espresso using their one-cup expresso maker, and Betony put hot chocolate and marshmallows into a thick ceramic mug full of water she'd heated in the microwave. The four of us met with Conall in the living room, where he sat with a tall glass of ice water on the coffee table.

"Is your mother aware that you're staying with us, Betony?" LaDonna asked.

Betony shook her head. "Not from me. Maybe from Ericka. Did you ever bring her over here or tell her I was staying with you?"

"No. I told her I had a pupil named Betony, but not that you stayed with me. We did visit Conall's father's house, though." Her brow grew worried wrinkles as a thought occurred to her. "Conall—"

"I'll call him and make sure he's alright," Conall said, his hand already snatching his phone from next to his water glass. He rose from the couch to make his call away from our conversation.

I leaned in to grip my teacup and sized up Betony's energy by attuning myself to her aura. Her gray was in a positive place—so light it was nearly silver; good. Her mood was receptive, and she'd likely take my following statement as I intended.

"Bet, what did you mean earlier when you said, 'I'm going to give them chaos?'"

Her eyes lit up. "I can't believe we didn't think of this earlier. Why not work with Pan as my deity? Luke, you know how Pan can totally scare the crap out of an army? What could be a better way to stop them? We wouldn't even have to physically hurt anyone, just scare the living daylights out of them. Make them freak out and panic. And since I'm a Gray witch, it'll probably come naturally."

His warning to his father completed, Conall returned and took a seat next to me. I cupped my hands around my mug and sat back on LaDonna's lush brown couch as I mulled over her idea. "Would we not be adding to their own chaotic energy if we did that?"

"Not necessarily," LaDonna said. "We could appeal to Pan's more positive nature—animals, plants, sex, music—"

"Music?" I perked up. "Like, loud, chaotic music. Like—"

"Like Jake and Lorina's band!" Conall exclaimed, slapping his hands onto his thighs. "This is brilliant! If we do that, we won't be giving the Stygian any particular spell to easily deflect our efforts. We could encourage witches across the planet to engage in activities that Pan would love, but are also positive. Volunteer to clean nature. Help at an animal shelter. Play with other witches in the woods or in a pasture. Throw a huge middle-of-the-week concert."

"Have sex in the supply closet," I joked.

"Have sex in the supply closet!" Conall crowed. "Or better yet, have it out in nature if they can do it without freezing their balls off. And the whole time, they can focus on sending that energy out to Pan. To a chaos god."

A small smile played at the corners of Luke's mouth. "I like it. Murph, do you think Jake and Lorina could make up some songs that people could spell with before the big day?"

I scoffed. "Luke, they could write an entire album's worth of music by then. Those two are *prodigious*."

"Get them on it, then. Instead of broadcasting a single spell, this time, Rita's going to share the first ever Worldwide Witches concert."

)O(

The following day, after calling Jake and Lorina and tasking them with their musical assignment (which they accepted with zeal), LaDonna worked with Betony to prepare her for her upcoming challenge: weaving her chaos within the world's natural, already unpredictable, energy. LaDonna, a green witch who worked with plants and animals, was a natural choice to help Betony wind her chaos magic with nature—and appeal to the god Pan for his aid. I followed along so I could tap into Source power and attune myself to Betony's chaos and balance it out. We wanted to petition Pan, but not destroy nature along the way.

We took the lesson onto LaDonna's wooded deck behind her home where the Lughaidh had held the spell. Gods… had it only been days before? It felt like weeks. So much had happened since then. Although the cold lingered, the air was still, and the sun shone through the trees and clouds. I raised my face to the bright sky and inhaled a crisp lungful of air that smelled like leaves and winter.

Staying clear so Betony could extend her energy beyond her physical body without interference, LaDonna said, "Close your eyes." Betony complied. "What do you sense around you?"

Betony's eyes moved under her lids as if searching for the answer there. Her hands and fingers opened up like feelers extending to taste the air. "Cold. Air. I can smell the forest around your house."

"Good. Can you think of ways to summon Pan's chaos energy in the forest?"

Betony licked her lips as she thought. "I could use air to blow the branches and leaves. That'd make some noise, and it wouldn't hurt the trees."

"You could," LaDonna said encouragingly. "What else?"

"I could… stir up the animals."

"Yes. Be cautious if you do that. We don't want to harm them, just cause a little disruption to their lives. Anything else come to mind?"

Betony's hands relaxed to their natural position at her sides. Her shoulders drooped a little. "I can't think of anything."

"Can you bring him music?"

Betony's eyes opened, and she grinned. "I can sing to him. Does that count?"

Small smile lines appeared at the corners of LaDonna's eyes. "Absolutely. And what else is Pan known for?"

"Sex. That's out. For me, at least. Oh—and drinking," Betony laughed.

"We could bring him some wine. Sure. That'd be a good measure to take."

"What about dancing?" I suggested.

Betony's nose wrinkled. "I can't dance."

I gave a half-shrug. "All the better. Big, crazy, arms pinwheeling around, literally dancing like nobody's watching. That'd be perfect."

Betony did a wonky pirouette with wavy arms and her tongue sticking out. We all giggled. Betony's face lit up when both feet were back on the planks. "Oh! What if I wore, like, woodsy smells when I do this? I could put on like a pine essential oil or… is there an oak oil?"

"There is, but it's pretty thick. Maybe oak moss oil. Another one that smells nice—it's made from the camphor tree—is ho wood oil."

Betony's face contorted as she suppressed another giggle. "Did… did you say *ho wood* oil?"

One alternate translation of the phrase came to my mind. Then another. Apparently, I wasn't alone. Soon, all three of us were overcome with gales of full-bellied laughter. I nearly choked on my spit, which triggered a coughing fit so bad LaDonna had to smack me on the back a few times so my lungs worked the way they're supposed to. Our laughter died down to titters, and we all grew somber when Betony pulled at her lower lip with her teeth, concern painting her pretty features.

"Y'all, what if I can't do it? Or worse, what if the chaos I spell up makes everything worse, or feeds into the Stygian's chaos?" Her shoulders tensed up. LaDonna stroked Betony's back this time, soothing the tightened muscles.

I pushed at a pile of crispy winter leaves with the toe of my thick gray slipper. "LaDonna, have you explained to Betony about chaos theory yet? The way you think it works, anyway?"

LaDonna shook her head. A breeze blew a heavy strand of brown hair across her face, and she tucked it behind her ears. "The short version, Betony, is that even in chaos, there is an underlying pattern, relationships within patterns. Sometimes the pattern is too large for us to see, but ultimately there is a…a…."

"Method to the madness?" Betony ventured.

LaDonna performed a gentle nod. "Yes, exactly."

"You mean even if I fuck things up, the universe won't let the world get completely fucked up?"

"It might seem fucked up to us, as humans," LaDonna said, "But the universe, the force behind it, has an inherent beauty and perfection. What is right will ultimately prevail, although it might not be 'right' as we think to define it. You won't ruin the world, Betony. I promise."

Betony sniffled and regarded LaDonna with her hazel-gray eyes. She pulled in a deep breath, steeled herself, and gave a resolute bob of the head.

"Ready to continue?" LaDonna asked.

"I'm ready."

Chapter 40

Between the freezing cold weather and years of lonely Valentine's Days, February has been my least favorite month for years. Now I can thank the Stygian coven for yet another reason to hate this gods-forsaken month: they decided it was a great time of year to end the world as we all knew it. OK, technically, the plan isn't until March, but still.

Tromping through the gray early-morning woods with my coven and Conall by my side made the chill a little more bearable. The frosty air moving through my lungs gave me an annoying cough that I buried in the crook of my elbow as I plodded down the path overgrown with thick, leafless branches. My toes grew numb in the tips of my Doc Martens. Two pairs of socks were inadequate in today's nippy temperatures, and I wiggled them as I walked to get the blood flowing again.

The clan, plus Cadence and Lorina, carried various supplies: backpacks full of spelling equipment, cables, computer gear, and ladders. Jake pushed a wheelbarrow of resin speakers made to look like rocks, and Lorina helped him lift the wheel over branches and other obstacles they encountered. Cadence kept glancing over her shoulder with a worried, distracted expression, as if she expected the Stygian to arrive early and catch us in our preparations. LaDonna and Betony took up the rear, using their power over nature and a bit of gentle chaos to stir up the path we'd taken and disguise any human footprints.

LaDonna's outfit that day was so perfectly high-priestess, so naturally her, it warmed my heart: flowy skirt over thick leggings, tall leather lace-up boots, and a voluminous moss-green sweater covered by a hooded cloak the color of willow bark. Next to her, Betony looked very next-generation in her baggy jeans and oversized hoodie. Even for a trip to the woods, Betony had added black winged eyeliner to complete her appearance, and she'd tucked her long, bright red hair under a loose beanie. They both appeared delightfully how I pictured what the words "divine feminine" meant.

My style took up another side of the feminine: boots, dark jeans, a double-breasted black wool coat, and a black beanie pulled down over my ears. The "boyfriend" style is more my thing. Thankfully, Conall seemed to find it adorable.

Wrapped up in my thoughts as I was, we reached the clearing much sooner than I'd expected. The air here was still, almost reverent, and we all stood momentarily and observed the space like hallowed ground. The ring of yellow poplar and chestnut oak trees stood fairly equidistant, leaving an empty area of about thirty feet between them. None of our coven's rituals had taken place here since the night Hanna, Conall, and I had lost our mothers to Betony's crazed, knife-wielding parents. It hadn't changed much, the only difference now being the lingering daylight and some slightly taller trees.

I heard a shuddering breath and was surprised to see that Betony was the one making the heartbroken sound. Fat tears fell down her cheeks and left dark spots on her hoodie.

"Y'all… I'm… I'm so sorry." Her voice broke, and I moved to her side to comfort her. Conall and Hanna joined me.

"I'm so sorry," she said again, her voice thick. "I can't believe they… I just… they…"

"Not your fault," I asserted. "Not at all. You are not responsible for your parent's actions, Bet. You had nothing to do with their crazy coven and what they did."

Betony's eyes flitted from my face to Conall's, then Hanna's, and saw nothing but love there. It broke my heart that we were able to love her so much more wholly and profoundly than her own parents.

"Hug?" I offered.

She nodded, her eyes welling with tears, and sniffled. The three of us surrounded her in a gentle embrace.

"We love you, Betony," Hanna said. "We kinda love the crap out of you, actually."

"You've grown on us, kiddo," Conall added.

"Really?" Betony choked. We nodded and hugged her harder. "I love you too, y'all."

Lorina, Jake, and Cadence joined the group hug with youthful enthusiasm, and Betony let out a throaty laugh when Jake wrapped almost all of us in his massive wingspan and squished us all together.

When we let each other go, I noticed how everyone had already started taking steps to prepare for our campaign and hurried to join them.

Although the coven wouldn't physically interrupt the ceremony unless we had to, we planned to do everything possible to disrupt them so their spell lacked the focus it needed to attract the Sovereign Darkness. Which meant hidden speakers resembling rocks to broadcast Jake and Lorina's concert. It also meant sachets of herbs and stones, specially combined to encourage positive energy and deter negativity, were concealed in the union of branches and tied discreetly to limbs. (No hammers—LaDonna didn't want us to damage the trees.)

I accepted a handful of dark burlap sachets and twine and set to work finding hiding spots, blessing each with an additional push of energy as I put them in place. Rita worked with Terry to place hidden cameras in the nooks of trees and used her laptop to ensure she had an uninhibited view of the empty clearing. They sprayed each lens with an ice inhibitor as a precaution. Once everything was in place, Hanna meticulously circled the clearing, enchanting each hidden object with a glamour spell to augment its camouflage. Mercury, god of thieves and tricksters that the Stygian undoubtedly planned to use to assist them in their endeavor, would be proud of our tactics.

When the gear was distributed and our presence sufficiently erased (right down the buried cables connecting the speakers and portable generator), Luke called us all to the center of the circle.

"Come on, come on. This has been thirsty work. And I have just the thing."

He opened his leather ruck, pulled out amber bottles of brew, and passed around an opener.

"This was made especially in honor of our efforts. Well, not *made* for us, but bottled and blessed for our efforts. The brewer had a name picked out, but they changed it for us to add energy to our spelling."

I cracked the metal cap off the bottle and passed the opener to Hanna. Tipping the bottle slightly, I read the label. *Faunus' Favorite Fermentation.* Cute.

Recognizing that this was a moment for commemoration, we paused before taking our first sip. Once all the bottles were opened, Luke raised his and led the toast.

"To Faunus in your home of trees, and Father Pan, we toast to thee. May your power bless our work that night, and our chaos feed your appetite! *Slainte*."

We echoed his toast, and I took a sip of the brew. I had learned enough about beer over the years, thanks to my home-brewing foster father, to recognize it as a wheat beer. It tasted pleasantly of cinnamon and oranges with a hint of saltiness.

"Not bad," Conall said. From him—the ale connoisseur—it was a compliment.

We stood in place, our Lughaidh coven, sipping tasty witch-made ale and enjoying the peace in our togetherness.

An idea came to me, and I leaned over and whispered into Conall's ear. "Do you know the way back to the car if it's just the two of us, you think?"

"Yeah, I should be able to. Why?"

I paused and sipped my ale, thinking I must be crazy. It was too freaking cold to do what had occurred to me, and yet...

"I think I have one more idea of a way we could... um... consecrate the area and get Pan's attention at the same time."

The wicked smile that crossed Conall's face at my suggestion should be illegal in all fifty states.

"Oh *really*?"

I felt my cheeks grow warm at the heat in his eyes, and then the rest of my body felt warmer as well.

"It can't hurt."

"Not unless we wind up on top of a rock or something."

"You're not afraid that it's too cold?"

He chuckled. "I have a feeling we won't notice after a minute or two, but if it gets chilly, I'm sure your witchy skills can warm the air around us."

I nodded, feeling my own sly grin grow. "I can do that."

He slung an arm around me and pulled me close, and I was grateful for his body heat. We stood silently as a coven, the reality of our coming battle settling heavily on us as we finished our beers and eyed our work. One by one, Luke collected the empty bottles, and after the final clank in the bottom of his backpack, the group gathered to walk back to the vehicles.

"You coming, y'all?" Rita asked when we lagged behind, our hands intertwined.

"We'll head out on our own," Conall said. "We're going to give Pan one last offering to make sure we have his attention."

They met this announcement with a lively howl, a whistle, and a few knowing, merry, teasing sounds of appreciation and encouragement. My face grew as red as Betony's hair.

Once the last footstep was out of earshot, Conall touched my neck and tipped my head up. I licked my lips and met his eyes, which were ablaze with passion.

"Let's give Pan something to remember us by."

Chapter 41

The weather promised to take a sudden upturn for the better when the month changed, but not before an evening threatening tornadoes the night of February twenty-eighth. I guess March decided to come in like a lion. Hopefully, it would go out like a lamb. If it went out at all, I guess. If the Stygian didn't blow the whole damned world up.

LaDonna's home in the Appalachian foothills was less prone to be in a tornado's path. Still, I watched the internet news stations with concern as the green and red pixelated clouds on the screen developed rotation as they approached Gryphon. Thankfully, the storm dispersed before I was forced to use untried skills to scatter the clouds. Not being a meteorologist, I did not know how the consequences of taking control of the weather might ripple into the environment. I had no urge to see how the butterfly effect might spread.

Nerves frayed, I expressed concern to Jake and Rita about the wires connecting the speakers and other electronic equipment and was assured they were weatherproofed and sturdily emplaced. I thought of our sachets and wondered if any had suffered from the wind and rain. If so, it was too late now. The ceremony was to take place early tomorrow morning, and the dark coven was likely deep into their preparations. I was glad for Hanna's extra precaution of the glamour spells; if any of the sachets had fallen out of place, her protection would keep them hidden from unwanted view. We'd been thorough. I'd have to trust in that.

March first passed both too quickly and too slowly. Impatience hounded me, the urge to engage in the looming faceoff and get it over with. Yet, a nagging fear consumed me as I doubted whether our actions could match the Stygian coven's unknown power. And that dread hated the passing of each minute.

Most of the evening before the big day was spent quietly. LaDonna played peaceful classical music—Bach, Debussy, and Mozart—and most of us lounged like lizards. The stars had peeked out for a moment after the storm, but with the new day came new rains and long, low, rumbling thunder.

I sat cross-legged with Conall on the upstairs bridge landing. We watched the storm through the cathedral windows and listened to the drumming of fat raindrops on the roof and windows as a backdrop to the strings issuing softly from the speakers. As a child, I'd been thin enough to slide my legs through the balusters and watch Luke and LaDonna conduct their life below.

"I need some outside time," I said.

"Need some company?"

"As long as you don't mind letting me focus."

"Focus. Got it. I'll keep my hands to myself. For now."

"You're incorrigible."

"You're irresistible." He waggled his eyebrows. He stood, offered me a hand up, and we headed downstairs to the porch that connected to LaDonna's expansive wooden deck.

The temperature had jumped significantly in the past forty-eight hours; spring had finally arrived. The moist air still brought a chill to the skin, but wasn't a wintry chill. A set of black wicker chairs with red cushions were nestled under the eaves, and Conall took a seat without a word. The rain pattered on the leaves and the deck so hard I barely heard the chair creak under his weight.

Water has always been my favorite element. Stretching an arm beyond the roof's protection, I offered an upturned hand to the downpour and gathered a palmful of rainwater. I spread it onto the arm on the opposite side before switching hands and repeating the process. I cupped my hands and collected another small pool, which I splashed on my face before sitting across from Conall.

Earth… air… fire…water…

I pictured each. The earth that gave us the wood beneath our feet and the ground under that wood. The air moving in and out of me, caressing my wet skin. The water pouring from the sky, blessing the dry earth with moisture, and waking the seeds for the coming spring. The fire of the sun, hidden now behind the clouds but still strong enough to shine through and give us daylight.

Earth… air… fire… water…

With each word, I pictured the elements in various settings. The smell of turned earth for spring planting. The air blowing through car windows on hot summer days. The bonfires we gathered around for spells as a coven, and the smell of smoke in the air. River water on my feet gurgling like nature's music.

And I… I was part of it. We were all part of it. Every cell in our bodies sprouted from the same life source. I consumed the energy that sustained the plants' growth to nourish myself. The water I drank and bathed in has been present in one form or another for millions of years. It returns to the earth in a new shape: ponds, clouds, lakes, rain, fog, and mist.

My body thrummed with energy as I encouraged the power of the earth and sky to enter me. To use me as a vessel. To assist me in keeping this precious earth alive and in harmony. In keeping humanity alive. I felt the touch of each element fueling my spirit, and the feeling was so intense I believed I could float from the chair without intentionally tapping into Source energy.

I slowly brought my awareness back to my body, to my position not within the cosmos but standing as I was on the porch. As I did, the door behind us swung open on soft hinges. I opened my eyes. During my meditation, the evening had crept in. Luke stood in the doorway with an expectant expression.

"You ready for tomorrow?"

Oh, I was ready. I'd be lucky if I slept at all. And from the spark in Conall's eye, that was fine with him.

Chapter 42

The early morning hours of March second arrived. The Lughaidh coven and witches everywhere, from Atlanta and Nashville to New Orleans and Little Rock, had gathered at the Whelen's Alabama treehouse just after midnight. On the surface, the house looked as frenzied as a kicked anthill, but there was a purpose to our scuttling that fueled our anticipation and determination.

Hanna's computer screen showed Jake and Lorina setting up on a stage at a witch-positive bar in the neighboring town of Stony Spring. The owners had agreed to lend their facility for our broadcast free of charge.

My favorite musical duo was joined by a colorful bassist with a short 80s haircut nearly as gangly as Lorina and a compact young man built like a fireplug with curly brown hair. Rita was also there, prepared to record, broadcast, and troubleshoot should anything go haywire during the transmission. Cadence's frizzy curls occasionally appeared from the corner of the screen, and I was glad she could be there to support Jake. I imagined the plot she and Lorina had concocted to sneak out at such an ungodly hour. I guessed they'd each claimed to be staying at the other's house.

Everything assembled, the squat man took center stage and gripped a microphone as someone switched on a spotlight. He flinched and covered his face with his hand to block the light until his vision adjusted. "Check. Check. Um… How are we coming through?" His voice was throaty and robust, and I loved his energy immediately.

I fumbled with a headset and slipped it on. "You sound great. Loud and clear." *Loud and clear? What am I, a Marine?*

"Loud and clear," he said with a friendly chuckle. He dropped his hand and stood full in the spotlight. His eyes were bright green, his face broad and youthful. "Good stuff. Um… is that Murphy out there?"

"It is."

"Murphy, I'm Cash Keaton, and I'm borrowing the center stage to help y'all out so Lorina can fuck up those drums today. I hope that's alright."

Cash had star energy; he'd be the perfect frontman tonight. I'd miss Lorina's gorgeous, soulful vocals, but even through the screen, I could tell when it came to chaotic singing that would attract the power we needed that Cash was the man to deliver.

"I believe in Jake and Lorina, and if they say you're the one, then you're the one, Cash."

Cash's humble grin toward his shoes as he rocked back and forth with pent-up energy won my heart. This was going to be… what was the word Lorina liked so much? Lit. This was going to be lit. My spirit felt it already.

"Murphy—Oh. Oh, we're live?" I saw Rita's head bob up and down at the corner of the screen. We'd let the kids start their show a little earlier than our spelling to set the tone for the day.

"Oh, cool. Well, to Murphy and Rita here and anyone else out there who might tune in to the Worldwide Witch Web show… Lemme give y'all a quick intro before we get started. This here is Lorina." Cash pointed to the back of the stage, where Lorina picked up a subtle drumbeat on the snare and high hat. "And here you have Robin on bass." Cash directed attention to the right side of the stage, where Robin plunked out a tune reminiscent of Fleetwood Mac, their head bobbing up and down with the rhythm the bass and drums kicked out. It appeared they'd found a camera operator for the event; the view on screen moved to follow Cash and his introductions.

"Over here to my right, your left, is Jake on guitar." Jake picked out a lightning-fast riff that complemented the drum and bass riffs already in motion.

"And I'm Cash Keaton, and together…for today, at least… we're Shrewd Monkey."

I shook my head, amused. *Shrewd Monkey. Sure, why not?*

The music took a turn, and within seconds the band was playing a metal punk version of Tears for Fears' *Everybody Wants to Rule the World.*

Well, maybe not everyone, but the Stygian sure as hell does.

With any luck—and quite a bit of magic—we'd stop them.

☽◯☾

Some of those present opted to take a purifying bath or shower before the ritual. I was too nervous to think about sitting in a tub of hot water. And while it might have relaxed me, I clung to that energy, as well as the vigor I'd held onto from the storm and the sexual energy Conall and I had created earlier, hoping I could direct it later into a force for good.

For this ritual, the Lughaidh did not dress in ceremonial robes, opting instead for more practical clothing in the colors of winter woods that allowed us to move freely and be somewhat camouflaged. Ideally, the ceremony would be completely magical, with no physical confrontation necessary. Realistically, however, there was a better-than-average chance we'd be called upon to confront our opponents bodily.

We donned lightweight clothing and shoes, divvied out handfuls of blessed salts, and anointed ourselves with protection oils with a quick plea to Hecate to watch over us and our mission. We packed items effective for protection: quartz crystals, garnets, and lava. We carried sage, basil, juniper, and pine in our pockets. The silence that had prevailed over LaDonna's home the evening before was replaced with nervous, hushed conversations and a lot of reassuring one another that we did, in fact, have this. We were ready.

As we prepared, I watched the monitors Rita and her mother had set up for us. One showed the performance on stage in Stony Spring. Though I couldn't tell from the sound coming through the tinny speakers Rita gave us, the band must have been doing a bang-up job riling up those present. They were only a few songs in, and a crowd surrounded the stage and were dancing and raising their arms with abandon.

Rita had divided the other monitor into six different camera views of the clearing where the ceremony would occur. The perspective reminded me of what security officers viewed when monitoring a building.

"Just wait until he gives them a good mosh pit song," Luke said with a fond grin and a motion with his head to the screen relaying the band's performance. "That'll bring some serious chaos."

The plan was to wait until the Stygian were in place and uttering the beginnings of their incantation before flipping the switch on the speakers, disrupting their ceremony. Our plan was to surround them and keep them contained so they couldn't regroup elsewhere and fulfill their plan while the planets were still aligned. It wasn't a one hundred percent solution—they would undoubtedly formulate a new plot soon—but it would put a pause on their scheme for today, at least.

We loaded the group into several cars—joined by every positive-magic-wielding witch in the Southeast. I piled into the Whelen's vintage Mercedes with LaDonna, Luke, Conall, and Hanna. Betony had opted to ride with Miriam and a few others from our coven. It seemed appropriate for the five of us to be riding together to confront the coven that had torn Conall, Hanna, and me from our mothers. As if things were about to come full circle, somehow.

At least, I hoped it would.

Chapter 43

The time had arrived for us to put our plan into action. No other cars were in the parking lot when we arrived at the path leading to the clearing where the ceremony would take place. Few people took the muddy footpath in the middle of the night—not even die-hard trail runners or cyclists with mountain bikes.

We parked our cars farther from the lane than practical, so they were semi-hidden behind a wall of shrubs in the circular gravel lot. To further disguise their presence, Hanna cast a glamour on the cars, muting bright paint and preventing any shine from the overhead lights that could draw attention.

The conjunction would be at its fullest at 3:35 a.m., and our assumption was that the Stygian's plan was to have the ceremony at its peak then. We needed to be in place, ready to disrupt, long before that happened, long before they had the ear of their Sovereign Darkness—whatever that was.

The first part of our walk felt normal, except for the massive non-stop fluttering in my stomach. Owls hooted in the trees. A handful of stars broke through the scant gray cloud cover. The day promised to be warm, a welcome change after the winter cold.

As we made our way along the winding trail, Hanna and Conall kept me updated with live feeds of witches around the world doing their best to stir up joyful chaos. Turns out "Shrewd Monkey" weren't the only ones having an atypical Wednesday morning concert. Across the globe, people were having rooftop concerts, flash mobs, raves. Witches on Essex Street in Salem, Massachusetts, had chosen that time to hold a special nighttime ceremony. There was video of someone starting an impromptu sing-along in a city subway—I wasn't sure where. A few bars on Bourbon Street had opted to stay open through the night, ignoring local ordinances, and allowed patrons to party as long as they wanted. Television stations were flushing their standard format, instead opting to broadcast funny, humorous, chaotic scenes from movies. Several people had gotten married the night before and were celebrating until the early morning hours. Better go get married before the world ends, I supposed.

What really got my attention, though, was when someone tapped into the feed of several Times Square electronic billboards and broadcast Shrewd Monkey. I hoped there was sound. We had been keeping our phones silent to prevent detection in the event the Stygian were getting into place when we arrived. Rita was supposed to notify us when she detected movement on the hidden tree cams.

My phone buzzed, as did everyone's near me. I pulled it from my pocket and read the text, even though I knew what it said.

Rita:
Stygian approaching. Take caution.

My mouth pressed into a tight line as I darkened my phone screen and put it into a pocket of my jeans. Prickling goosebumps rose on my skin, and immediately I went on alert. Motion at the tree line caught my eye, and I held up my hand. We all froze. All of us were in a cluster, making us easy prey for anyone with directional spells. Dammit, we should have thought of that sooner. I pulled on Source energy until my ears thrummed and scanned the trees for whatever had gotten my attention.

A white-tailed deer emerged from the wood. The gray-brown winter coat on its thin frame was shedding. Great black eyes studied us as it chewed on something and flicked an ear unconcernedly. I let out a pent-up breath.

"Ryan? Is that you?"

The deer made a few up-and-down motions with both head and neck. Maybe it was coincidence—it wasn't like we had anyone able to translate his messages with us—but I took it as a sign that my father was there.

"I really hope that's you. We need all the help we can get."

Done with whatever it had been eating, the deer flicked its ears and did a quick tail flick before strolling away.

I took in a deep breath and let it out slowly. "OK. Let's go."

Without uttering a word, Betony and LaDonna stirred the wind to hide the sound of our footsteps on the dry winter leaves. I loved how they had reached that level of spiritual communication.

We reached the clearing and separated, each witch of the Lughaidh taking their predetermined location around the perimeter, leaving the trail open for the Stygian's approach. Once they were ready to begin, we'd strike.

$$\supset\!O\!\subset$$

The planets would be in their peak position at 3:35 a.m., so we arrived two hours early. We guessed they'd want time to prepare for the ceremony. They also wouldn't want to be fatigued when the Big Bad—I'm sorry, the *Sovereign Darkness*—appeared.

Sovereign Darkness? *Really?* Were they planning to call it royal highness? Your majesty? SD? My dude? They made it sound like this entity was an actual being—like a ghost or something. But no spirit alone could let chaos loose in the world. I was still unclear how they planned to use the SD to do that, but since we planned to disrupt the ceremony before they accomplished that, I figured we'd devise a "Defeat It" plan if the "Thwart It" plan fell through.

I speculated on how long the SD would take to conquer the world if we failed to keep it from materializing. Poor Rene. Even if he was on board with the Stygian plan, how long would his body be able to sustain an otherworldly power like that? Not long, most likely. And he was so young. Betony's parents were willing to kill on the chance their daughter might become the Summate. Now Ericka was throwing her son on the altar of darkness. What the hell was wrong with these people that they valued life so little?

The Stygian coven members who arrived on our heels had been sent ahead to prepare the site. Two lugged an empty metal fire pit, and four more carried armfuls of wood and sticks for starting a fire. A sixth used a wide rake to pull leaves from the center of the clearing until she'd cleared a layer of exposed dirt and dead winter grass about fifteen feet around.

"Fire," Conall noted in hushed tones. "Destructive power."

"They sure don't need it for the heat anymore," I agreed.

I hated waiting. The longer I waited, the louder my heart pumped, the sweatier my palms felt, and the tighter my chest became. I fidgeted cautiously, careful to not make noise. Reminding myself to breathe, I focused on my inhales and exhales, on the power of the earth and air and the godly spirit surrounding us.

No pressure. We're just here to save the world.

The sound of footsteps on gravel announced the arrival of the rest of the Stygian. It was game time.

Chapter 44

The entrance of the dark coven into the clearing was nothing like the spooky, smoky, gray-robed evil thugs in my vision. I couldn't believe the folks approaching the center of the circle, now aglow with the beginnings of a fire, had nefarious intentions at all. They could have been there for a picnic. In fact, they'd brought their spelling equipment in a picnic basket. *All the better to kill you with, my dear.*

Instead of midnight snack material, they withdrew a red-hilted athame, black salts, and their own brands of spelling herbs. They placed black pillar candles at five points on the circle, and I understood now why they'd raked the space free of leaves. Wouldn't want to start a forest fire before you burn the world down.

Standing with one hand cocked on a hip, his body presenting to everyone he hadn't a care, Rene examined the woods. His brow furrowed slightly as he panned the tree line. Searching for the Lughaidh, no doubt. Did he have faith that we'd save him? What if our entering the clearing was part of their plan? Too late now.

Conall's body twitched as if something had stung him. He inspected the area around him as if hunting for something.

"You OK?" I asked. "Did something bite you?"

"I… something. I need… shit. No mirror. No cards…"

It wasn't a bug that had caused his agitation. He'd been struck with a bizarre and pressing need to divine.

"Um… book?" I offered the novel I'd brought along to kill the time and distract my racing mind.

"Bibliomancy?" he said with raised eyebrows. I shrugged.

"You're the orange witch. Ever tried prediction with a book before?"

"Surprisingly, no. Think it will work with a book that's not sacred?"

"No time like the present to find out," I said as I pushed the book toward him. "I could give you a boost?"

Accepting the book and holding it in his right hand with eyes closed, he said, "Yeah. That's a good idea. We don't have time for my inexperience to muddle this up."

I hadn't fully let go of Source energy since the night before on LaDonna and Luke's porch, but now I let in a fuller measure of power. The edges of my surroundings grew crisper, the moonlight brighter, the smell of earth and leaves and fire on the wind more apparent. Reaching out to touch Conall on the thigh, I pushed a yarn-thin strand of Source through the fabric into his body. His breath caught, and his eyes grew brighter.

"Never gets old," he said, his voice shaky with new liveliness. He gripped the book in both hands, his confidence in his ability stronger now.

"Show us. Guide us. Help us."

He closed his eyes and thumbed through the book, first in one direction, then another, his hands following the impulses of spirit to detect the right passage. After a few seconds of flipping back and forth, he came to rest on a set of pages. Keeping his eyes closed, he allowed a finger to trace the page as if reading braille until they came to a stop.

"There," he said with certainty. He leaned forward and read the passage. "A father's love can be a mystery, but there is one thing I knew beyond the shadow of a doubt: my father would always be there for me, even if it meant walking through the fires of hell."

"It *was* him," I whispered. "The deer. It was Ryan. He's here." I chewed my lip, frustrated that talking to Ryan was damn near impossible. "He must be planning to help us somehow."

The sound of chanting drew my attention back to the Stygian. While Conall and I distracted ourselves with his bibliomancy, the dark coven had assumed their positions around the circle. The ceremony was about to begin.

)O(

I had to credit the Stygian coven for one thing (other than their insane urge to make the world chaotic): they could sing far better than the Lughaidh. Perhaps the group had discovered each other in a musical theater or choir. Then I realized their coven had a blue witch—a witch of music—who took any discordant sounds and blended them into perfectly harmonious vocals. A blend of harmonies so magically strong it surpassed consciousness and dug into the coven psyche—likely that of anyone standing nearby. The effect even mesmerized me momentarily, but I caught myself as I wavered back and forth. Blinking and shaking my head, I rid myself of the hypnotic pull of their melody.

"Shit," I hissed. I grabbed my phone and started pressing buttons as quickly as my cold, stiff fingers allowed, praying the Lughaidh coven members watching were not getting sucked in by the enchanting siren song stirred by the blue witch.

Start the broadcast. Quickly!

Rita:
On it.

Within seconds, the uproarious double bass drums and shredding vocals of "Shrewd Monkey" tore into the morning air. Cash's voice sounded fantastic, now airing through speakers that did better service to his wide-ranging voice than the tinny speakers at LaDonna's house. I was impressed by the music's quality, considering the impromptu arrangement of the inexpensive rock-shaped speakers and the lack of a sound check.

The beatific expression on Ericka's face melted like a popsicle on a hot August dashboard. Her raised arms drifted to her sides as she blinked and sought the source of the commotion. It would have been funny under other circumstances.

"Keep singing, dammit!" she bellowed. "The melody doesn't matter. Just the words!"

At least, I'm pretty sure that's what she said. It was hard to tell over all the heavy metal racket.

That's when my coven revealed itself. Rene noticed LaDonna and Betony. Then his eyes swiveled through the group until they settled on me. The tension in his face eased, and relief swam over him.

He was genuinely glad to see us. Ericka, however, picked up on her son's readiness to defect, and her body stiffened in fury. Everything in her overly made-up face twisted and bugged in frustration, and she dug into a pocket for something.

Does she have a gun? Is she going to shoot us?

But it wasn't a gun. It was a hypodermic needle. And Rene, his back now turned to his own coven, never saw it coming. I raised a warning hand, but before I could get Rene's attention and caution him, Ericka had flicked off the cover to the needle and injected her son in the back of his thigh. Rene's eyes grew in surprise and he turned to discover his attacker, only to find it was his own mother.

The injection took effect, and Rene collapsed to the earth.

Chapter 45

Nope. No, that is not how this is going down.

Seeing Rene's motionless form, helpless against his mother's malicious attack, infuriated me. What kind of cruel mother was she? She treated her child like nothing more significant than a voodoo poppet—a rag doll made solely for spelling, nothing more.

It was the same way Betony's parents had treated her. Their child, a living, breathing human being with their own thoughts, dreams, and emotions, was created as a means to an end. That end being ruling over all the earth.

I caught the furious way Betony glared at Ericka, and I knew she was thinking the same thing. Her pale jaw was tight with anger, her nostrils flared, and her hands tightened and untightened. She anxiously watched Rene's body, hope painted on her face as she waited for him to rise. When she was certain Rene was down to stay, her hands splayed open at her side, the muscles in her arms rigid, her fingers curled like talons.

"Je contrôle les vents forts, je contrôle la nature…"

I couldn't understand what she said since French was her spelling language, one she was learning from Luke. Some of us chose languages other than English to spell in, as it allowed us a special place in our minds reserved for that unique purpose. It doesn't matter what language a person uses to spell; intent imbues the invocation with power. And Betony had every intention of protecting Rene.

The barely there spring breeze whipped into a frenzied microtornado that pulled dry tree limbs from their trunks and stirred up the dusty ground. The furious gust wedged itself between Ericka and Rene, separating Ericka from her coven. It then encased Ericka within its fierce rotation. It reminded me of those wind tunnel games that challenged contestants to gather prizes or money in the swirling air. Only Ericka was contained within the twister by a terrifying mix of whirling branches, leaves, pebbles, and pine needles.

The rest of the Stygian refused to be dissuaded. Their focus stuck to Rene, still unmoving in the dirt, the strength of their spell increasing, shimmering in the atmosphere like heat waves in the desert.

I pulled on Source power to amplify the boisterous music coming from the speaker until their spell was utterly drowned out by the clattering tornado and the furious sounds of Shrewd Monkey. It wouldn't take away from the intent of their invocation, but it might weaken their focus. Concentrating on a spell intensely when you can hardly think is nearly impossible.

I turned to my coven. "We have to protect Rene from their energy!"

Hanna, who stood just over my shoulder, had a defiant gleam in her eye, and a corner of one lip turned up. Her fingers wiggled subtly, telling me she was doing some spelling of her own.

"What are you doing?"

"Making us look scary as hell." Her half-smile grew into a malicious grin.

Glamour spelling for intimidation. Excellent.

Meanwhile, Hanna's father, Rafael, motioned his idea to Betony. Bet replied with an understanding bob of her head and moved Ericka and her tornadic tunnel farther to the edge of the clearing. In a flash, she released Ericka and switched her focus to create a bubble of chaos around the Lughaidh and Stygian covens, effectively creating a shifting, floating dome of debris that trapped us— and any destruction we were about to unleash—inside.

Whoa. Cool trick.

Rafael took a bold step forward, tapping into his potent white witch abilities. In that instant, the energy within our chaotic dome surged, blazing with intensity like the peak of a scorching midsummer day. The atmosphere resonated with a palpable hum as he worked to expel the lingering negative energy from our surroundings. No doubt he knew he'd never keep the Stygian from summoning the Sovereign Darkness on his own, but he was pouring every ounce of his being into trying.

The Stygian moved as one toward Rene's inert body, their hands extended. The next portion of their plan involved physically touching Rene's body.

Uh-uh. Nope. Not happening.

"LaDonna!" I cried. "Imagine Rene protected by the earth!"

I had no idea how my foster mother would accomplish my request, but I sent a bolt of extra Source power her way to aid her in whatever idea she dreamed up. In my haste to protect Rene, I may have been a tad generous when I pushed my energy out. Her eyes bulged when we connected, and she pulled in a sharp intake of breath.

Sorry. I grimaced, but LaDonna's eyes were fixed on Rene and narrowed with determination.

To my amazement, tree roots swelled and broke forth from the ground. They crept around Rene like shuddering brown snakes cocooning him within a vinelike grip and blocking him from the Stygian's touch. It wasn't what I had in mind, but her idea was better—burying Rene would have only suffocated him. The protective roots kept him above ground, but inaccessible.

The Stygian, however, weren't going down easily. One of the Stygian troupe, a rangy, tanned man with short white hair and bright green eyes, came forward and laid a hand on the roots. His peaceful countenance revealed nothing about his designs, but the winding roots blackened and withered within moments. He must have been a black witch capable of pushing a curse into another person's spell. That was some scary shit.

And the scary shit kept coming. The Stygian descended on Rene like turkey vultures on a deer carcass. They gripped him so tightly their hands became clawlike, and Rene's head drifted from side to side. Was the motion merely a result of the eagerness of his coven members, or was he stirring from whatever Ericka had dosed him with already?

Meanwhile, Rafael continued to mouth his incantation, urging waves of positive energy to fill the entire dome. I considered boosting his power like I had LaDonna's, or giving LaDonna another boost so she could grow vines that would imprison the Stygian.

In my frustration, every spell I knew fled from my mind. And given the Stygian black witch's skills at reversing another's effort, I was afraid to try anything. So, I refrained from using any of them. Instead, I crossed the ground in long strides and kicked the first person I reached with the toe of my Doc Marten boot. Then I kicked another.

"Get. Off. Of. Him. You. Assholes!"

My feet kept flying, and they, expecting a metaphysical battle, not a physical one, toppled like bowling pins clutching their ribs and backs. In seconds, I was joined by Conall, who started in with his fists instead of his feet. His skills as a prophetic witch wouldn't come in terribly handy during the spell-casting portion of the fight, but the physical strength he'd accumulated over years of construction work sure would. Luke joined in, then LaDonna, and we were in an all-out brawl. But it didn't help.

After receiving a disorienting punch to the jaw by Creepy Black Witch, I pivoted in a complete about-face and discovered Rene on his feet, his eyes a hellish swirling of red and black, power radiating from him as he stood, prepared to strike.

Oh, shit. The Sovereign Darkness. We're too late.

Chapter 46

Rene—or the thing that used to be Rene—lowered his chin, a malevolent expression painted on his handsome face. His piercing gaze scanned the group as if deliberating on which unfortunate soul to claim first. The red and black in his eyes curled and twisted, first appearing like flames, then smoke, then like a furious colony of bats, and back to fire again. No glamour Hanna conjured could have terrified me more. The worst had happened. The deafening clamor of Shrewd Monkey tore through the air, surrounding us as if the end of the world hadn't just announced itself in this tiny Alabama clearing.

And the battle surrounding us continued. Witches channeled their collective energy into various support for their respective covens. Some focused on maintaining protective barriers, weaving intricate layers of defense, guarding against the onslaught of destructive forces, erecting invisible shields, or deflecting and nullifying hostile magic. Some who shared similar spell-casting abilities bolstered the spells cast by their fellow witches, enhancing their effectiveness and potency. Others sought to tip the scales by disrupting the opponents' concentration. They wove illusions or attempted to distract and disorient their opponents.

At the heart of it all was our little group, the few who had witnessed that the worst had already happened. I had to do something. After all, as the one witch on Earth possessing the power to counter the Sovereign Darkness, the responsibility to confront this menace fell on my shoulders. Yet, my mind, overwhelmed by terror, became incapable of coherent thought. If I failed to halt Rene's rampage now, the extent of the havoc he would wreak remained unfathomable.

Taking a deep breath, I strove to center myself amidst the chaos. My goal was to shut out the external and internal racket, from the cacophonous metal music assaulting our ears, to the raucous commotion of battling witches, to the erratic dance of debris swirling in the ceiling of Rafael's protective dome.

A savage, guttural scream pierced the commotion and broke my reverie. Betony stumbled backward, crashing into me with a startled grunt, propelled by the forceful shove of a scrawny woman with unkempt mud-colored hair, yellowed fingernails, and weathered skin.

Virginia Yarborough, Betony's mother, had joined the fracas.

I staggered to keep my footing, forced to deal with this new predicament. The two women engaged in a savage clash on the ground, their struggle mirroring wild beasts vying for dominance, driven by untamed instincts. I couldn't help but spare a brief thought about Virginia's fighting skills, and how much they may have been honed during her stay in prison. Conall and Luke inched closer, cautiously searching for an opportunity to intervene.

As Betony grappled with Virginia, Ericka brushed at her disarrayed hair and clothes, her countenance reminding me of every chilling photo of a serial killer I'd ever seen. Ericka's eyes fell upon Rene, noting the swirling vortex of red and black within her son's stare and the malevolent expression on his face. She grew manic with joy.

"Your Majesty," she crooned, bowing her head in a display of reverence.

Rene regarded her with undisguised contempt. "You dared to summon me and imprison me in this mortal form?"

His tone dripped with disdain, hinting at the repercussions that awaited, but I wasn't about to stick around to see how the SD would mete out his punishment.

We needed a solution, an advantage. I weighed the scales. Our side had the World Wide Witches. They had a global reach as well. We had the Lughaidh and every coven within driving distance, and then those in the clearing to assist with physical and magical combat. They had the same. They had the Sovereign Darkness trapped inside Rene. The Lughaidh had me, an only partially trained Summate, on their side.

I backed up to regroup with my coven and nearly tripped over Betony, who was rising now that Luke held Virginia's arms behind her back in his muscular grip. I supposed it wouldn't be terribly hard for Betony, a gray witch, to subdue a lifelong smoker with a history of hardcore drug use. But if Virginia had learned to fight in prison, or had been hopped up on drugs, the odds might have been closer to balanced. Poor Bet was covered in Alabama red dirt and had a cut dripping blood across her cheek. She shook out her hand from some sort of injury and made an "ouch" face.

"Traitor!" Virginia growled. "Fucking traitor! Benjamin Arnold!"

I think you mean Benedict Arnold, but whatever.

"Victory!" Ericka crowed. "We have succeeded! The battle is ours!"

The Sovereign Darkness had decided not to kill Ericka, and from the sound of it, the SD was begrudgingly cool with whatever plans the Stygian had for it. Great.

Chapter 47

"Your Majesty, the dome. It is suppressing our power and your reach."

The being within Rene regarded the swirling ceiling overhead for a moment, his piercing gaze filled with otherworldly intensity. With a simple wave of his hand, a surge of supernatural energy crackled. The force struck Rafael, who doubled over as if hit by a heavyweight boxer. Debris rained down on everyone below, a storm of our own making. I protected my head with my arms as a heavy branch crashed over me, bringing me to my knees.

And I stayed there as the air grew thick, and a powerful wave of depression incapacitated me, both physically and mentally. It pressed upon me like an invisible hand, physically and mentally rendering me helpless. The world around me seemed to crumble, and I curled into a ball, overwhelmed by the sheer weight of despair. The dark forces of Stygian spells, which had been kept at bay by the dome, now poured over us all. At that moment, it became painfully clear this could be the end, the act that would seal the fate of the world. The Summate and the gray sat helplessly beaten to death by the coven that had killed my mother, Conall's mother, and Hanna's. The weight on my chest brought on by the heavy depression felt thick and physically suffocating.

Virginia Yarborough, suppressed by Luke's powerful grip, fought like a wet cat in a sack to get loose, grunting and kicking fruitlessly.

A twisted smile curved upon Ericka's lips, a mix of pride and possession akin to a demon mother cradling her newborn child. But beneath that veneer of dark maternal affection, a chilling question nagged me. Was Rene still inside, imprisoned by the Sovereign Darkness that now puppeted his body? Again, I wondered what kind of asshole would do this to their own child?

They were all so different. Betony's mother. Rene's mother. Conall's mother. Hanna's mother. My mother. And my father, Ryan.

Our ancestors.

That was the secret. Ancestral magic. Calling on not just the witches of the earth, but the spirits that had gone on before them, those in the place where universal knowledge resided.

"I have to stop this. I have to…" I murmured, my voice barely audible amidst the cacophony surrounding us. My determination surged, pushing me forward despite the suffocating weight of despair inflicted by the Stygian spell. Rising from my knees, the outcome of the world pressing heavily upon my body, I shuffled to LaDonna's side and spoke in a whisper barely loud enough for her to hear.

"Venerated ancestors, we bid you to hear the voice of your daughter and come forth. We, the bone of your bone and blood of your blood, desperately need you to lend us your assistance. We pray for your strength and your divine wisdom. We pray the bond between the living and the dead to be one of fortitude, magic, and trust."

As my words pattered on, the Lughaidh rallied around me: Hanna, Rafael, Conall, Terry, Joey, and Conall's father, Paul. They understood that the power I needed to draw through me could not be conjured alone, and thus, they stood by my side. Facing outward in a protective ring, their focus unwavering amidst the chaotic battleground.

Before that day, my existence as a Summate had granted me glimpses of something greater than myself, something more significant than my physical body. I had ventured into the ethereal realm, glimpsed prophetic visions, and tapped into a tiny sliver of the vast cosmic energy that courses through all things. But the adversary we confronted that morning topped anything I had ever faced—a menace that called for an equally momentous counterattack. Everything I drew through me had to surpass the limits I had previously experienced, too.

Trusting the Universe and my coven to protect me, I closed my eyes and envisioned pathways around the Earth for the ancestors to enter the earthly realm. Doors—hundreds of thousands of otherworldly portals—opening, and spirits of protective family, friends, and well-meaning forces descending to protect not just us, but everyone. Even the Stygian. Protecting them from whatever they may fall prey to at the hands of the hostile forces that drove them. Protecting them from themselves.

The ethereal beings sought their loved ones and countless other souls yearning for the solace of love and embraced them with boundless compassion. They built unbreakable psychic barricades around their loved ones, spiritual bulwarks shielding them from harm. Faced with the Stygian coven, whose goal was to plunge the world into chaos, these spirits strengthened their understanding that, while imperfect, humanity possessed a divine essence. They nurtured the wounded spirits in their embrace, mending their brokenness and offering solace. They illuminated the boundless potential for human goodness that far surpassed the limited character assumed by the Stygian coven.

My body radiated with billions of cells absorbing and emitting Source energy. My head fell back as my spirit swelled with love, compassion, gratitude, empathy, and forgiveness. I understood now why positive energy would always defeat negative. Humankind, overall, sought connection. We desired unity and stability, not chaos and uncertainty. Despite our inherent imperfections, we possess a divine spark, a glimmer of transcendent goodness. Love can transform us into better beings. Love gives us the resilience and courage to face death and destruction. It converts fear into fuel that allows us to rise above our limitations and to sacrifice ourselves for those we care for. Love is timeless and knows no cultural bounds. Love creates life.

"Do you really think you can beat the Sovereign Darkness?"

Ericka's question stirred me from my reverie but did not break my bond with the Source. As my eyes fluttered open, it felt as if I beheld the essence of the world itself revealed in its elemental beauty: the trees, the ground, the sky, and the people.

Rene.

It was Rene, and yet it wasn't. Relief washed over me that the young man's spirit hadn't been evicted by whatever entity he contained. However, when I grasped the entity he *did* house, it didn't appear "dark" or "sovereign" at all. Not like it had presented itself, anyway. Yes, it had a vast power to influence nature and the ability to hop a ride inside someone, much like I could share Conall's body when I astral projected. But this… this whole Sovereign Darkness thing was a front for something else.

Rene shuddered, blinked, his body bucked, and the swirling hues of red and black within vanished. His chin lifted, and the sinister smile across his face transformed from hateful to downright friendly. The abrupt transformation was unnerving, akin to seeing Hannibal Lecter morph into an embodiment of Mr. Rogers.

"Hello there, Murphy."

Skepticism hung heavy on surrounding faces, revealing my coven's doubts about Rene's sudden personality shift. It would have been too easy to believe that attitude shift was a deceitful trick. Had it not been for the power running through me, I might have doubted its intention.

"Who… *are* you?"

"He's the Sovereign Darkness!" Ericka cried, her serial killer demeanor indisputable now. "And *you* are an absolute fool."

Rene cocked an eyebrow in response. "Yeah, no. See, that's where you're mistaken."

Ericka's jaw dropped, and the moment was delicious. However, it didn't answer our questions.

"Rene?" I ventured cautiously.

"Not entirely," Rene confessed. "He's in here, and you'll have him back in a second. But to keep that terrible dark thing from staying inside of your friend here, he needed… a little assistance. Kind of helped that Rene and I have a common goal in mind."

Finally, things fell together.

)O(

I had summoned the ancestors, and one had arrived who'd been helping us all along. That pins-and-needles feeling returned, and I knew for sure.

"R-Ryan?" My mouth hung open, and I slapped my lips together. I kept blinking, as if expecting to see him physically appear.

Rene's face lit up, and Ericka's crestfallen expression worsened. She took one step away. Then another.

"Who. The fuck. Is *Ryan*?" Ericka's tone carried a mix of confusion and irritation and rose with every syllable.

"That would be her father." Rene's finger jutted in my direction. "The man she loves more than you love your son. And she barely even knows me."

Ericka's nostrils flared, and her jaw jutted as she clenched her teeth. Her feet continued to edge away from the being she no longer recognized as her deity.

"Where is the Darkness?" she demanded. "*What* did you *do*?"

Rene's shoulders shrugged. "It headed back to wherever y'all conjured it from, I imagine. Rene was more than happy to let me help him evict that nasty thing from his body. I'd be glad if I were you. From my brief contact with it, it didn't seem thrilled with being summoned and shoved into a measly human body. My guess is that it would have wiped you and your little coven off the face of the earth before taking on your plan to unleash chaos. Fortunately, we dead fae carry a bit of magic into our afterlives. That helped."

Did he say dead fae? My father was fae? Holy shit... that means... I'm half fae. Was that how Summates were created? Was that why Terry was leaving offerings for the Seelie fairies at my house? Did she know? I waggled my head back and forth and forced myself to push that puzzle back to solve later.

Ericka's body shivered so intensely it was apparent from where I stood several feet away.

"No," she murmured. "No. We did everything correctly. *We did it all right! All of it, damn you!*"

"And yet, you lied to your own coven so your child could host this thing to have power by proxy."

Rene's suspicion was correct. Ericka's bleached-blond hair, unkempt and dirty from her time in her personal twister, moved from side to side. Her lips pursed. She had clearly never considered the possibility of defeat and was at a loss about what to do next. After several long moments of deliberation, she pivoted in my direction and glared at me.

"This isn't over," she snarled. Motioning to her coven, most of whom were now limping or cradling other injured body parts, she stormed from the clearing. Luke finally released Virginia, who took one final half-hearted swat at him before chasing after the rest of her coven. Clearly, struggling for her freedom had worn her ability to fight down to a nub.

Perhaps I could have pursued her, but I didn't. I would not kill her—not while she fled. Undoubtedly, if the Stygian lived to fight another day, they would take advantage of their escape. Regardless of my feelings toward the dark coven, the Source still loved them and wanted to offer them the opportunity to return to the love and light that is the greater power. And who am I to question that?

Epilogue

There are many beautiful things about Sweet Home Alabama, but it's hard to deny that some of its laws are peculiar. For instance, the age of majority is nineteen. So even though Rene was eighteen, he had to file for emancipation to sever his legal ties with Ericka and the rest of his coven. We may have stretched the truth a bit, claiming his mother had abandoned him for over a year, but she didn't put up a fight. And let's face it: she'd abandoned him ages ago when she decided he was her ticket to the Sovereign Darkness. Rene was finally free from her—legally, at least.

We witches were still closeted, but that was probably for the best. We still weren't sure what the ultimate consequences would be from pissing off the Stygian coven. Or how long it would take for Rene to heal from the realization that his mother was willing to sacrifice him to bring chaos to the world. But we had hope.

Three months later, we had heard no word from Ericka or the dark coven. Perhaps they were still nursing their wounds, or maybe they had gone underground and created a new website, intentionally dropping a few posts on the old site to mislead or confuse us. Rita diligently monitored the Stygian's website, but other than a handful of posts, usually concerning the pagan holiday get-togethers, not much was said.

I was back in Blackwell Manor. My once dull, very white spare room was now totally rebuilt in more ways than one. Vibrant lime-colored walls, a spray-painted black bed, a luxurious black faux fur rug, and a desk with a high-speed computer now defined the space. Overlooking the neighbor's backyard and Titania Street, a black altar cloth adorned with Ouija planchettes, crescent moons, and spell books added an extra layer of darkness to the room.

"You good up there?" Hanna called up the staircase.

I descended the stairs with a box of dried lemon and orange rinds borrowed from my Room of Power.

"I'm good," I replied. "But sometimes it's still so hard to believe."

"That you're a foster mom at almost twenty-seven to a kid that is a legal adult in forty-eight other states?"

"I'm not a foster mom. He's emancipated."

Hanna cocked her head at me. "Murphy, I'll bet you're more of a mother to him than Ericka ever was."

The front door to Witch's Brew burst open, and my favorite group of teens trouped inside. Betony, Lorina, Cadence, Jake, and Rene beamed with the joy of freedom. A blast of hot, soon-to-be summer air followed them.

"Last day of school!" Betony crowed, her excitement filling the room. "Senior year next! Woo-hoo!"

"You're homeschooled, shut up," Cadence kidded.

"LaDonna said she'd consider letting me go to Gryphon High next year. I might graduate with y'all!"

I hadn't heard that yet, but LaDonna's confidence in Betony's gray witch skills didn't surprise me. The young woman had come a long way since last Halloween.

Rene made his way to the glass cake tray, offering pastries to everyone before helping himself. He slid the record book from its place next to the cash register, grabbed a ballpoint pen, and noted the inventory he'd removed. Then he gave me a wink and joined his friends as they all tromped up the stairs to his room.

"Y'all are eating me out of house and home!" I shouted jokingly.

Hanna chuckled in response, her adorable nose wrinkled. "You love it, and you know it," she said, and she was right.

Life had taken unexpected turns, but amid it all, I had found a new family member and now lived where love and magic intermingled in new and pleasant ways. Sweet Home Alabama was where wounds were healing, and the future held the promise of brighter days.

Coming soon from Iris Kain:

Offshoot: In an astonishing twist of fate, Wade Beringer, a devoted police officer, is transported to an alternate universe. There, he crosses paths with Sergio, a street-smart doppelgänger, who helps him learn about this perplexing realm. As Wade's friends and family embark on a desperate mission to bring him back, he strives to use his detective skills to find a way home—no matter how improbable the odds.

Salty. Murphy and the Lughaidh coven are caught in a global surge of anti-witch hysteria. Together, they search for solutions to quell the rising panic and protect their kind from persecution.

Support Indie Authors

Buy
Read
Review

www.ingramcontent.com/pod-product-compliance
Lightning Source LLC
Chambersburg PA
CBHW010553170726
48285CB00011B/2885